DATE DUE

MAY 2 0 2021		
JUL 3 0 2021		

Dogwood Crossing

DOGWOOD
CROSSING

a novel

STEVEN FRYE

BATHCAT PRESS

Dogwood Crossing
Copyright © 2020 by Steven Frye

This book is entirely a work of fiction. All characters, and their names,
are from the author's imagination. Places, events, and incidents, while
often based on reality, are used fictitiously. If there is any resemblance to
a real person, whether they are living or dead, is purely coincidental.

Cover and interior design by Lance Buckley

ISBN: 978-0-578-59822-2 (Hardcover)
ISBN: 978-0-578-59820-8 (Paperback)
ISBN: 978-0-578-59823-9 (eBook)

Library of Congress Control Number: 2019916802

Publisher's Cataloging-in-Publication Data

Names: Frye, Steven, author.
Title: Dogwood crossing / Steven Frye.
Description: Ashland, OR: Bathcat Press,
An Imprint of Academic Services Partnership, LLP, 2020.

Identifiers: LCCN: 2019916802 | ISBN: 978-0-578-59822-2 (Hardcover)
| 978-0-578-59820-8 (pbk.) | 978-0-578-59823-9 (ebook)

Subjects: LCSH United States–History–18th century–Fiction. | Southern
States–History–1775-1865–Fiction. | Family–Fiction. | Frontier and
pioneer life–Missouri–Fiction. | Frontier and pioneer life–Tennessee–
Fiction. | Frontier and pioneer life–North Carolina–Fiction. | Historical
fiction. | BISAC FICTION / Historical / General | FICTION / Literary

Classification: LCC PS3606.R928 D64 2020 | DDC 813.6–dc23

For Kristin, Melissa, and Thomas

Love – is anterior to Life –
Posterior – to Death –
Initial of Creation and
The Exponent of Earth –
-EMILY DICKINSON

There is a Within to things.
-PIERRE TEILHARD DE CHARDIN

Samuel: *Son of Elkanah and Hannah, judge, priest, Nazirite. Most frequently, however, he is called a prophet.*

Elisha: *("God has granted salvation"), son of Shaphat, a native of Abel-Meholah in the northern kingdom of Israel, was a prophet during the reigns of Jehoram, Jehu, Jehoahaz, and Joash (846-785 BC).*

KENTUCKY

Hunting Creek

▲ Standing
Stone

Clinch River

Johnson's
Stand

White's Fort
(Knoxville)

Brushy Mountains

NORTH
CAROLINA

SOUTH
CAROLINA

1798 — 1799

───── Rivers, Creeks

───── Avery's Trace

━ ━ ━ Natchez Trace

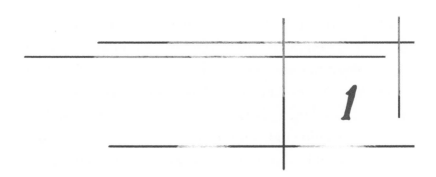

*B*lue flames gripped the kindling and melted the bark to cinder. Sam Rolens leaned gaunt and naked against a table leg tapping his feet on the dry-cut logs. He took in the chill quiet and the whiskey. His thoughts were a haze and he could feel his own breathing. He scratched the top of his head and followed the fire as it tapered into translucent webs of smoke. Lucetta moved in bed. He took another drink from the clay jar and standing heard a footfall near the door. Elisha walked in and tossed his hat on the table.

"Pa don't look like himself no more," Elisha said.

Sam looked over at the old man lying dead on a plankboard in the corner of the room.

"He don't fill that suit of clothes like he once did," Sam said.

"No, he don't. Noon's when they're all coming?"

Sam nodded and slid the jar across the table. Elisha took a mouthful and cast his eyes on his older brother.

"Together in death?" he said, thinking of his mother.

"I don't know. I guess."

Sam saw the lines under his brother's eyes. "Take another drink."

Elisha took in the last of the jar then picked up his hat and went to bed. Sam dusted the fire and walked through the breezeway to the other side of the cabin. Lifting the child he set him between Lucetta and the wall. He lay next to his wife and looked up at a strand of straw in the rafters and he knew sleep would elude him yet again. With his share of the tobacco he could cover the cost of travel and he imagined the cradle scythe working as the tall grass lifted from his own land. He was sure it would feel different. His mind rested for a moment on his wife and children.

Everything he did was bound to their needs and unspent hopes and no sacrifice was unworthy of them. But still his days were a void and no amount of loving could fill them and with his father on a plankboard death seemed unsanctified. He took in a breath and closed his eyes as the war came back clear and vivid, the sound of the cannon and the smell of the powder in the mist and the trim worn coats of the British infantry crimson in the dust. On cold mornings in the frost near places like King's Mountain and Guilford Courthouse they would mass forward to an entrenched line. The musket fire would fall and the artillery was like a dull axe cutting the lines and when he came away safe he never knew why. In a trance he would step to the pace set by the whistler and when it was finished he would lay the moment out straight and visible. It worked for him sometimes to think this way, since there were no questions then only memories. Pa died Tuesday. He heard Lucetta's voice singing sweetly in his head.

"And wish a woman's hand to close, my lids in death and say, repose."
Sixty-two years. Laid out for the wake.

Sam woke glassy-eyed from the liquor as Raymond rolled
a plump leg onto his belly. Lucetta was at table with a skin
blanket over her shoulders. She had built the fire and
in the mottled light of the flame he could see the shape
of her breast and her face near the wall. Her skin was
still smooth in places untouched by sunlight. She worked
around the table and tossed wooden bowls and spoons in
front of the chairs. She went back to the fire and bending
hooked the Dutch oven above the flames. Sam went to her
as she secured the oven and he reached under the blanket.
She began to turn as Ray let out a whimper. Sam noticed
the tangles at the bottom of her hair and reached up to
touch them.

"Witches been at me," she said.

"Appears so," he said as he turned toward the door.

"You ought to put something on before you go out there."

On a bed nearby Little Charlie sat up and seeing the fire
elbowed Eve Mary and Ewan.

"Get on up and help Mama," he said, looking at Eve Mary.

"I'm still tired."

"Get on out the bed before I throw you out naked."

Lucetta turned to them.

"Eve Mary, bring Ray over here and fetch me the whey.
Charlie, go on outside and get what's left of the sour milk."

Charlie stood. She saw the dark line of new hair above his
mouth. The boy nearly a man now slipped into his leggings

3

and looped on the shoulder straps and passed Sam coming through the door.

"There's some milk still in the bucket, enough for today," said Lucetta.

Charlie walked around to the side of the cabin and dropped the wooden bowl into the bucket under the side window. He spun the bucket on itself mixing the separated milk and cracking the frost then filled the bowl and went back inside. Eve Mary had given Lucetta the bucket of whey and holding Raymond at her hip she poured it into the pot along with the milk and curds. The fire burned small. Touching the base lightly Lucetta mixed away. Charlie took hold of Ewan and swung him around toward a chair. Sam slid into his leggings and shirt and buttoned the collar to the top. Lucetta looked over at him.

"You ain't wearing that are you?"

"I got time to work a while before everybody gets here."

She stirred the clabber until hot and dished the blend into the bowls and pouring whiskey into the cups she sweetened the children's with a pinch of sugar.

"Y'all best get over here and eat. Unless you want it iced over."

Elisha came in from the door and sat at the table and Charlie looked at his uncle and found a chair. Eve Mary stumbled from the fire still dense with sleep and struggling not to whimper. Ewan shoveled in the clabber with his bowl half empty before the rest of them had settled.

"Slow down there, boy. There's plenty left," said Lucetta.

Sam took his seat and Lucetta filled his bowl and sat down looking at Ewan. The boy tried to keep the clabber in his bowl the same as the others and to pace himself by tapping his feet three times between spoonfuls. But his wrenching gut got the best of him. The clabber felt warm in his throat and good in his belly but once down he wanted more.

"No wonder you're growing, you little shit," Lucetta said. "You want another bowl?"

She reached at him and pulled the boy into her. Sam let his eyes rest on his wife. She was beautiful but with a hint of mystery in her profile, the line of it angled and her cheeks full and olive and her eyes moss green and penetrating. She made her own small world and kept it tight and ordered with plates and jars and herbs in rows, a web spun over the abyss of her mind. She let the boy go and stood to fill his bowl.

Sam glanced across at Ewan then set his eyes on Charlie and couldn't remember raising the boy. He thought on his answer to Rupert Baxter's taunting out near Stallsburg.

"You sure are lanky, boy," Baxter had said. "Time comes old Gilchrist will boot you off his land as useless."

"At least I don't suck in more food than I grow, you fat fucker."

Sam had stood back quiet as Charlie not ready to leave off fighting gathered up the supplies slower than he would have otherwise.

He kept looking at the boy as he ate from his bowl.

"You stay away from Rupert Baxter today."

"I will if he stays clear of me."

"You do as I say, boy," Sam snapped. "Or I'll strap your ass. I ain't having you ruining your grandpa's wake."

"Listen to your pa," Lucetta said.

"Give me some more food, Lucy," said Sam.

She returned to the table and filled every bowl but her own. They ate almost as fast as she dished it but today it was all she could do to get the clabber made. The whiskey and the sugar made her ill as well. She went to the fire again and lifted the pot from above the flame and walked through the door setting it on the dirt near the porch.

"Eve Mary, finish up and help your ma clear up these here dishes," Sam said.

Eve Mary took up the bowls and spoons and followed Lucetta outside. She tossed them into the pot and with her mother carried them down the twisted and tick-ridden footpath to the inlet pool in the creek just beyond the implement shed. Charlie and Ewan left the table and Sam sat alone with his brother, looking across at the old man on the plankboard.

"Do you remember how much Pa could eat, back when he was healthy?" said Sam.

"Hell, he ate more than any man his size I ever seen."

"When I was young and hungry like Ewan, I'd be afraid he'd eat so much I'd never get none."

"He used to pester me was I done yet so he could clean my plate."

Sam picked at his teeth and looked away at the wall. There was a lot about the old man that eluded him. His father always took to things with ritual calm. Being told how to live didn't shake him. In his last moment he held Lucetta's hand and gathered in dying like a sleeping child takes in the air. The old man had taught Sam all the details of a day. But there was something he held back. He had a gift for music. He could pick up any instrument and before long some lilting melody would spring forth. Sam knew anger and fear and hope in depths the old man never did, and the music was a silence between them.

"Do you remember Pa's favorite tune?" Sam said.

"I don't know as he had a favorite."

Sam took a drink of whiskey and reached for the clay jar and filled the cup again. Then he ran his hand down the back of his neck and gazed out the open door.

"I wish there was some way we could get word to Uncle Burley about him."

"I can't think of any," Elisha said. "Burl's somewhere on the river now, or up on the Natchez Trace maybe. We'll see him soon enough."

Elisha looked down at the table and tapped his fingers on the edge. His brow was creased and his eyes wide and Sam could hear him breathing. His words came out hollow.

"When are we leaving then?"

"As soon as the tobacco's in and we get paid. Gilchrist may get slow with the money if he finds out he's losing another family. So I ain't told him yet."

"Might be better to hold onto that forty-two dollars when we get out to them territories. There's plenty of work around Ste. Genevieve in the lead mines."

"I'm tired of being owned," Sam said. "The land there's free for the cost of a survey. A man named Bollinger over at Charlie Cole's heard it from the governor."

"I don't trust no damn Frenchman, governor or not."

"We'll get our land," said Sam. "Six hundred arpens will be enough if we all work it. We'll need all of us. It's you and me have to keep this family safe and together."

"I ain't sure leaving's the way to keep together."

Sam looked hard at his brother and Elisha turned away. Elisha didn't take well to change and his capacity for anguish was shallow, thin and opaque, almost imaginary, like the green on fallen tree limbs or dust on still water.

"We'll cross the Blue Ridge and winter at White's Fort near Knoxville. From there we can start out in spring," said Sam.

"You think Burley will get there near the same time?"

"I guess."

"I don't fancy traveling any length of Avery's Trace without him."

Sam reached across the table and picked up the whiskey and taking a long drink he handed it to Elisha. They walked toward the door. Sam could hear Lucetta yelling into the trees at Ewan. Charlie carried planks from around the implement shed to set up for the wake. Mist was rolling from the tops of the trees and lifting from the creek pools onto the distant ridgelines. There had been a light but early frost this year. Sam remembered the old man as he looked across the Brushy Mountains and death seemed an insult to thinking. He stepped from the porch and walked down the thin path to the implement shed. Elisha joined Charlie and began wedging a split log plank into a posthole. He opened the door of the shed and entered the room and took in the smell of hickory and leather and mule sweat. The frost hadn't been severe enough to burn away the smell of green that made the tactile world almost palpable in the air. He went to the corner and lifted a pawl and carried it outside to the stone. He began scraping along the edge of the blade.

It took him a minute to get his rhythm but once it was set a flat calm took over behind his eyes. He continued to move to keep the feeling going as the bugs let loose in the woods and his young son's laughter rang out from behind the tree-line.

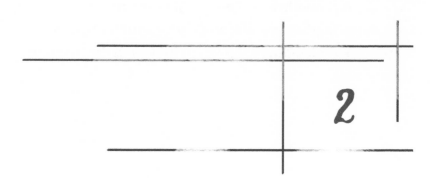

2

*T*hey stood out washed and groomed at the crest of the hill beneath the cabin looking downward at the footbridge over Hunting Creek. People sifted through the trees.

"There's Arch and Druscilla," Lucetta said.

"There ain't no struggle picking Druscilla out of a crowd," said Sam.

"I got good eyesight."

"Hell, you can't miss Druscilla if you ain't blind."

"Samuel."

Elisha wiped the dust from his collar and lifted a jar and washed his mouth clean. He spit the bitter liquid into the grass.

"That's damned ungracious of you, Sam," he said. "I bet a healthy woman like Druscilla is a real comfort at nighttime, if you're short on skins."

"Come to think of it, it was dead winter when Arch married her."

The crowd moved up the knoll along the thin grass pathway cut from the brush. Before the people reached them they turned to the cabin and walking in stood near the wall. When the old man died three days before, Sam and Elisha had lifted him from the bed and laid him on the rough flooring planks. Then Sam ran his eyes across the line of the old man's back and saw the ease with which his father in death seemed to form himself to the boards, sinking evenly into the uneven contours of the rough wood. Lucetta had begun singing over him, first speaking in whispered breaths.

Listening to her Sam couldn't make out the words but he guessed at their meaning. They were a dimly uttered prayer in common verse. Moses and Elijah and even Christ played into them but they took breath from mystery. They danced reverentially near something bleak and impenetrable within and around the old man, something underneath the planks out amongst the dust and weeds and moss-covered rocks between the cedars.

When she was finished Charlie had walked outside and brought in a man-sized plankboard. Eve Mary followed with a wood platter holding a handful of salt and another of moist earth. Lucetta took it from her and made sure they remained there unmixed. She placed the platter on the old man's chest, the salt his spirit and the earth his flesh reclaimed. She stepped back and Sam and Elisha lifted the body from the floor onto the plank. Elisha claimed the first watch. Charlie Cole took over in two hours.

The cabin was thick in heat as people crowded in quiet reverence around the body. In the morning after breakfast Lucetta and Eve Mary had cleared the cabin of the kitchen

utensils and covered the dial plate with a small linen cloth.
A woman's voice began almost in echo and lifted wing-like
into a psalm - *In thee, O Lord, do I put my trust; let me never be
ashamed: deliver me in thy righteousness* - Another trailed in as
the other finished with a second verse - *Bow down thine ear
to me; deliver me speedily: be thou my strong rock, for an house of
defense to save me* - then a third - *For thou art my rock and my
fortress; therefore for thy name's sake lead me, and guide me.* The
room was filled as people spilled in from the yard and from
down the slope of the hill near the footbridge. Sam watched
as they moved past the body, each bending over the old man
and touching him, the men on the chest and shoulders and
the women sometimes on the cheek, all of them taking care
to leave the platter upright. An old woman took hold of a
young girl who placed a milk-white hand on the old man's
face. Sam held his eyes hard on the doorway as two Baxter
boys came through. He looked to see if the old man bled
when they touched him. Elisha glanced away without concern
since his father was old and the events of his passing made
the death seem natural and unsuspicious. The crowd slowed
as the old woman placed a thin and skin-draped hand on
his forehead and ran her fingers down his cheek and took
hold of the collar on his chest and sobbed. A big man heavy
in the shoulders lifted her away and took her to the door.

The body rested on a plank and a gray cat slid through
the legs of the mourners and leapt over the old man toward
the corner of the room. Lucetta's eyes widened and Elisha
touched her shoulder looking across at Charlie Cole who
drifted to the back of the room and picked up the cat. He
stepped outside and walked down the path toward the creek

out of earshot. He ran his hand back over the cat's ears around its muzzle to close its mouth and with the other hand snapped its neck. Then he tossed it into the brush for the dogs.

When the touching was complete and the line of folks finished passing over the body they gathered outside with the men sifting into groups and the women around the table. There were bottles and jars filled with whiskey and long leaves of dried tobacco next to cut strands ready for smoking beside a stack of pipes. Arch Chandler took one and filling it struck a thin stick against a flint. He drew on it long and handed it off to another who took a mouthful of whiskey and traded Arch for the pipe.

"Arch, you help me keep Little Charlie apart from Rupert Baxter," Sam said as he walked up to them. "That fat bastard likes to pester the boy when I ain't looking. I don't want to scrap with that son-of-a-bitch the same day I plant my pa."

Arch nodded and Sam took a long swig from a jar and walked around to help Elisha, who was straightening the skin tarp that protected the table from rain. Lucetta picked up another jar and handed it to Druscilla who gave her a lit pipe in trade. Charlie seemed to drift and as if without knowing it began an orbit around Rupert Baxter. Arch was too intent on the whiskey.

"Elisha, you tail Little Charlie while I get Arch to help me with Pa," Sam said. "Damned Archibald's too dumb to do what I asked him. It's likely as not he'll get a fight started."

"Likely as not I will."

"Not today. Or there'll be more than one ass gets whupped."

Elisha half-smiling walked over to Charlie and took him from behind the neck and playfully wrestled him away.

"Come help me get more tobacco," Elisha said. "Folks will be wanting more after we bury your grandpa. We need to get some more of Charlie Cole's whiskey on the table too."

People gathered around the table to drink and smoke as Arch and Sam entered the cabin with Lucetta and Eve Mary. Lucetta took the platter from the old man's chest and placed it on the table. She walked to the end of the room and picked up a long linen cloth from a shelf near the low ceiling. The men stood at each end of the body and when Lucetta returned they lifted him off the plank just enough so she could spread the linen beneath him. She smoothed all the folds as the cloth lay flat on the floor. Sam's eyes fixed on the waxen wrinkles on his father's face. They were heightened by the gray-white linen framing them. He could feel his insides twist and his head pound and the moisture well behind his eyes. He gathered in the silence near his father's body and pain surged like some viperous thing within him. He knew this moment would come but he didn't know when. He looked toward Lucetta, fearing most of all her seeing him this way. She walked over to him and helped him sit. His eyes stared wet through the door as the sound of voices drifted from the outside.

Lucetta walked toward the old man on the plankboard. Arch eased back as Eve Mary began wrapping the body. Lucetta lifted a fold of cloth over him and covered his face as her daughter placed the ends underneath. She worked her way around making sure the linen was wrapped tightly. With the cloth secure she bound it at the chest and ankles with thin strings of hide. Sam stood up conscious of the weakness in his knees and looked across at Arch who began lifting the body. Then he took his father by the shoulders and carried him outside.

Elisha and Little Charlie were the first to reach the top of the knoll and they stood near the flattened plot of graves. There were twelve there with slabs of limestone thin and rough cut with blades of busted stone near the edges. Lucetta followed with Ray at her side along with Eve Mary and Ewan. She slowed near the small stone of a grave and tightened her jaw. Then she moved forward. Sam and Arch carried the wrapped body and trailing them the crowd moved in ritual procession, the men and women within it lost in a rhapsody of commemoration and unity, the whole of it a mystic embodiment of embattled mutability and devotion. Sam motioned to Arch to wait a moment longer then he moved toward the grave holding his father for the last time. He felt his gut rise and his throat tighten and he could barely breathe. Elisha stepped forward to straighten the old man's back as they lowered him into the ground. Sam took two short breaths and stood. Charlie Cole carried the gravestone. As they lowered the old man he wedged it into the ground. It read:

HUR LYES
THE BODY OF
JOHN SAMU
EL ROLNS WAS
BORN JUNE 13 1736
DESEST SEPTEMBER 27 1798

Lucetta began singing with Ray still in her arms and Sam tuned his mind to her voice. She lifted it on the first word and set it low on the third as the ballad measure sifted through the trees. He felt his throat loosen and his breathing slow to pace and he pushed back a surge of anger, staring down the slope to the cabin and upward toward the Blue Ridge. For the moment he turned away from death and from the knowledge of himself thinking. He took in the song and the dark angelic rhythms of Lucetta's voice and the slow tones of her drifting words. Standing there he eased a bit from the old man's dying and settled into his wife's psalmic reverence.

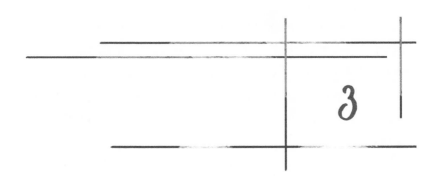

3

*T*hey were in deep water and this far south the river was narrow and dark and shrouded in cane. With his hand on the steering oar Burl Rolens could ease up and take in the horizon as the low bow of the *bateau* rode the current and the *engagés* and *voyageurs* sat sleeping. The breezes were chilly across the bow. He pulled up the collar on his bearskin and took in breath and stared across at the canebrakes as they rolled from solid ground into the river. He leveled his eyes across the shoreline and could see the separations in the trees, and he knew that between them slow bayous cut bankless into the backcountry. There the broad-stemmed grasses and cane stalks lined the shores and the flatboat men had to hunt for places to land. Shoreline on the bayous rolled steep into the water, and in the mud under the surface hand-sized crabs scuttled sideways, making it a painful prospect to wade without boots.

Burl looked down at the men. He didn't envy their sleep. The best kind of rest was waking rest when there was little to command his attention and the noises were distant and sweet. He liked being patron, leading the *bateau* downriver and giving the orders and seeing them obeyed, and he kept his mind off the rich loads that filled the keelboats that more and more were crowding the river. In spite of them he was proud to work the *bateaux*. Even onshore he watched big boats like his own, as their tall sides and low bows passed by languid men on slow rafts that drifted oarless with currents unpredictable and sad.

He steadied himself and cut the boat to midriver to catch the fast water. The bow slid into the swift current alongside a flat raft with three men aboard. The water was too deep for poling and one of the men steered with a long paddle. The other two sat cross-legged with knives bared and hands bloody to the wrists. They were cleaning a pile of channel cats.

"You boys got you a passel there, don't ye?" said Burl.

"Got them mid deep, about fifty yard offshore," one of them said.

"Sitting on that old raft, I guess y'all got plenty of time to take fish."

The men ignored the remark as best they could. One of them slid his knife along the belly of a fish and cleared out the guts and tossed the body to the other who slowly and with method loosened the skin and removed it from tail to head. The man at the paddle looked up at Burl.

"You got any whiskey?"

"Our whiskey's too damn rich for you rafter boys," Burl said. "You best wait. You can rot your gullets in Natchez. With whatever you can afford."

The rafters were silent as they kept cleaning and the man steering looked away. The *bateau* moved past them with the bow taking to the current more swiftly than the fat logs of the raft. There was a mile of visible river ahead of him before it drifted westward and wandered to narrow and approached the delta. Burl's mind drifted. He steered the boat with greater ease than he did his own thinking. He remembered leaving the Brushys after the war and making enough money to be brash and loud when he visited Carolina again. He also remembered the deep waters of the Ohio and rumors of the Mississippi and knew there was something remote and essential in the dim specters at the edge of seeing. It soothed him to think he would see his family again and guide them across the Trace. He knew Sam would leave someday with or without his father, and he wasn't sure if the old man would ever go. He didn't know how many he would meet at White's Fort.

An *engagé* began to stir as a garish light sifted through the trees. He was a big man in a thick skin overshirt creased with grease and cut with holes. Burl kicked him on the back.

"Get your big ass up front there and get me some flat-bread," he said.

"Kiss my ass," said the *engage*, in accented English.

"Get on up, you old bastard."

The big man stood and stumbled through the other men as he worked his way to the bow where the food was kept. The flatbread was in a basket covered in soiled woven burlap and he lifted it and pulled out four cakes and made his way back. He handed them to Burl and reached under his seat for a jar of whiskey. Pulling the cracked cork from the top he took a swig and handed it to Burl. He sat facing him and pulled a slab of tobacco from a soiled pocket in his shirt. The tobacco was solid and round at the edges where the spit had soaked and dried hard again. He took a chaw with the back of his teeth and stared up at Burl.

"We're moving quick in this low water," he said. "You think we'll make Natchez by dark?"

"I expect so, if these sons-of-bitches wake up and get their backs into the oars."

"Those ladies on the bluffs won't take long to dig into to these boxes," the big man said, pointing to the wood cartons of dresses, scarves, garters, and parasols they had carried from the wharves in St. Louis. "I heard some of these garments come all the way from Paris."

It wasn't every trip Burl carried clothes for the gentlemen merchants and plantation highbreds on the bluffs above the shore in Natchez. He had been up the hill on an errand or two and marveled at the buildings the Spanish left, at the curved and fluid iron grillwork and the high ceilings and ornate galleries and long vaulted corridors. It was another world to him and interesting for a moment, but if he stayed he found himself taking short breaths and tightening behind the eyes.

"One or two of them dresses ain't going to make it up the slope," Burl said.

"You might just get a rare little piece up at Madame Aivoges's for one of them," said the big man.

"You're speaking to my purposes," Burl said. "I seen me a little toe-headed one peeking from behind the window last time I walked by there. But I wasn't highborn enough to get let in once they seen me through the peephole."

"It'll take some convincing to get in, even with something sweet to offer. That old madame keeps her girls mainly for them hilltop boys."

The men began to wake and stretch their arms and two of them stood and moved to the bow for flatbread. Burl picked up the jar and handed it past the big man to an old Acadian named Marsal who yawned and pulled the cork free and took some whiskey and passed it on. A low rumble of words lifted from the *bateau* that rose to muffled laughter then to aimless banter.

"You boys get that bread down quick and get into them oars," Burl said.

A few men lifted their heads while the rest went on eating. Marsal twisted the straw on his hat and picked his teeth with a spiked fingernail. The old Acadian took another bite and leaned back against the stern. He looked forward at the younger men.

"You fellas chewing away like that reminds me of a story I heard down on the Acadian Coast," he said. "You ever hear the one about Bouki and Lapin in the smokehouse?"

A few heads lifted.

"Bouki and Lapin spent lots of time together. Bouki was a poor old boy, and he never had much to eat. So he'd go to Lapin's who always had food and a lot of meat, especially pork. One day, Bouki went to Lapin's for the day, and while he was there he asked Lapin about it.

'How come you always have good meat?' Bouki said. 'I can't never get none.'

'I ain't telling you.'

'Tell me.'

'I can't.'

'You got to,' Bouki begged.

'Well, I take it from a smokehouse of some Frenchmen up-creek. Come by later but not before the rooster crows for midnight. Come when all them French boys are sleeping, or they'll get us.'

'I'll be here.'"

Marsal picked out an *engagé* and stared hard at him. He stood up in the *bateau* and set his feet shoulder wide and bent forward animating his words with his hands, pointing them and moving them and miming like a clown.

"Bouki went on back to his house. But he come back too soon. He was hungry and nervous and wanted to get to the smokehouse soon as he could. He went into Lapin's henhouse and got a stick and started poking the rooster to make him crow.

'Crow, you rooster. Crow for midnight.'

"But the rooster wouldn't crow, but only just clucked away but louder than normal like someone was bothering him.

'Crow, I said!'

"The rooster just clucked away, pestered. Lapin come outside, curious about what was bothering his chickens. But the noise stopped, and he went back inside the house and went to bed. After a while the noise started up again. Bouki kept saying, 'Crow rooster, Crow for midnight! Damn you!'

"Lapin come outside again. 'What's after those chickens? Bouki, go on back home! It's too early. The Frenchmen will bag us and we'll get cuffed. Go on back home for now.'"

"So Bouki left but went only a ways away and hid himself in the grass behind the henhouse. He stayed there until midnight when the rooster crowed and Lapin stepped out. They got everything ready and made their way. Bouki took his blanket. He thought, 'I'll steal as much as I can fit into this blanket.'

"When they got to the Frenchmen's smokehouse, Bouki laid his blanket on the floor. He began piling up sausage and hams and everything. Lapin only cut one piece of meat and left, leaving through the busted-out plank they come in by, which was the best part of the secret he didn't want to tell."

Marsal's body changed. As Lapin, he stood tall and moved slow, but as Bouki his shoulders were slouched and his movements sharp.

"Bouki stayed and filled the blanket with everything he could find and tied it together. He tried to leave by the hole, but the blanket filled with meat wouldn't go through. He tried but it wouldn't break out. He kept pulling until the sun rose up."

"The Frenchmen came outside and after a while saw him tugging at that bundle. 'What is that?' one of them said. They saw who it was and caught him. Bouki only said he was real hungry. They got out a big rawhide whip and give him a good thrashing. Then they give him a slice of meat and sent him away, another one of them saying, 'Go home and chaw on this, you bastard!'

"So Bouki ruined it for Lapin. They weren't ever able to go back to the Frenchmen's smokehouse to get food. Bouki spoiled the trick."

Marsal sat down again and leaned against the side. The *engagés* and *voyageurs* turned their faces to the food and Burl looked down at them, then over at the old Acadian.

"What do you expect us to do with that one?" Burl said. "You made this bread taste worse than usual. It's dry as hell anyway."

"Ha!" the old Acadian said, "I expect it'll be the second rather than the first dollar that gets spent on whores under the hill. The first will go to a slice of pork."

"I expect not. It's morning, and these boys is randier than they are hungry," Burl said laughing. He looked at the young men. "You boys, listen here." He tossed the steering oar over to the big man.

"There was a bad man once that died and went to hell. But when he got there it looked like paradise. There was flowers and lawns trimmed down pretty and white chairs to set down on and green leaves blooming out and pretty girls everywhere."

Burl flailed his hands and thrust his face at the men as they ate listlessly.

"'It ain't what I figured,' said the bad man. 'This place is prettier than any place I ever been to.'

"He set down on a nice chair in the shade and thought about it, trying to figure it out. Before long he knew he got put in heaven by mistake because some clerk got the names down wrong."

'I better act natural,' says the bad man, 'or else I may get throwd out of here.'

"He kept to himself for a long time, till a fat man from up north set down next to him on another chair. The bad man looked over at him.

'Mister, what's the name of this here place?' he says.

'You must be new,' says the fat man. 'This here's hell. You're setting right in it.'"

Burl lifted and shook his hands and mimed the flames. Then he twisted his face and lifted his hand to his chin.

"The bad man looked around and seen how beautiful everything was.

'I don't believe you,' he said.

'This is hell, friend. If you don't believe me just wait.'

"Then some pretty girls walked by with dresses riding up their asses. Never in his whole life had the bad man seen prettier women. They was soft and fat around the ass, with white skin everywhere. They pranced down in front of him showing him their tits and laughing and saying for him to come on. Pretty soon he couldn't remember a time when he wanted a woman more, they was so fine. Then he got one of them to go behind some bushes. She went on with him, them sweet tits bouncing, and he knowed he was in heaven not in hell. In about a minute he come out angry and dragged another one behind them bushes. She was about as pretty as the next one, sweet and white and fat around the ass. Then he come out and grabbed a third one, but she didn't do no good for him, neither. The fat man set there laughing and finally the bad man give up and set down on the bench next to him.

'You old son-of-a-bitch. The girls here ain't got no cunts,' he said.

"The fat man from the north just shook his head and the bad man knowed he was the devil.

'Nope,' he said. 'I said you was in hell.'"

The old Acadian leaned back and laughed. One of the other *engagés* looked across the stern and spit a mouthful of dry flatbread into the river. Another stared blankly at Burl. Two others picked up the oars and set them in the oarlocks and faced forward.

Burl lifted his eyes to the bow point and took hold of the steering oar as the oarsmen leaned down current. Their rhythms set and the *bateau* moved at a pace hard to scale on the river. The *engagés* and *voyageurs* looked down but Burl scanned the horizon to the bank a quarter-mile away. The hanging tree branches slipped past as the speed of the boat became clear to the eye and the slow water near the banks seemed still and stagnant. The boat cut the water to midriver and the current made way and the river thinned and deepened. They passed by rafts that used the current as well but kept to the side for the keelboats and *bateaux*. Far off they could see brown specks on brown water that were other moving vessels and Burl yelled at the men to lean in and holding the steering oar he bent down breathing. The current was fast in some spots and slow in others as swirling eddies of stale water faded to glass. He kept his eyes low and looked hard to find quick water for the oarsmen. In the shallows logs and branches and rotted cane were hidden but he could make them out from the way they stilled the surface. He knew to watch for the mudflats this close to Natchez and to be careful of the big logs, soaked and swollen, that would skate the current and hide like snakes. He saw a still circle and pushed the oar veering away from the slick stump of a longleaf pine cut and dumped into the river. He looked forward again and thought on the cutting and the groundbreaking that were changing the river and choking the Trace. He kept to the steering, partly because of the danger and partly because he had never been able to tally the stark glory of the tree-lines and canebrakes along the river with the slim majesty of the buildings along the bluffs in Natchez. He moved the *bateau* past branches and the water narrowed and deepened as the men leaned into the oars until evening, when the firelights on the docks in Natchez broke through the fading light.

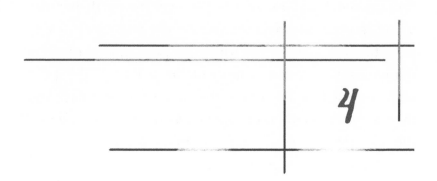

4

*T*hey arrived at sunset with the last wagonload of harvest and settled with Gilchrist's agent for eighty dollars. Elisha and Little Charlie jumped from the wagon and lifted the bundles free and stacked them on the crates near the landowner's storehouse. Charlie's old sheepdog sniffed at the waste near the wheels. Sam counted the bills.

"You're five short," Sam said, looking at the agent, who stood staring waiflike and carbuncular.

"You can count, I guess," the agent said.

"Hand them over," said Sam, looking past the thin man's shoulder at Elisha. "Ain't you boys tired. Let's get us a drink. Let old Bob here work himself over them bundles."

The agent counted out five more bills and Sam took them and turned away without speaking. A bridge of logs crossed the creek and three buildings hung together atop a knoll faced by a manure-strewn road. They walked in the mud along the tall planks rising toward the bustling middle of Stallsburg. They passed the dry goods. The town seemed to take hold of Elisha as he navigated the fences and made a path through the tobacco and indigo and rice all stacked in woven bundles against the walls. The livery was new and the logs on the buildings were freshly daubed and a short man bow-legged and leaning strung a chalk-line down the length of another, setting it to be scored into a plank for fencing. Another man stood on a cut log and was hewing to the line, cutting loose the eight-inch notches and bringing the board to square. They walked with the sheepdog behind them and turned the corner from the livery and faced the tavern. They could hear the sound of an ill-tuned fiddle and the wail of someone singing and the rough hum of voices and laughter and argument. The smell of burning leaf drifted across the road and mixed with the manure and grain and moisture from the dogwood thicket behind the buildings. As they came in the smoke hung heavy but Elisha's face lightened and Little Charlie followed him to the corner where Charlie Cole sat with a group of men. Elisha looked at him.

"You're sitting in my seat," he said.

"Sit down," said Charlie Cole, as Elisha and Little Charlie took the chairs across from him.

"I like that one because it leans up against the wall," Elisha said.

"You got here too late."

"I'd have to get here damn early to get here before you do," said Elisha, swiping the clay jar from him. "Quit pulling on that jug and save some for the rest of us."

He took a long draw on the jar and handed it to Little Charlie. Sam walked across the room to a table near the wall where Gilchrist sat. The old man wore a white high-collared shirt and light deerskin leggings tied with a rope belt and his paunch hung over and his face was puffed red. He was bald on the crown but his gray hair hung in thick strands down his neck. He looked up at Sam with a thin smile and kicked a chair away from the table so he could sit down. Sam stood a moment and then set the chair sideways to the table and leaned with his elbow on the edge.

"Old Bob settle up with you?" Gilchrist asked.

"Not to his satisfaction, I expect."

"You going to give me my rent?"

"Hell, no."

The old gentleman leaned back and laughed so hard he nearly busted the chair leg.

"I hear you figure to be leaving?" Gilchrist said.

"I do."

"What do you think you're going to get by going elsewhere?"

"Something that's ourn and ain't yourn."

Gilchrist rose in his chair and his face turned inward. Sam had seen the look before when he was thrown under his command at King's Mountain against Ferguson and when the old man stood over a dead Granville County boy at Guilford Courthouse.

"There's rules, boy," said Gilchrist. "Some folks own and some don't. Things is balanced out that way."

"They'd be the rules you make along with them bastards in Raleigh?"

The old man's face darkened and his eyes were thin slits of black coal.

"I was in the Regulators with your pa," he said. "We was both at Alamance. Do you remember that, boy?"

"How could I forget with you reminding me every four breaths."

"The point is, I weren't no friend to William Tryon or his government," the old man said. "What do you think owning your own plot west of here is going to get you?"

"It'll get me shut of being a slave to you."

"Nobody's gets shut of being a slave. There's interests pouring west with money that'll put you to work just like I did."

"Not if we get us some land."

"Land will work you quicker than you'll work it," Gilchrist said. "If the good land ain't all grabbed up by the big money before you get there."

Sam looked across at the old man's bulging gut and gray hair and staring into him a slow ache took hold in his throat. He could taste his own quick breathing. Gilchrist rose large in his mind as some black incarnate thing that haunted him. He remembered pieces of the past handed to him in fragments by his grandfather. Rack renting in Ulster and contempt from the good Quaker ladies in the Delaware Valley and closer in time the Whiskey Rebellion and Indian Wars. But in his presence the old man became fleshy and absolute, iconic in his power sift circumstance and order it to his taste. Sam stood and turned away.

Elisha sat drinking whiskey with Charlie Cole and the other men and as Sam joined them Elisha slammed his hand on the table and looked up, smiling.

"I got one for you," he said. "Once there was a boy who was poor and wanted to get married to a girl, but her folks figured he weren't good enough. His grandma was a witch, and she said she'd help them change their minds. She made

up a horsehair witchball, and she put it under the girl's
porch. The girl stepped down the porch and walked over
the witchball when she come outside. Then after a while she
went back in the house. She started to talk, and just as she
did, she let loose a hell of a fart, and every time she spoke,
she'd let another'n fly. Her ma told her to stop or she'd shut
her up good. Then her ma went out for a while, and when
she come back, she let loose too, every time she tried to talk.
The girl's pa come in and farted away whenever he opened
his mouth. He thought they was all sick, so he went for the
doctor, and when the doctor come up the porch, he started
to fart every time he spoke out, and they was all talking and
farting away. The old witch come in and told them God
had probably cursed them because they wouldn't let their
daughter marry. They changed heart quick and told her to
run and get the boy so he could marry the girl that day. The
old woman got him, and on her way out, she picked up the
old witchball from under the porch. Then the boy and girl
got married and lived happy after that."

"There's shit and farts in near every tale you tell," said
Arch, as he pulled up a chair and sat.

"I'd expect you to direct your thinking to the shit part,"
Elisha said. "It ain't about shitting and farting."

"It's about looking out for witchballs," said Charlie Cole.

"You boys are dumb as hell. That's why you both married
nasty, loud-mouthed women. Here's one for the both of you,"
he continued. "One Friday, an old farmer went to town. He
was near as dumb as you. He met some of his friends, and
they all talked him into shaving off his whiskers and getting
his hair cut short so he didn't look like himself no more. That

night, he went on home. It was late, so his wife was already sleeping, or at least he thought she was. He slipped out of his clothes and got himself in bed. She turned toward him, and he was surprised cause she hadn't given him much in the way of tail in years. She ran her hand over his smooth face and said, 'Young man, if you're gonna put it to me you best get at it, because Old Whiskers will be home soon.'"

"I wish I had me more whiskers," Charlie Cole said. "They don't never grow in right."

"Story works the same way the other way around," Elisha said.

Sam smiled at his brother only slightly and looked over at Little Charlie.

"Go on out there and check the team, son."

Charlie stood and walked from the tavern and thick smoke hung to the rafters and the room gathered in a collective drunk. In the corner an old man played a reel with his fiddle but the music was softer now since the hum of voices in the room had lifted higher. The song was long and they listened through it. The man who was singing when they entered had gone outside to piss in the creek. Elisha looked at Sam.

"I'll never understand why you let yourself talk to old Gilchrist since he riles you so much."

"Didn't intend to."

"You never intend to, but you always do."

"He started up with me first."

"Seems to me you planted your ass on a chair in front of him."

Sam took the jar from the table and lifted it to his lips.

"Old Charlie's whiskey," he said, looking at Charlie Cole, who was smiling from across the table. "There's one thing I'll miss from this place."

"There's a lot I'll miss," Elisha said, looking across the table at the blurred faces of his friends.

Sam turned to the door as a rush of voices from outside flooded the room. Men moved to the door in a single body and Little Charlie's voice lifted out of the crowd outside as Sam pushed past the men moving. In front of the livery eight men formed a circle around Little Charlie and Rupert Baxter. The boy's fists were swinging hard but missing and Baxter held him at arm's length laughing, his hand grasping hard at the back of the boy's collar, a trickle of blood dripping from his smiling lips.

"Let loose of me, you bastard!" Charlie yelled.

"Ain't you a scrappy little fucker?"

Sam saw them and sent his voice over the men gathering.

"Baxter, cut him free!"

The big man turned as his expression lost its mirth. He tossed Charlie a safe distance away and landing on his knees Charlie moved at him again. Elisha had sifted through the crowd and took hold of the boy and held him back.

"Your pa's here," he said, grasping him tight around the waist until he felt the boy's forward movement slacken.

Sam stepped out as the crowd formed snakelike into a ring. Gilchrist came from the tavern and with no signal he took hold of the moment as the other men deferred. Baxter remained standing. His feet were set shoulder width and his back was curled forward and his hands were fat and claw-like. He was well over six feet. Sam looked up and seeing him knew he was at least two hundred and sixty pounds. Much of it was fat and bone and his gut hung over the waist strap on his leggings but his arms were strong and he kept the nails on his right thumb and second finger long and carved to points. In the pale light Sam could see them. The big son-of-a-bitch had hardened them with a candle flame and they gleamed under the fire as blood dripped from where he had punctured the palms of his hands. Baxter's face was still hard as he began to smile.

"I was having me some fun here, throwing your boy around."

They stood facing each other as Gilchrist stepped between them.

"You boys been at this longer than I can remember," he said. "Rolens, I expect you'll want to settle this before you leave?"

"I ain't here to settle nothing that happened before," Sam said. "I'm here to kick this fat bastard's ass for taking after my boy."

"You men want to fight fair or rough and tumble?"

"Rough and tumble," Baxter said.

"All right," Sam responded.

"Rough and tumble!" Gilchrist yelled and the crowd let loose a piercing roar that lifted into the trees. Sam began to circle and his thoughts were a cloud and he remembered he had figured ways to avoid the big man in the past. On even footing most days he knew Baxter would win, though the fat bastard was mostly too lazy to fight and too prideful to take on risk. But now he was drunk and stupid, and the liquor in the big man's brain might even the odds.

Baxter shifted sideways, and Sam moved with him, a rage gathering behind his eyes and in his chest and rising to his skin. He knew to harness his own anger and to rile his stone-skulled rival. He watched and circled waiting for him to move, and Baxter seemed to do the same, pressing his nails against his palms.

"How many years did your ma spend fucking hogs out back of your house? Must have been a few to grunt out a prize like you," Sam said.

Baxter was drunk and mad and as he charged Sam stepped aside and kneeled and slipped a leg out dropping him to the dirt. He flew onto the big man's back and reached around at his eyes but Baxter got hold of a loose fold of his shirt and threw him to the ground. Sam spun to his knees but was addled from the fall and before he could find himself again the big man was on him. He shielded his face as Baxter clawed at his ears ripping at the soft flesh of the lobe and slicing at the base with a thumbnail, tearing the ear from the side and dropping a piece into the dirt. Sam felt nothing save the wetness and the warm blood and a strange repose in knowing he had protected his eyes. Baxter's legs were set wide and Sam slipped free and rolled beneath them to standing.

The big man came at him and Sam moved sideways. He circled and let loose a laugh and knew how to madden him and keep him stupid and how to get the crowd yelling for him, since they were animals anyway and like yoked oxen would follow the thinking man instead of the brute. He looked aside at the crowd and Baxter charged again and took him. The big man pressed his arms around his chest and

Sam felt his lungs thin to nothing but Baxter was covered in sweat and Sam slipped free enough to lean back and arch his arms to the front. Baxter was dumb enough to figure himself the winner too soon and he left his eyes open. Sam plunged a thumb into the big man's left eye and gouged at him as blood spewed in a swath down his cheeks. Baxter roared in pain and let loose. Sam took breath lamely and dropped the eye into the dirt. He felt sick from the lack of air and he gagged and took in breath then fell to sitting. The big man stepped forward to rush but his legs were weak and his face sheathed in blood. He took two steps and dropped to his knees. Gilchrist moved between them.

"I think these boys is finished," the old man said.

The crowd moaned and three men came up and helped Rupert Baxter to his feet. They carried him to a wagon at the side of the livery. Sam still gasped for air as Elisha, Little Charlie, and Charlie Cole lifted him to a bench a few feet away. Charlie Cole soaked a rag in whiskey and handed it to Elisha who dabbed it against what was left of Sam's ear. Sam's face drew inward in pain.

"Go find something clean to wrap his head with," Elisha said, looking at Charlie Cole. Then he looked at Little Charlie. "How'd it start?"

"The son-of-a-bitch kicked my dog."

Elisha dabbed Sam's ear again as Sam lifted his head and began breathing more evenly.

"Well, I guess he lost an eye for it," Elisha said, looking at his brother.

Charlie Cole came out of the tavern with a piece of clean linen. Elisha wrapped his brother's head then lifted him onto the flatbed of the wagon. Little Charlie checked the harnesses on the team then climbed into the seat and took the reins. Sam lay silent tracing the silhouetted roofline of the new livery with his eyes. Elisha looked into his face. Sam's eyes took hold of him and held him firm then let him go. Elisha stood still for a long moment. Then he drifted slowly backwards into the shadows, moving toward the tavern to have another drink with his friends.

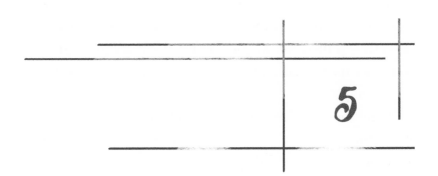

5

 am sat in the chill near an indented plot in front of a thin limestone marker. Diphtheria took the boy just when he was old enough to grasp a jack hook, and when he died Sam defied the convention that the dead be interred in linen, delaying the burial to build him a cedar casket. He remembered hewing the boards, running his palm across the thin surface of the wood, staring down the line along the edge to ensure it would seat properly. He remembered setting the planks in a row, measuring them to the length of his son's body, carefully cutting them large enough so the optics would conform and the boy lying clay-like would look like a child. Sam had sought out the image in his head and sculpted it in anger. It seemed wrong to let him go any other way, with any other image pressing, impossible to bring him back to life even in memory. When the boards were ready, Sam and Elisha placed them together and carefully sunk the corner nails. Then they set the rest into the siding and the casket was complete. Stepping back when they were finished, facing his brother and looking at his face, Sam let go and lost himself. But Elisha took his shoulder and pried his fingers from the Roman claw hammer he held at his side.

From atop the knoll Sam watched Elisha and Little Charlie as they pulled the wagon toward the cabin to load. Eve Mary was inside feeding Raymond and Ewan was somewhere out among the trees. The air was clean and his senses were crisp and the sound and scent of home was heavy in his chest, more now because he knew he would never hear or smell them again. The chill lifted from the hollow and the sun capped the elms and the grasses swayed dry near the grave plot. There were reasons for leaving and he had laid them out clearly and the others had listened. Lucetta was afraid and free enough to say it but still willing. Elisha's silence was a tome. Sam had been sure of himself and until now certain he would climb the wagon and lash the team and roll through the glades toward the Blue Ridge without a backward glance. There was life enough beyond the settlements and possibility and hope he saw more than anyone. It was right to leave, but in the stillness and silence near the grave of his boy he knew it was never right to leave home. He wanted to believe in time and its pre-woven threads and contours, to think that all he had to do was move and when he reached the end he could bow down to a silence that shaped even his own will. But his thinking slipped at the base as he straightened the headstone and tapped it deeper into the ground. Lucetta walked from the cabin to the top of the knoll and joined Sam next to the plot. Sitting down behind him she rested her cheek against his shoulder.

"It ain't easy when it finally comes down to leaving," she said.

"It ain't easy, but it's best," he answered, turning around and standing and facing her for a painful moment. "I was thinking a minute ago of taking him with us."

"I never heard of nobody doing such a thing." She stood up looking at him, slightly stunned.

"I never did, neither."

"It don't seem right."

"No, it don't. But it don't seem right to leave him here."

He pressed his foot downward on the soft sinking ground in front of the stone and he looked down the hill at Elisha who was stepping out of the implement shed carrying a cooper's adze and a barking axe. Charlie was atop the wagon bed, situating goods.

"I guess it ain't practical. We need the space," Sam said.

"We could find us some more space somewhere."

"We can't do it, though."

"No, we can't."

She laid her head against his chest and he came back to her as he rarely did in the light of day by pulling her toward him. She felt his chest heaving. She thought on the boy again, and a wave of cold fear passed through her and she felt her mind waver and hollow. She began breathing hard and Sam felt her and held her firmly by the shoulders and she looked up at him and took hold. She was more in danger of losing herself when her mind crept in from behind. But here there were no surprises and here she could fend off thinking. They began walking down the hill. Lucetta turned and loosened in his grasp.

"You ought to sit again," he said.

"No, I want to get off this hill."

Lucetta went into the cabin, and Sam joined the others packing the tools in the implement shed. He came in and saw Elisha in the corner lifting the reaping hooks from the wall and setting them on the floor.

"We ought to set them somewhere in the wagon where the water won't get to them," Sam said.

"I guess I could have figured that one out."

Sam stepped over and lifted an axe and a hewing hatchet from a stack on the floor and went outside to the wagon. He handed the tools to Little Charlie.

"Put these here tools somewhere where they'll stay dry. I don't want them too rusted out when we get there."

Lucetta had wrapped all the clothing in linen and skin and the bundles sat stacked outside the cabin door. She stepped out of the cabin and yelled out to her son.

"Charlie, step down here and get these bundles and stack them where we can get to them easy."

Little Charlie jumped from the wagon and Sam went back to the shed. Down past the footbridge Charlie Cole came through the trees carrying two sack-like clay jugs in his hands. Behind him were Jim and Helen McGregor and Arch and Druscilla Chandler. Elisha came out of the shed with the last of the tools in his hands and looked down the slope of the hill. He could barely make out Charlie's face and he was sorry to see him now with both of them sober. He was glad Charlie had been there when they delivered the last of the tobacco, when the liquor was there to hold him up. He bit down the back of his teeth and fixed his eyes upward on the tree-lines to level the wrenching in his gut.

He pushed away the thought of leaving. When Charlie Cole was in earshot he shouted down at him.

"Only two jars, you stingy bastard!" he yelled, smiling painfully.

"All I could carry. I only got two hands."

Trudging the pathway Charlie Cole came up and set the jugs down on the dirt near the wagon.

"Them for us?" Elisha asked. "Or are you figuring to just set there and drink all day?"

"They's the last two jugs of my whiskey you'll get for nothing."

Charlie uncorked a jug and handed it to Elisha as Sam came out of the shed. Arch and Jim stepped up and Lucetta came down from the cabin to greet them. Druscilla let out a bovine bellow reaching her arms out at Lucetta.

"Now, honey," Lucetta said.

Helen stood behind her weeping and Lucetta met her eyes. The four men stood in a circle not knowing what to do with their hands, each reaching for the bottle with relief when it came to them, digging into the moist ground with their shoes and carving senseless swirl patterns in the dirt.

"You think that wheel will last you all the way across the Trace?" Jim asked, looking at Sam.

"I guess it'll get us to White's Fort, at least."

"You sure got that wagon packed full up," Arch said.

"That's everything we own and some of Gilchrist's implements to boot."

Elisha managed to get down four long swigs and took a fifth when the jug came around again. He began to feel his chest free up and his stomach loosen. Sam tried to keep his mind from ranging and narrowed his words to the basic matters of travel. But Jim and Arch and Charlie Cole stood in front of him. The familiar taste of Charlie Cole's whiskey and Arch's mild stammer and Jim's beardless grin were familiarities that worked hard at him.

"You boys ever figure to come west?" Sam asked.

"I suppose, maybe," Jim said.

"Someone's got to stay here," Charlie Cole said as Arch stood looking.

Elisha took another swig and thought about telling a long joke but felt the knot cinch again. He managed only to force a smile.

"Charlie figures to be a Carolina whiskey baron," Elisha said.

"I'm losing half my market."

"Not the one that pays."

Lucetta sat down on the porch chairs with Druscilla and Helen, and Eve Mary came out of the cabin and joined them, setting Raymond down on the porch-planks. Helen looked at Lucetta.

"How you feeling?"

"Tired till midday, like always. Nothing different."

Helen turned her eyes to Eve Mary.

"Evie, somebody's going to want to marry up with you soon," she said. "When that time comes, Lucy, you find her a good Scots preacher."

"They ain't so easy to find no more," Lucetta said.

"There's always some fancy-mouthed bastard from the English Church trying to take us in," Helen said.

"Well, there won't be none of them black-gowned sons-of-bitches on any land we own. That much I'll tell you sure," Lucetta said finally.

Druscilla laughed and took a drink from a jar. Helen lifted Ray to her lap and Eve Mary rested her back against Druscilla's legs as she sat in her chair. Helen looked over at Eve Mary again.

"Sweetie, you could get rid of some of them freckles. Just wash them in cobweb dew."

"What time are you leaving?" said Druscilla.

"Morning, first light," Lucetta said. "It'll take us three weeks to get through them mountains, if we don't have no trouble."

"Maybe Arch will get a mind to follow, someday."

"You'll have family in the French territories."

Setting Ray at her feet Helen pulled a pipe and a skin pouch from the pocket in the front of her blouse and stuffed and lit it. She took a long draw and handed it to Lucetta.

"On one of Uncle Burley's visits he said the tobacco tastes different out west," Lucetta said. "He told me it was better here."

"It just tasted like home. I think old Burley was mixed up on going to them territories," said Helen.

"I don't think he ever felt right about leaving Ma and Pa," Lucetta said. "But he met folks from all over during the war, and afterwards some boys come around from out west with all kinds of stories. Set him dreaming."

"And he's too full of piss, too hotheaded and contrary to be around people for long," said Helen. "I ain't never known a man could move from a joke to an angry word and a fight so damned quick."

"Samuel's a lot like him. The dreaming part anyway."

"Sam?" said Helen. "It always seemed to me Elisha took more after him than Samuel. Sam never took after nobody I could see."

"Elisha and Burley like to spin yarns and joke, that's sure."

"Arch always comes home with Elisha's jokes," said Druscilla. "But I get the feeling he ain't telling them right."

"There's a gift to it, I guess," said Helen.

"I worry some about Elisha. He's going to miss them boys more than he lets on," Lucetta said.

"He could stay here. But I guess he wouldn't," said Helen.

"He wouldn't leave Sam and us. But he ain't got Sam's faith in what we're doing."

"You can keep off the homesick for him. Sew a good charge of gunpowder on the inside of the shirt near the neck."

Lucetta took a long draw from the pipe and stood.

"Y'all want to help me get supper?" she said.

They entered the cabin, except for Eve Mary who took Ray and stepped from the porch and walked around the footpath to the truck patch. She set Ray down and kneeled to the ground and reached under the green rich leaves, picked two cushaws, some cress, poke, and two stands of bear's lettuce. Then she plucked ten roasting ears and carried them to a straw basket at the end of the row. She put the rest in the basket and picked up her brother and walked back to the cabin.

Lucetta had set a piece of pork loin to boil and she checked it as it sat swirling in the pot. Fat gathered in a thick layer at the top and spattered against the side as the heat bubbled through. Druscilla lifted a sack of potatoes over near the fire and reached in and pulled out four handfuls and began slicing them skin on and setting them in a pan at her feet. She dipped her hand into a wooden bowl and with three fingers lifted out a palmful of lard and set it onto the cut potatoes and hung the pan next to the boiling roast. She took a handful of salt and sprinkled the pan. Helen took the greens and set them on the table and took to cutting them for sallet. Eve Mary laid the cushaw and the roasting ears into the fire, far enough away so that they would roast and not burn. When she was finished Helen picked up eleven wood plates and went outside. Druscilla took some cups and followed.

The men stood smoking with Little Charlie standing next to Charlie Cole. Elisha was drunk enough to be calm. Sam and Arch and Jim looked at the right rear wheel of the wagon, which was loose at the axle joint and split in spots near the spokes.

"We could get you another one if you could stay on a day," said Jim.

"No, I'm more worried about the weather," Sam said.

"I expect you're right. I've seen a lot of folks traveling on ahead of you."

"If we have trouble, I expect there'll be help along the way."

"This country's thinning out on people. Everybody's leaving."

"Why ain't you?"

"I don't know."

Jim reached down and wrapped his hand around the wheel, running his finger along the thin iron band that covered the wood.

"I think she's solid enough," he said.

Lucetta and the others had gathered the food at the table and the men snuffed their pipes and walked over. Elisha was shaky but kept himself steady, taking a seat slowly at the end of the bench. Lucetta began passing the food around. Sam took small portions and ate them slowly, looking at each of the others one by one and in the end resting his eyes on his brother. They ate in silence with the sun sinking under the elms and the fireflies sending sparks of cold light onto the creek pools.

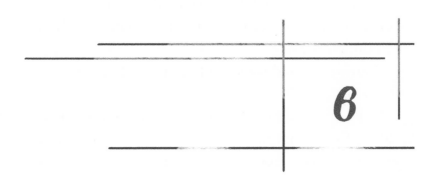

6

*B*url stared hard at a thin man in a tall hat who looked to question him about the dresses and parasol he took from the crate. He walked past the man, brushing him enough to clarify his resolve. He stepped off the dock and began walking down the mud path that led to the taverns and storefronts that lined the slope. He took in the odor and knew there was no place that smelled like Natchez Under-the-Hill. In St. Louis he could smell the green into September but as fall came so did the frost. It chilled the odors and bit hard against every sense but sight. In the south though, where the river was narrow, the moss hung from the trees and the marshes sent a muddy sweetness through the docks that mixed with imported spices and the smell of fish and rivermen and unwashed whores who smiled from open windows. Old Annie Christmas's floating house was moored against the peer, and as he passed a tall woman leaned out and looked down at him, her small wrinkled breast protruding from an undergarment that hung from the bones on her shoulders.

"What you got there?" she said wryly.

Burl looked up and didn't stop walking as he shifted the garments from the crook of his right arm to his left as if she might drop a hook.

"Nothing you old sluts wouldn't make look like trash before long."

She let out a laugh as he passed her and crossed to the building fronts that lined the slope. They were pressed together and black moss from the river gathered on them. The windows held dim glass darkened from the smoke of oil lamps and tobacco, and paint chipped from the panes and dropped and dissolved with runoff from the steep rooflines. The door fronts were short and leaning with no symmetry to them and the latches rusted brown. He passed by them and worked his way through town hoping he wouldn't see anyone he knew. He kept his eyes low and his hat dipped, and at the edge of town King's Tavern rose large against a hill that sloped down with windows facing the Trace. It was the last stop of wayfarers from Nashville and the upper territories and a gathering place for lies and degradation and brute nature unvarnished. A narrow side door was cut into a tall brick foundation mortared against the moisture to allow for an easy route to the taproom. Two floors stood above it made of plankboards cut thin and layered. They held the kitchen and rooms for men with money who wanted to and could afford to enter from the garden stairway. There they could stay clear of the river-men and trappers and whores that gathered in unseemly bundles of laughter and drinking.

Burl came in from the side door and stood in the familiar room with its stone bleakness, to him its easy lack of adornment. Thick beams held the upper floors with wooden pegs and insulated the lower tavern from elements outside that seemed less a threat than the elements within. The open fireplace took up the whole wall and the tall fire burned. Burl had waited for it on the colder nights on the river. He walked up to the bar and set the bundle of garments on top. The man behind the bar was vaguely familiar and Burl felt like talking.

"I'll have me a beer to start off," he said. "Then give me some of that whiskey."

The man turned from him and filled a wooden mug and handed it over, spilling the thin foam down the edges.

"You're dripping it. Fill her up all the way."

"You're awful particular," the barman said.

"I'm thirsty."

The man topped the mug and wiped the bar with his sleeve. Then he filled a cup with whiskey and handed it over. The room was near empty with only three men at a table by the fire and Burl knew he had made it in before the nighttime crowd.

"Y'all got you a lot of guests upstairs?" he asked, searching for a line.

"Some."

He sensed the barman's silence and took his mug to the fire and finding a tall-backed chair near a table he sat down to rest in the warmth. The room began to fill with people as the flatboat men stumbled from the rising chill outside into the lower taproom. Soon there were rafter men from the Carolinas wet and cold in worn skins and French keelboat men and leftover Spaniards and Acadians from the shores near Baton Rouge. There were free blacks and Creoles and lost souls of mixed blood from the Indies as well as Chickasaw traders, and Burl took in their speaking as they sidled to the bar and argued over the chairs. He lifted the whiskey to his lips, savoring the sweet rise in temperature that sifted through his brain.

Laughter came from a corner across from where Burl sat and the sound of voices rose in the room and the smell of sweat was thinned only by the burning leaf. Burl watched and after a while turned toward the door as another man entered. Burl knew him.

"Bill McCoy! You look damn near wore out."

Bill saw him and smiling wryly walked toward his table and sat down.

"What's got you looking so tired?" said Burl.

"Just got up."

"Rough trip this year?"

"I come down from Louisville alone this time. Did you hear about my predicament?"

"What predicament?"

"I cut a man five month ago and got called up for it," Bill said. "The recessing court called for more bail than I could give. Ten thousand bond. Then old Colonel Wilkins paid up on the promise I appear on the day of trial, which was two week ago."

"Why you so haggard?"

"My boat got caught in low water, and I'd have never made it if I stayed with it. So I cut out a canoe and rowed here fast as I could."

"Thirteen-hundred mile?"

"I got here on the day of trial. Old Wilkins was damn relieved when he seen me walk in. I guess they figured I worked enough because they let me off. I still ain't right yet. Damn tired."

"I'll buy you a drink."

Smoke hung to the rafters and drifted in strands along the beams as Burl came back with a full bottle of Monongahela.

"You're spending big these days," Bill said.

"I'm feeling good. I'm to see my family soon. And no whiskey's too rich for my friend."

Bill took the bottle to his mouth and the door swung open, and a big keelboat man pushed through the door.

"Hang on there, you foul-smelling fools and cowards!" the keelboat man said as he stumbled already half-drunk toward a table across the room. "You no-tooth bastards what can't say your own name right to one who don't already know it! I'm here now, and you best listen up if'n you want to breathe into tomorrow! Keep your mouths shut so's I don't have to smell your insides and hear what I got to tell you. I'm the one that can single-handed take on the task of ten men anywhere on the river. Bigger and more raw-boned than any of you and better to look at. I've kilt more men and hauled more stuff and done more damage than any twenty of you together, and if any of you bastards say no to it, and is given thought to testing me, you best look around and take in all you can of living."

He sat down hard amongst a group of loud men at a big table and grabbed the bottle in the middle of it and poured the liquid down with his mouth wide open.

"Might have known that big son-of-a-bitch would show up tonight," said Bill.

"Mick Flanagan," Burl said. "There's a bastard that's made more of himself telling lies in taverns than anywhere else."

"He's got himself a reputation. King of the keelboat men."

"You ever see any proof of it, or talk directly to anyone who did?"

"I always heard it third or fourth hand."

"That don't surprise me."

The taproom was full of smoke as four whores walked through the door. One of them was monstrous in stature, over six feet three in height with a wreath of wilted flowers in her hair and a soiled white hoop dress cut uneven with the lower hoops busted out to knee high. Burl looked at her clothing. She wore thick brown stockings to mid shin with frayed garters tied to bind them. Her fat veined thighs hung over her knees and two rotten teeth hung tight to her lower lip. But her eyes were big and as she scanned the room they seemed kind and he searched her features to find a past in them. It wasn't hard to picture an awkward thin-skinned beauty under the years. The other three were similar in dress but one seemed out of place. She was young and part black, slight of build and not too tall, with dark skin and blond hair cut boyish close to the top of her head, not yet nineteen, perhaps some lost daughter of the Indies brought upriver and left to make her way under the hill. She moved her head in stilted gestures and didn't know what to do with her eyes. It seemed to Burl they looked for someone they didn't know they wanted to find glancing up and quickly down again. She was a bit too thin for his taste and he liked women as white as he could get them. On another day he might not have looked at her. But something in her manner seemed lost and struck him. A tall rafter man from the northern territories, long beard stained in black spit, smiled hard at her as she turned her head from him and looked for something to hold her gaze. Burl fixed his eyes on her, knowing if he stared long enough he could command at least a glance. She turned to him and in a moment saw him. Her eyes stayed with him and her mouth rose to a thin smile. Burl stood and walked toward her and brought her to the table.

"Set on down there and make yourself comfortable," Burl said, moving over and finding another chair for himself. Bill shifted his seat and smiled at the girl and slid the bottle across the table. She took it desperately and lifting it to her lips took a long draw. When she opened her eyes they seemed knowing and relieved, as if they were seeing something they had seen before.

"Is this where you come every night?" Burl asked.

"No, just sometimes."

"You don't look like you been here long," Bill said. "Under-the-Hill, I mean."

"About a year. A rafter man won me betting on the cocks in New Orleans, but he drowned upriver."

The dresses and the parasol were sitting wrapped in twine across the table and she saw them. Burl noticed and nervously picked them up and set them at his feet.

"Where do you stay, nights?" Burl asked.

"A house along the banks across from Annie Christmas's. It ain't got a name."

"It's cool down there," said Bill.

She shifted in her chair and settled as her nerves calmed under the whiskey and the gentle tones and soft words unmixed with laughing. Burl looked at her again.

"You look like you could be hungry," he said. "How about you, Bill?"

"I could eat."

Burl waved a hand at the bartender who in a moment walked up to them.

"Tell the cook we want us some pork steaks and a big pile a taters."

"There's venison and catfish tonight."

"Venison then, but make sure there's plenty of taters."

The bartender left and the young girl took another mouthful of whiskey and Burl smiled and patted her on the hand. Bill leaned back in his chair and the three of them sat quiet. The taproom was full now with noise and laughing. They could hear the sound of bottles slamming hard against the tables and the wood beams and rafters were thick with a layer of smoke that creased the hat brims of the tallest men. The bartender worked briskly from behind the bar and sometimes walked with bottles over to the tables, staring hard and firm at men slow to part with their money. Mick Flanagan sat with five men at a corner table and Burl could hear his voice above the rest but couldn't make out the words. He felt a rich hate rise within him, knowing how reputations were made on the river, as chance events grew beyond themselves in the telling and retelling.

The barman brought their food. There were three venison steaks on a wood plate, smothered in rich red gravy mixed with flour and coffee and spices. There was a pile of fried potatoes unskinned and dripping in lard. The girl looked nervous but Burl invited her with his eyes and she grabbed a steak and began eating with her hands indifferent to the heat. The two men both took a handful of potatoes and putting them on plates began eating. The venison was well cooked and the gravy melted and made it moist. The girl ate fast.

"You best slow down, sweetie. There's plenty. Me and old Bill don't eat much."

She calmed for a moment, chewing and swallowing then taking another bite as Burl took a small piece of venison for himself. Bill lifted the whiskey bottle to his mouth and took a handful of crackling potatoes from his plate. As she filled up she slowed down and with less shyness took another drink of whiskey again, glancing at Burl's feet and the package of dresses.

Burl ate the venison slowly and took the potato slices one by one as the noise of voices in the room rose louder. Amid them he could hear the tapping of feet and the sound of a harmonica and he could see in one corner a group of three Acadians beating out rhythms on a table. But the heart of the noise centered on Flanagan, sometimes laughter and sometimes voices, and Burl could feel his appetite thin at the thought of him.

The girl's appetite too began to slow as she finished her meat. Bill worked his way steadily through the potatoes and whiskey. The sound of argument could be heard again from Flanagan's table but muffled again to talking. Then Flanagan stood up and held his hand out to another man.

"Carpenter, are we settled?"

"I reckon."

"Do you trust me then, as your friend?"

"Yeah."

"Then you got to prove it," Flanagan said. He lifted a tin cup full of whiskey from the table and handed it to Carpenter. "Set that on the top of your head and stand up straight."

"What?"

"Set that cup up there. I aim to shoot that cup from off your head."

"No, you ain't."

"Prove you trust me as your friend, or you're damn sure my enemy."

Carpenter stepped back six paces and placed the cup on the top of his head. His eyes were blood red and his face white and his hands shaking visibly. Burl could see that the man knew his choice was simple. His eyes stared glassy toward the wall for a moment and then closed as Flanagan stepped back on legs unsteady and leveled his pistol across the room. The voices thinned to nothing and the harmonica stopped playing and the men at the tables sat silent. Flanagan took an unsteady aim and pulled back hard on the trigger. The powder lit and sizzled and the ball let loose across the room. The cup fell but so did Carpenter, a stream of blood flowing down his cheeks.

"Why, Carpenter, you spilt the whiskey," Flanagan said, laughing.

The men sat down and the bartender walked over to the man lying on the floor. Burl felt the blood behind his eyes and the hate welling as he rose to his feet. He walked steadily toward Mick Flanagan who was still drunk and laughing.

58

Burl didn't present himself but sent a heavy blow to the big man's jaw lifting him over a table and into the corner of the taproom. Flanagan was startled and confused and began to rise but for Burl the room was hued red. He walked over to Flanagan in the corner and throwing him down again grabbed his head and began slamming it hard against the hard plank floor. He could feel the hair on his arms rise with the big man's pain and he kept on as blood from Flanagan's skull flowed like a crimson glove around his fingers. In an instant he felt the sharp blade of a knife as it creased the top of his collarbone. He stood and saw the knife buried handle-deep in Mick Flanagan's chest and the man who threw it staring past him in grim repose. He then looked across the room at Carpenter sitting at a table, head tilted down as two men daubed the thin wound. Burl walked over to his own table and reached his hand out to the girl.

"That other boy must have had him some friends," Burl said.

The girl took his hand as Bill McCoy stood up. Then the three of them walked out into the street.

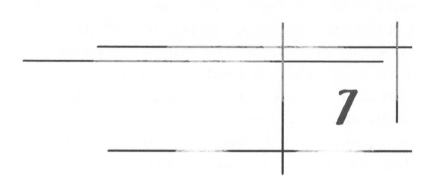

7

They were three days out and Elisha and Little Charlie carried the long-barreled flintlocks Sam and his father had used in the war. They walked together on the right of the wagon with Sam in front keeping an eye on the team. Lucetta drove them with her legs spread wide and one foot on the plank in front of her. The Brushys rose calm and misty and beyond them the Savannah Road and the Blue Ridge. The sun had yet to rise above the peak of Stone Mountain and Lucetta envied the men walking since the chill cut through the skin blanket draped around her. The team pulled the wagon smoothly but this early in the day the wheel ruts were frozen hard and the ice between them made the wagon slip and bounce, lifting her from the seat and sliding the blanket from her shoulders. The tired within her had an insidious smiling life of its own and she felt it creeping into her too early, but she knew she was due a reprieve mid-morning. Still, the cold bit into her and made her angry. She called back into the wagon.

"Eve Mary, you keep them kids well wrapped, you hear?"

"They're warm, Ma," Eve Mary said, holding Ray against her with Ewan wedged between her and the clothes bundles, asleep again in a bearskin.

Sam walked from the team to the back of the wagon and looked at the wheel as it dropped hard and lifted out of the ruts. The length of the Savannah Road crept into his mind. He knew he had been more than foolish in starting out when he did. It would have been better to wait and sturdy up the wagon. But leaving was tough on them and as the time came the wheel seemed sturdier than his own resolve. Near the axle it held fine and he looked up along the thin line of the mountain range in front of him. The Brushys were a landscape of dreams, and when he was no older than Raymond, sitting on the porch of the cabin looking at them, they were etched in memory. They rose oblique and strange and beyond him. His eyes drifted along the ridges and downward to the road. Elisha and Little Charlie had walked ahead with their musket barrels hanging downward, stocks wedged under their shoulders.

"You boys look out for rabbits," Sam yelled.

Elisha waved his hand upward without looking back. The wagon rolled as the sun rose over the ridgelines and the frost melted and the ruts flattened to a muddy palate that caked the wheels. The trail to the Savannah Road creased along canyons and hollows and crossing them they passed small farms and tenant plots wedged between creeks and stands of dogwood and cedar and mountain laurel. Since the harvest the color had broken in the tree-lines and the leaves of maple and alder had turned to dim gold and blood red. Along the tops of the dogwoods bright bands of yellow twisted like brushstrokes amongst the evergreens and long-leaf pine. Cut fields rolled up the hillsides and wedged against small stands of trees, and Sam chuckled as always, struck by their beauty and contradiction. The more hilly and rolling the fields the more picturesque and fine, but with the flatness went the fertility, as the good topsoil would wash from them with the rains leaving them weak and thin of crops.

"Pa," Charlie yelled back. "I'm going on into them woods to see if I can scare up something."

"Follow along this here trail when you break out, and don't be too long."

Charlie ran up a rocky slope of tall grass across a cut pasture and into a stand of trees. Elisha turned and walked toward Sam. As he passed the wagon he called up at Lucetta, who had relaxed into the reins and leaned backwards against the seat.

"You doing all right, Lucy?"

"Yeah, since the trail melted we're smoother," she said, and yelling back to Sam, "Honey, how's that wheel?"

"Fine, so far."

Elisha walked next to Sam with the musket in the crook of his arm. The cold at dawn and the chill of leaving had made him silent for a while, not angry silent, but unable to form words and say them. Now the warmth cycled him upward making him talkative and even inquisitive. The idea of settling west had been with them since they were boys. But after the war talking about it made Sam uneasy and only after their mother died would he speak of it again, and then not to muse but to lay out the when and where.

"There's a whole pile of Chandlers settled up in Kentucky near Boone's Camp and Harrod's Town," Elisha said. "It's well settled there in a band of towns near the Shawnee villages."

"I heard that's pretty country. Lots of trees."

"What's set us on the French territories?"

"I told you before," Sam said, irritated. "I talked to a man said we could get good bottom land for the cost of a forty-dollar survey."

"I expect there's arrangements like that all over, in places with more people in them."

"That's the point, ain't it? More people, less good land?"

"I bet there's enough land for us in a place near a good town with people that like to talk a bit, maybe tell a joke."

"I'm more sure of what I been told by people that's seen it."

"We're headed well beyond the settlements that are set up good."

"There's already a lot of people up near Ste. Genevieve, farmers and miners to boot."

"It's far out."

"It's where we're going."

Sam knew not to reason too long on it, and that his brother wasn't wrong, but he knew also the danger of changing plans and the tenacity of his will when he once set it hard on a vision of his own interior shaping. Only when the leaving was final had he begun to grasp his brother's heart, and he felt a tinge of guilt in calling on his loyalty. But he stuck to what seemed to him true beyond words. The way they lived was all sadness and degradation, and out among the settlements they could make something and live without compromise and with a dignity grounded in work and striving. He was sure that if Elisha didn't see this now he would when they arrived, when they set up a cabin and an implement shed and hung fences on ground they had cut and took in a crop and kept all they were paid. He looked at his brother and nudged him with his elbow. Elisha returned a curious smile.

The wagon rolled on smoothly enough with the rear wheel holding steady. Lucetta sat atop the wagon with her arms beginning to sag at the elbows as she hung onto the reins. The oxen swerved and she caught herself and pulled them straight. Little Charlie came out from a stand of maple and ran toward them.

"I struck on some new deer track about a mile from here."

"We're short on meat," Elisha said, looking at Sam. "That second hog's about half gone. Me and Charlie could bring in a deer and catch up."

"No, I'll go with the boy. You stay here and keep an eye on that wheel. Get the flintlock out the wagon and keep it in your belt till we're back."

Ewan woke and heard them speaking. He jumped out and ran toward them.

"Pa, I'm going too."

"No, you ain't," said Lucetta. "You spend more time in the woods than you do anywhere. We might need you here."

"Pa?"

"You stay here and help your uncle for now," Sam said. "This will be a hell of a long trip. There'll be plenty of hunting for you before it's over."

Sam and Little Charlie and the dog stepped out and cut through the trees into the tick-ridden underbrush, moving toward a beam of light that opened into the meadow where Charlie had seen the tracks. The weeds and grasses and infant trees reached to their knees and upward to their necks and Sam knew that even this late they would be standing naked near the fire tonight burning off the ticks and chiggers and fleas. The brush darkened the woods and muted the light in front of them allowing it only to shine dimly above their heads through the branches. He could hear a wren sing somewhere out to his left, and the music carried into the rhythmic humming of bugs and the swaying of grasses and all of it melted into dark waves of sound. They struck the end of the stand into an uncut meadow of knee-high grass, where the trail of the deer was clear as a creek bed. The grass was trampled and the track was stamped in the mud. From its length it was probably a mid-sized buck of a year or two and large enough to push them to kill him quickly so they would have less distance to carry him.

He was ahead of them and they didn't know the country. They would have to track him rather than wait for another. His was the only sign on the mud path and they were unsure if they were walking a well-traveled game trail. Sitting quiet in a stand and waiting might be a waste of time. Charlie sent the old sheepdog forward as they walked side by side traversing the grasses with the sun now rising above them. Charlie looked ahead of them on the trail.

"Look up there, Pa."

"Droppings. A half-hour old, maybe."

They passed them walking steadily, knowing they need not hurry since the dog had its own work to do. Charlie looked over at Sam.

"You ain't never told me what it's like where we're going."

"In the French territories?"

"Yeah."

"What do you want to know?"

"I don't know. Is it different?"

"I ain't never been there."

Sam knew the boy's mind and the winter and the slow trip across the Trace would do little to ease him. He could tell Charlie nothing that was true beyond guessing, and he didn't want to frame hope too neatly or promise a living he couldn't make happen alone.

"I heard from more than one man that there's good flat land there for the taking, and that there's trees and rolling hills like there was just east of the Brushys."

"I heard you and Uncle Elisha talking about the mines."

"There's lead mining there too, around Ste. Genevieve."

"We could work them, couldn't we?"

"We don't know nothing about mining."

They stopped at a horning bush where the deer had paused to rub the velvet from his antlers. Behind the bush the tracks deepened and spread apart and it became clear that the animal had begun moving more swiftly. Charlie kept talking but Sam was uneasy. He couldn't quite define what was wrong but something had unsettled the deer and it wasn't them. When the tracks were made they were too far away. The woods were silent and they could hear nothing of the dog in front of them. The trail led into what appeared to be a deep stand of chestnut and Sam looked into them.

"Keep alert, boy. Let's find old Tom."

"What's the matter?"

"I can't say as yet."

They began trotting slowly toward the trees, which appeared thick at first because of the underbrush but revealed themselves as only as a thin stand that split two grass meadows. Sam felt the hair on his arms rise and began running faster as they entered the woods. Something was clearly amiss. The deer was running now and frightened and the dog wasn't barking. They opened up into the meadow and at first saw nothing as Sam's eyes scanned the tops of the grass. Then the panther let loose a scream. It stood over the carcass of the deer, its long teeth barred and its shoulder blades piercing the brown hide behind its neck. The old sheepdog stood not ten feet away growling with his lips creasing above his teeth and the black of its mouth in clear sight. Charlie saw him.

"Tom, get back here!" he yelled, running toward them, but the dog didn't turn and stood facing the panther as if he didn't hear. Sam planted the musket stock firm in his shoulder and took aim just as the panther struck. The shot missed. The old dog crouched low and met the cat nearly halfway knowing the wild animal would go straight for the big vein beneath his neck. He managed to get underneath the panther but missed the tender and vital part and got hold only of the thick skin above the breastbone. The dog held with tenacity, his growls strong and steady. But the cat knew it was safe, that the dog couldn't let go this close, and

it swiped hard with its big paws at the old sheepdog's head.
The dog held its eyes closed tight but the cat's big claws were
barred to their full extent and slashed indiscriminately into
its skull and face, clearing out the eye sockets easily and
quickly. Blood flowed in thin rivulets only slightly from the
cat's neck but streamed out of the dog in a dark blanket of
red across his back and shoulders. Charlie aimed his musket
but didn't want to hit the dog. Sam kneeled and reloaded,
dropping the powder and ball down the muzzle as quickly
as he could. The dog held tight and the panther screamed
again slashing at the dog's sides and upward again at the
head. Charlie could see the dog's legs weaken at the exertion
and blood loss but it held as the panther swung him to
standing. The old sheepdog didn't let loose until he died,
and as he dropped Charlie fired. The musket sizzled at the
stock and the ball flew between the two animals as the dog
dropped to the ground. The big cat turned quickly away and
Sam fired, the ball slicing into its shoulder. But the animal
managed to twist into the underbrush alongside the tall
grasses into a thicket out of sight.

Charlie ran ahead up to the two dead animals the panther left behind. He stood over the old dog, all blood and
hair, his head nothing now but teeth and muzzle. He kneeled
down and reached under the body and picked him up and
stood, looking downward. The old sheepdog was limp in his
arms and he felt a shock of recognition at the grim materiality of it. The fur was wet and warm but the body heavy
and yielding. Sam came up behind his son and stood at his
back. He knew to give the boy his moment but was unsure
really when to speak.

"He was your good old dog, weren't he?" Sam said, after a long moment.

Charlie said nothing. Then he turned with the animal still in his arms.

"You got a ball into that painter."

"Not good enough to make him worth tracking, son."

"Reckon not."

"Let's bury the dog," Sam said. "Then we'll see if we can't save what's left of the skin on this here buck. Your ma can find a use for the pieces."

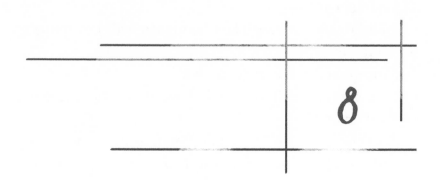

8

*E*ve Mary lifted the Dutch oven from the slow-burning coals. She placed it in front of Elisha who took a draw on his pipe and leaned backwards against a stack of cut logs. Lucetta lay asleep in the wagon with Ray. Sam and Charlie and Ewan gathered foxfire from a rotted stand of trees near the camp. Eve Mary lifted the top from the oven and took a hot biscuit and tossed it to her uncle.

"I expect it ain't practical to make biscuits while we're traveling," Elisha said.

"It ain't much. They keep good for later, if you don't mind them hard."

Elisha couldn't help but see she was filling out around the edges and looking less like a girl. Living at the cabin with each day the same kept her a child. But they had been on the road two weeks and hard traveling stiffened her and Lucetta's weak body and orphaned spirit seemed to awaken her to necessity. She hung the oven high on the ring above the fire to keep it warm without burning the biscuits and then went to the side of the wagon where the food was stored. She lifted the thick woven tarp and cut a piece of fat from what was left of the cured hog. Then she took it over to the fire and lifting the lid from another oven sitting in the flames dropped the fat into the cooking potatoes. She then sat down cross-legged in front of her uncle. The sun had set and twilight was fading and the foxfire glowed rich from the rotting logs at the base of trees. She stared across the flames into the woods.

"Them logs look like they're staring at us."

"Maybe they is," said Elisha with a wry smile. "You don't never know. A lot of times when the moon is out, with the clouds hiding it and changing it, it'll put you in a mood. You may be out walking and see a hanging rock or a stump, and if you're scared of seeing something you'll get to looking at it and think maybe there's a head or a dim smiling mouth with teeth just behind the light, staring away at you demon-like. Then you study it a little more, and you're sure of it, then a little more and there's a body and hands. So you run like hell on home and tell that you've seen a ghost."

Sam and the boys came up holding armloads of rotten logs with foxfire glowing. They set them around in a circle sending a rich red hue through the camp across the faces of the two sitting at the fire.

"Is your old uncle telling stories? From the look on your face he's telling about a haint," Sam said.

She smiled at her father and looked at her uncle again. "It ain't real, though," she said.

"Not a haint," said Elisha. "But a ghost is. A ghost is different. A ghost is a spirit creature that sets around a pile of money. And God will sometimes want folks, poor folks usually, to find it. If the poor folks ain't too skittish and don't run, they can stay there and talk with the ghost and after a while it will tell them where the money's hid so they can dig it out. That's a ghost. Now a haint is something you conjure up in your head. But a ghost is an actual thing."

"How do you know the difference?" Charlie said.

"You don't at first. You got to set and talk to it."

"What if it's a painter ready to rip your throat out?" said Sam playfully.

"Then you run like hell," Elisha laughed.

Eve Mary stood up and walked over to the fire and brought them the biscuits. She did the same with the potatoes setting them down and handing spoons to all of them. They each took two biscuits and sitting cross-legged ate the potatoes together from the Dutch oven.

"I guess your ma's real tired?" Sam said to Eve Mary.

"She dropped soon as the wagon was set still. Her face was drawn down some. But I got Ray fed before he went down."

"She gets like this early on, but she'll be better later, after winter when we're on the Trace. At least she don't get sick like some women do."

"Maybe I ought to drive the wagon and let Lucy set in the back till we get across the mountains to the fort," Elisha said.

"I don't reckon she'd take to it. She gets jittery if she ain't got nothing to do."

They could hear the rhythm of her breathing from the wagon. She was sleeping hard and Sam hoped she would gather herself enough so they could get through the rest of the pass in the morning. If she walked she would worry about the wagon on the steep ridges. If she rode in the back she would worry more. The best thing for her was to drive the team while the men kept a close eye on the wheel. Sam stared into the fire then over at the cold glow of the rotting logs. Whenever he wanted something with a passion too intense the weight of it seemed to level him, as if some malevolent thing more real than sense could capture had set itself unmitigated against him. Lucetta with child at this of all times. But they were here and alive and events always seemed to sort to a purpose that eluded him until it took hold. He knew he could do nothing now but stand against anything that would slow them up or turn them back. He stared across at his brother, who took a swig from a clay jar and handed it to Little Charlie. Eve Mary stood up and took the oven and hung it unwashed on the high limb of a tree. Then she walked to the wagon and climbed in to sleep.

Lucetta woke to the sound of a hard rain against the canvas. The drops fell heavy and popped like musket balls. It had been raining steadily since midnight and the men had crawled beneath the wagon but were well soaked anyway. Lucetta nudged Eve Mary who rolled from underneath the skin blanket and rose to her knees and yawned.

"Evie, get some biscuits out the bag, and give them to the men. I think we got enough milk left for two days for the boys, which ought to get us there. Give the men a jar of whiskey and ask them if they want some water."

"I guess water ain't their favorite thing right now, Ma."

"Well, ask them anyway," Lucetta said with a forced chuckle.

Eve Mary climbed from the back of the wagon. Little Charlie and Elisha were pissing against a tree. The rain began letting up and the moisture glistened against the leaves and dripped from the branches. She wondered what made men think they needed to pee against something. Why not just let loose on the ground? Her father was sitting on a log pulling on his boots and staring blankly at the rear wheel.

"Here's some biscuits, Pa. Ma wants to know if y'all are thirsty."

"No, we're wet."

He took the biscuits and the jar and set them down at his feet. Lucetta climbed from the wagon and stretched looking upward at the drifting clouds between the maple branches.

"You sleep good?" Sam said.

"Hard. How's that wheel?"

"It ain't no worse. But it was damn stupid of me not to get a new one before we left."

"You'll fix it at the fort."

She walked over and sat down at his feet leaning her back against his legs. He put his hands awkwardly on her shoulders at the base of her neck. She suppressed a chuckle at his confusion knowing that his worry about the wheel was displaced. It was really about her. She sometimes tried even now to traverse the daytime distance between them by leaning on him or touching him, and he would fumble and stiffen and struggle to find something to say. He was the same as every other man she had known.

"How much milk we got?" he said.

"Two days' worth. If we're careful with it."

"Ewan's been hungry for it. I'd hate to see them boys do without."

"We can all make it two days more."

She stood up and motioned to Eve Mary and they walked toward the trees lifting their knee-high skirts as they came to the grass. Sam leaned against the logs immune now to the wetness beneath him and remembered Lucetta just after they married, standing with her sister, her skin smooth and brown, naked to the waist near a bucket of bear oil, rubbing it against her with her skirt lifted above her thigh. Now she was lined a bit around the eyes like women always were with years but in other ways she hadn't faded much since then. She was still willful and prone to her own bleak interiors, but hard underneath a weakness he felt sure would fade with time.

Elisha and Little Charlie walked up to him and he handed them the biscuits and the jar. Elisha took a light swig and handed it off to Charlie who had stuffed his mouth full with dry biscuit.

"We'll climb a lot today," Elisha said.

"It will be rocky and the trail will be narrow in spots, I expect. We'll need to keep a close eye on the wagon. Charlie, you remember that."

"None of your thinking about them young women and dancing and such," Elisha said, elbowing him playfully as the boy looked around nervously.

"You're one to talk," said Sam.

They finished the biscuits and hitched the wagon. Eve Mary and Lucetta picked up the two dirty Dutch ovens and cleaned them in the rainwater that had gathered in pools in the fallen logs. Sam pulled the two long-barreled flintlocks from the back of the wagon and handed them to Elisha and Charlie. Then he placed the flintlock pistol into his rope belt. Lucetta climbed to the seat and slapped the reins to the oxen's back. Eve Mary walked with the men as the wagon slid awkwardly on the rain-soaked trail.

They had hoped to reach the end of the east-west road and catch the Great Trading Path late yesterday. But the weather loomed and the traveling had been slow on the narrow passes in the eastern Appalachians beyond the Blue Ridge. If nothing stopped them, they would reach the Great Trading Path mid-morning and once there the well-traveled road that led to White's Fort. The trail that came from the Cumberland Gap through Harrod's Town and Boone's Camp and the Shawnee villages would be peopled enough to help with the wheel if they needed it. Feeling the wagon bog in the mud Lucetta slapped the reins hard to keep it from stopping altogether. The oxen pulled them like a sled through the mire up the steep and narrow slope of the pass. Sam looked on. Rock walls rose high beside the road and out of them single stands of pine pressed out like orphaned roots from busted ground. Water had flowed over the rocks through the millennia and layered them with swirl patterns and circles and concentric shapes of bleak intent that from a distance seemed drawn to a purpose. Between the trees the ground was flat and solid, wet with the rain but firm from layers of pine needles. The wagon rolled into a thin pass in the hillside with Sam walking in front as if to guide them and Elisha in back near the wheel. Ewan was in the wagon with Ray, and Little Charlie walked along with Eve Mary beside him.

Sam regretted letting the boys ride in the wagon through the steep ridge country. But it seemed a long way to walk with Ray at anyone's side. Now it would be a grave mistake to stop and let the wagon bog in the mud and settle spoke-deep in the trail.

"Rein them, Lucetta! Hard, now!" he yelled.

She slapped at them again and the action needed only a little whip of her arm but she felt a hot wave pass through her from her stomach to the back of her neck. Her lungs were open and clear but the muscles around them lacked the strength to bring her air. She knew that the team did the work and things would be no better if she was walking or riding and that too much thinking was what plagued her now. She pushed as the wagon wavered forward to the summit of a hill and slid down into a flat canyon that drifted down to a ravine cut by a stream.

The mud was still heavy and deep and Sam knew the wagon should keep moving. With his eyes on Lucetta he failed to see the hard cliff at the side of the trail. Elisha looked at the wheel as the wagon moved forward. Lucetta's eyes fixed on the shoulders of the oxen as they rose up and down over the leather strap on the yoke. The wagon rolled smoothly enough onto the thin slope along the ridge and Sam walked backwards urging them forward with his hands. He lost sight of everyone but Lucetta as his eyes held hard on the wagon and the team. Only after she was committed did he notice with horror the sixty-foot drop to the rock-strewn water below. He steadied himself and the wagon seemed to move straight until Elisha's voice rung out.

He was sure it was the wheel. He ran forward heading straight for Lucetta whose face was white hot. Her eyes were fixed on the team and he flew past her into the back of the wagon over a barrel and past the clothes bundles where Ewan sat with Ray in his arms wedged against the gate. He could sense the downward slope of the wagon bed where the structure had given way, and he could feel the wagon slide backwards. The right edge of the opening was still on the road and he managed to work against the pull of the earth and scoop the boys up into his arms. Elisha and Little Charlie had found a foothold on a ledge beneath the ridge and were underneath the wagon trying to push it upward. Eve Mary was at the opening. She took hold of the boys as Sam dropped them and rolled into the mud.

"Hit 'em, Lucetta!" Sam yelled as he stood but she had already done it. The blood rushed and her head pounded as she slapped them harder. The wagon stood still for an instant and Sam slid underneath with the others and pushed. She didn't know that the boys were out or that the men were underneath the bed. She felt the wagon slide along the ridge and she hit them again pushing back hard at the thought of falling. She could see the shoulders of the beasts in front of her clenched and tight with the weight and one of them bellowed loud. The wagon still slid, for a moment it seemed into the vortex behind her. Then she felt something catch and the wagon began to rise. It rolled onto the road and across against a cliff. She let loose the reins and fell forward off the seat as the bluffs in front of her faded to gray mist and finally to black. Sam stood up from the ground. The weak wheel was solid. But the axle was busted like an old bone.

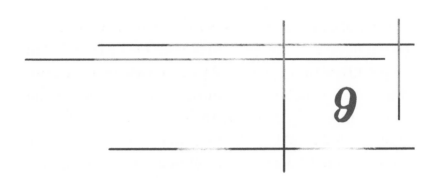

9

Burl lay awake staring through the dark glass of a window at the light of fires burning in the street. He was calm and content to feel the bed underneath him. The mattress was old and the slats pressed his back but they were evenly spaced and he could stretch out without having to huddle himself against the cold. The girl lay asleep next to him. She was olive skinned in the firelight and her hair a dim yellow and her narrow hips glistened as if she had just stepped from a pool of water. She lay sideways facing him, her lips sometimes touching his shoulder. He pushed away the thought that youth was damn near apocryphal under the hill. He looked down at her as she slept. She seemed satisfied, less by him than by a good meal and a warm bed. He stood up and walked to the window and looked through the dark panes onto the muddy street toward the docks. He could see Annie Christmas's house floating in the still water and even this late he could make out the moving shadows through the dim interior light. There was no music and the streets were silent save the sounds of insects between the buildings and breezes among in the eaves.

He looked far up the street to Madame Aivoges's, and though he could only make out an outline he could fill in the picture with memory and with stories he had heard. In spite of his doubts he let himself believe them. He had seen the white curtains from the street and the clean and newly painted plankboard siding, and he had heard of the richly carpeted flooring and soft beds and of the green-eyed madame who with theatre and courtesy served wine instead of whiskey. He had heard that she smiled as she introduced the young white and mixed-blood whores, who feigned innocence well enough to play into the conscious fictions of the most jaded men. Truth and falsehood were hard to distinguish and under the hill no one cared to parse them. When the only sounds around him were inhuman he thought on it and understood vaguely their need for the lies. He looked for a moment more at the house of finery and then into the room again at the bundle of garments under the bed. The girl still lay sleeping as he walked over to his clothes, which were strewn on the floor. He picked up his shirt and stockings and put them on. He stepped into his leggings and boots. The girl stirred a bit as he stood cold silent and in the lines of her face he saw the dim contentment of dreams. He knew it was a feeling that would come to her only as thin respite from the tobacco-stained beards and foul breath of the flatboat men and trappers. The garments still lay there. He looked at them for a long moment. Then he left them and walked out the door.

❦

He was nine days out riding an old gray he had bought for two dollars. The Natchez Trace was narrow in spots but always wide enough for a wagon. The moss and thin-stemmed grasses grew quickly between the wheel ruts forcing him to ride along the side. He sometimes crossed the green mound in the middle depending on the scenery and the old mare would stumble and catch her footing again in the hardened mud. The road was at its driest in the fall as it cut through the rock, slicing sideways to reveal contortions and twisted layers of earth. The limbs of willows and bald cypress hung across the trail and clasped each other like fingers in prayer as the moss hung in thick sheets downward at times to the level of his eyes. The trunks of the trees were thick and green and the shadows seemed to harbor a malignity present and real, manifest in the outer dark that dimmed the shape of things. Spending so much time on the wide river under the sky made him uncomfortable here, since the sun had yet to set but the darkness was pervasive under the thick branches. He kept his eyes ahead, knowing that somewhere out amongst the trees, between here and the Chickasaw Agency, there were men and women who would kill for a dollar and rape for nothing. But out there also, cloaked in the moss, was something beyond knowing that held the materiality of objects before it like a sacrament.

He continued forward running his eyes along the angle of a split rock and beyond it in the woods he heard a stirring of dried leaves. He straightened his back as the hair on his arms began to rise and he wrapped his hand around the grip of his flintlock. He pulled it smoothly from under his belt and rested it on his thigh. The rustling was still there and became louder, and he stopped the mare and pointed the flintlock toward the trees.

"Step on out of there!" he yelled.

The rustling kept up and he yelled again.

"Now!"

Out from behind the dogwoods stepped a tall man as thin as a branch wearing a black suit and tie. He appeared worn and out of place and his clothes were caked in mud and sap.

"Don't shoot, damn you!" the man shouted, lifting his hands and holding them palm up at Burl.

From behind the man stepped two Chickasaws dressed in skins with worn leather boots and tall black hats probably stolen or borrowed or bought cheap. Their hair hung to their shoulders and beads hung from the lower strands.

"Who are you?" Burl said.

"William T. Craig of Nashville," the white man said. "These Injuns is with me."

"What's your business here?"

"I trade produce. Just brought three boatloads to Natchez," said the white man. "I got other men dragging the keelboats upriver. We three went overland to get home quicker but our horses got stole." He paused a moment. "Are you a damned killer? If you are then get done with it."

He stood straight up and closed his eyes and pursed his lips tightly. Burl reached out his hand.

"Climb on up here," he said. "Your Injuns can walk behind."

The tall man's posture eased and he walked toward Burl and taking his hand spun upward onto the back of the mare as they began forward. The Chickasaws followed the horse staying back twenty yards or so, walking side by side on the hard wheel ruts.

"What's your name, mister?" the man said. Burl saw that in spite of his height and formal look the man was young, not much more than eighteen years old.

"Burl Rolens."

"What you down here for?"

"I'm patron on a river *bateau*," Burl said. "You don't look like you know the Trace too well. You'd have done better to stay with your boats."

"I expect you're right," the young man said. "This is my first time out. My pa sent me out on the family's business and I guess I was anxious to show him I done it right."

"This ain't the place to be traveling with money."

"I figured my Injun's would keep me safe."

Burl looked back and saw that the Chickasaws had disappeared into the woods. He held tight to the flintlock and sat up straight and ran his eyes across the trees. They passed the dogwood thicket and the trail evened out as they entered a stand of white oak that spread out for three hundred yards in each direction. The trees themselves seemed alive and knowing as they peered eyeless past them into the brush. Burl stiffened in the saddle.

"What's wrong?" said the young man.

"I don't know yet."

He heard a rustling again from the side and knew it was the Chickasaws. They stepped out of the brush. Burl stopped the mare.

"Well?" he said, looking at them.

"Two people following us," one of them said. "A big man and a big woman."

"You Injuns best hide yourselves. We got to move fast."

The Chickasaws began running off the trail past the white oaks into the thick brush beyond. Burl kicked the horse hard, incensed at himself for not spending more on a younger one. It was a mistake impermissible at his age. The mare stepped into a trot and then into her best guess at a gallop.

"What the hell's wrong?" the young man said. "Who's behind us?"

"I ain't sure," Burl said.

The mare hugged to one side of the trail near the cliffs and the young man held tight around Burl's waist. Burl knew it would be best to keep the horse away from the short cliff sides but held her where she was rather than risk her tripping on the mound between the wheel ruts. She seemed to pick up speed just as they came to a part of the road where the cliffs were four feet high. Suddenly Burl's sight went blank and he felt the weight hit him as he fell hard onto the ground.

He stood up still spinning and sick in his gut from the loss of air in his lungs. The young man was unconscious on the ground and his right leg was fractured. Two men were on Burl quickly holding him under the arms. Calmly walking up the trail was a big man on a dust-gray gelding and with him a woman of near equal breadth. The big man wore tight skin leggings of dark brown and moccasins tied upwards to the knee and draped around his shoulders was a thick wool overcoat with a wide collar once in fashion but now absurd and vainly theatrical. He seemed uncomfortable and slightly constipated, stiff and irregular in his composure. His hair hung in tight curls down to his shoulders and was braided around the ears and tied with red cloth. The woman was big-boned and ugly, with jaws that edged outward beyond her ears and whiskers that shadowed around the edge of her mouth. She wore a thick gown that conspired with her bulk and nearly hid the protruding girth of her pregnancy. Burl was still stunned from the fall and the figures before him floated like specters. He began to find himself, and as his mind regained balance it welled full in animal rage, not yet at the big man and his hideous wife but at himself for being so foolish. He should have sensed them without the Chickasaws. He should have hung far enough away from the cliff walls to avoid being waylaid. Instead he did the first thing that came to him and ended up flailing on the ground next to a green kid with a busted leg.

The big man sat atop the gray gelding, staring at him as the woman spit black tobacco-stained mucous onto the wet mane of her horse.

"My guess is you're Big Harpe," Burl said. "And that torturous lump a shit next to you'd be Susan Roberts."

"You heard of me?" the big man said, smiling cruelly.

"Didn't hear nothing to recommend you," Burl said. "Except that you're a sick murdering coward and thief."

Big Micajah Harpe looked past Burl to the men that held him and then down at young Will Craig.

"Pick that boy up and take these bastards back to camp," he said.

One of the men lifted the young man onto the woman's horse. She seemed not to notice. She began moving forward before they had a chance to set him comfortably. The other man stepped back from Burl as Harpe leveled a musket and commanded him forward. Burl began walking and in a moment felt a slow pain in his shoulder. But he stood up straight and kept his eyes facing front. He was becoming clearer and clearer in the head and he knew his nemesis now was fear together with the impulse to blood that had taken him at King's Tavern. The men before him were mostly stupid but they knew how panic took hold of people and they could use it to work them into anguish. He knew that defiance would give them pause and make them blink and perhaps bring him a chance opening to freedom.

The trail narrowed and widened as they moved forward, and he stuck to the left side of the road trying to walk steadily. He could tell the sun was setting as they passed from the grove of white oaks into a thick stand of cane that rose above his head. The moss hung from the willows above him and he felt for a moment the impulse to run but he mastered it and continued. As they passed through the cane they came to a clearing bordered parallel to the trail by a pool of standing water. He could see it was a wide spot in a bayou rimmed at the top by a cloud of hovering gnats and mosquitoes. In the center of the clearing a tall figure sat on a white horse and in front of him was a man standing, shaking at the knees, his hands held stiffly at his sides. At his feet was another lying dead with a single hole in the center of his forehead. Coming into the clearing from the other side was a short man and two women, both pregnant.

The horseman was refined in appearance, with tight-fitting riding pants and a long frock coat that fit him well. He wore a crimson hat of dull satin that came to a point in regal fashion above his eyes. His face was shaven close and he wore a powdered wig that dusted his shoulders only slightly. He held a flintlock firmly in his hand as he sat straight on the horse not in contrivance or pretense but from habit. He looked beyond the man shaking at his feet as if he barely noticed him and in a smooth motion lifted the pistol and sent a ball into his chest. The man fell with his arms and legs dropping like string as the blood trickled in a thin rivulet onto the ground. He turned his face to the small man and the women who quickly ran to the bodies and began rifling through the clothing. Both dead men carried pouches with money, which the three scavengers gave to the horseman.

Big Harpe pushed Burl forward with the stock of the musket toward a tall cedar at the side of the clearing. He held him up against the tree and tied him firmly. Burl lifted his face.

"I guess a dumb fool like you has got to get his orders from somewhere," Burl said. "I suppose the man up there's Sam Mason?"

Burl knew that to provoke the big man too much might move him to the knife. But he knew the greatest pleasure Harpe took was in slow pain, and that with each insult the captives became delicacies to be savored for when there was time for real sport. Harpe stayed silent and tied him snuggly to the tree. With effort Susan Roberts stepped from her horse and hauled Craig by the feet and dropped him to the ground. The shock of the fall woke him dimly and he sat up. Mason motioned to the little man who carried Craig and lashed him to the tree next to Burl. When they were tied he walked back to the center of the clearing where the dead men lay. The outlaws gathered in a circle.

"Who are these people?" Craig said, groggy, his voice vibrating and unsteady as Burl looked forward without moving his eyes away from Big Harpe.

"Sam Mason and the Harpe Brothers," he said. "The big bastard that brought us in is Big Harpe. The little one that tied you up is Wiley, Little Harpe."

"They look like they're part nigger," Craig said, wincing from the pain in his leg. "From them black curls."

"You ain't the first to speculate on that," Burl said. "I know they're Tories from North Carolina, which weren't a popular thing to be after the war. They took to murdering for pleasure all along the territories up in Kentucky and Tennessee. Consider yourself lucky. Your about to get kilt by some of the more well-known sons-of-bitches on the Devil's Backbone."

"I ain't dead yet," the young man said, his voice gaining in steadiness. Burl looked sideways at him. Craig looked forward.

"They got women working right along with them, by God," he said.

"That big ugly one's Susan Roberts, and the little blond one's probably her sister Betsy."

"Hard to believe they're sisters," Craig said. "The little one's kind of pretty."

"The other one must be Betsy Rice. I heard her pa was a preacher in Knoxville."

"How do you know so much about them? You seen them before?"

"Sick bastards like that get reputations fast." Burl said.

"What about that fancy son-of-a-bitch?" Craig asked.

"He's an odd one to be leading these bloody fools. He's a well-born Virginian that served with the Continental Army. He's a planner and a smooth talker but a damn killer along with it."

Sam Mason calmly turned the horse and walked into the trees out of sight with the two men that had been with Harpe following him. Wiley Harpe went over to a saddlebag on the ground and took out a clay jug. His brother saw him and walked over and grabbed it from his hands and uncorking it took a long draw. Then he walked over to one of the dead men. He laid the man straight on his back and extended his legs. He took from the side of his belt a long knife. It was silver and dull and curved from the base of the blade to the top and there were rough serrated notches cut at the tip. He stripped the dead man's shirt from his front and plunged the knife into his gut six inches below the navel. He pulled the knife out nearly all the way and began slicing with the rough edges up toward the chest. Blood flowed in a thin sheet down the side as Harpe moved the knife up and down. Big Harpe's eyes were wide and intent and his face was far away and blissful as his little brother came over and knelt down and began digging his hand into the cut, separating the abdominal muscles and revealing the insides of the dead man. The innards were white and wet and lined in red and since the air was cool they steamed upward past the faces of the assailants into the air. The three women gathered hand-sized stones at the edges of the clearing.

"Oh God," Craig said, gasping.

"Try not to puke," Burl said as he looked forward, grimly trying to hold his face steady in case the murderers glanced over at him. The sun had set and the stars seemed to float above the silhouetted tops of the cane stalks and above the oak groves behind them. They seemed the same to him as they did when they shined above the porch of his brother's house or on the river late at night or even as they danced above the docks in Natchez. They peered like witnesses and he imagined them the distant lit windows to a divinity remote and separate but discerning and aware. For a moment he found himself lost in the blood and killing and he looked from them over at Craig, who held his lips pursed and leaned forward averting his eyes from the scene in front of him. Wiley began to glance at the young man, looking up at him from the gore. Craig tried to keep from meeting the murderer's eyes, and Burl stared forward as the rage began spinning in his belly and upward behind his eyes. He saw the guts split open and the dead face of the corpse and he imagined with grim pleasure that it was Big Harpe's face staring lifeless into the sky. The big man took another swig from the jug and handed it to his brother.

"They may get drunk enough to hold off on us till tomorrow," said Craig.

"Maybe. Or the liquor may make them more bloody."

"Damn," the young man said, staring forward wide-eyed.

"You got to prepare yourself," Burl said. "If they start in on you, get into your own head. Pick out a point in the sky and stick to it. Remember, them bodies you're looking at are just meat. They ain't men no more. The men they was is somewhere else."

"A point in the sky?"

"Pick out a bright star or something."

The women walked over to the brothers with their dresses lifted high and immodest above their knees carrying piles of smooth stones. They dropped them to the ground and stood waiting. Together the Harpe brothers dug their hands wrist-deep in the dead man's insides and lifted the intestines from the abdominal cavity and dropped them in a pile. Big Harpe severed them and when the space was clear the women began filling the man with stones. Once the cavity was full big Susan went to her saddlebag and pulled out a large needle and some thin line. Walking back to the dead man she attached the needle to the yarn and began closing the cavity. Then the Harpes lifted the man by the shoulders and feet and carried him over to the bayou near the clearing. When they reached the edge they both stepped knee deep into the water and tossed the corpse into the center of a deep pool where it sunk like dull matter into the reeds and mud.

As they walked back to the clearing to start into the next one Craig began to take short breaths inward and the air spun in his brain and his eyes gathered upward around his lids. Burl thought he might lose him but lost none of his respect since most boys he knew would probably have wet themselves on the trail. It was best that some blissful delirium take him somewhere early, since the Harpes who didn't know much knew well the depths of suffering and that a victim's clear mind would lift him to staggering heights of pain. They would pay less attention to the boy now and maybe they would only toy with him a bit and save them both till tomorrow. The mist was evanescent in the starlight

and seemed the outer projection of memory, shaping itself
and altering its contours and sifting into his mind in images
of Lucetta bathing Little Charlie when he was small and
Elisha laughing and Sam wide-eyed and young around the
fire the night before the battle at Guilford Courthouse.
Damn these bastards, he thought, because he knew they'd
shackled his mind as well as his limbs. They forced him to
think away the best of things since with the thinking came
a fear exquisite and gnawing and too much even for his age
and studied repose.

After loading the second corpse and sinking it Big Harpe
walked toward them. He was bloody to the elbow and Craig
was still awake but had fallen into a dreamy babbling. Burl
emptied his head of everything and stared forward eyes
thin at the big man. Harpe stepped past him and drawing
a knife cut the ropes that bound Craig to the tree. As he
dragged the boy toward the clearing Burl could see that
the big man had been sloppy and sliced along the wrist but
missed the artery as blood trickled in trace amounts into the
boy's hands. Harpe dropped him to the ground in front of
a fire and his brother lifted him up and leaned him against
a stump. Then Big Harpe staked Craig's boot to the hard
ground and cut his pant leg to reveal the thin flesh above
the skin. Little Harpe held the blade of his knife above the
fire as the boy's head rolled in circles and the edges of his
mouth creased into a twisted smile. The women were tired
from gathering stones and had gone out for the night leaving
the men to drink. Big Harpe stood up and took another long
draw and stepped back. His brother kneeled down and took
the knife to the boy's lower leg, slicing first into the thin skin

and flesh in the front and then quickly into the bone. There was little blood at first and the bone cut too cleanly so Little Harpe slowed down and looked upward at the boy's face. The screaming rose from his gut upward but Little Harpe seemed unsatisfied since from the boy's expression its source seemed distant and undefined. He slowed the cutting still more and the screaming drifted to sobs that seemed more immediate to the knife. A thin smile grew on Little Harpe's face. Big Harpe looked over at Burl who forced himself to look directly at the boy and set his jaw tightly. The big man walked over to Burl and standing in front of him looked him straight in the eye.

"You see that, do you?" he said.

"I see the future," Burl said. "My guess is after you finish off with me and that boy, there'll be someone waiting for the both of you."

"Who'll that be?"

"Don't know. Don't matter."

"Well, if I figure right it won't be you or any of yourn."

"That don't matter, neither."

Big Harpe looked at Burl with an expression that stopped short of anger. It sent a chill into Burl since his best ally was the big man's rage. He stopped thinking on the possibility of escape. The only hope for rescue was the Chickasaws who were damned Indians anyway and were halfway to Nashville by now spinning lies in their heads about how they tried but failed to save the boy and the money he carried.

Little Harpe had worked through the bone and into the thick muscle behind it and the blood flowed in a stream onto the dark ground. When the leg was cut he pulled it from the stake and stood up unsteadily, holding it upward and smiling and howling over at his brother. Mercifully the boy had lost consciousness and his head leaned back like a weight and Burl looked at him as he lay in odd relief against the dim speckled sky. The stars seared his eyes now and the moon rested like inlaid granite above Little Harpe's shoulder. He tossed the leg off into the distance and dropped to sitting, exhausted and drunk. Big Harpe walked over to his brother and sat down next to him and Burl knew he had been spared at least until morning.

Burl sat up straight and passed his eyes across the tree-lines and traced the shapes of constellations and worked hard not to think about tomorrow. He could make out the shape of the boy's body and he knew he was either unconscious or dead from fear and blood loss. The brothers and their consorts were deep in sleep.

As his mind drifted into memory again he felt the tugging of a rope, and just as he did he saw a shadow shape move past him quietly toward the boy. The knife cut into the fat of his palm only slightly as the rope loosened and dropped to the ground. *Damned if it ain't the Chickasaws*, he thought, as the shadow shape and the boy drifted toward him. He knew that to take on the brothers without weapons was foolish, even with them drunk. But it ate at him to leave without seeing them dead and sightless in the moonlight. He stood up steady and slow and quietly followed the Indians into the canebrakes.

10

The Chickasaws worked at the boy's leg as Burl held him from behind. The wound was fresh and moist and bled steadily. One of them held the thigh in the crook of his arm as the other washed the wound and tightened a tourniquet. He had already lost a lot of blood. The Harpes were craftsmen and suffering was their medium and if they had their wits they would have seen the beauty in severing the healthy leg and leaving the busted one complete. But drunk and stupid they cut off the fracture and left the boy lame but still able to work at something if he healed. Infection was looming though and the blood loss heavy. The boy woke and stared into the darkness at the silhouettes of the Chickasaws. Burl could see his pain and weakness and fear of dying. He felt the boy's breathing and sensed the stillness of a body losing itself and he held him tighter and pressed his face against his head. He could feel hot tears coming to his own eyes. They burned him and maybe he could hold them but they found their source in his own wellspring of contradiction. He looked across at the Chickasaws and whispered down at the boy.

"You calm yourself now, son," he said. "Your Injuns saved us both. We'll lay you out on a gurney and get you some-place safe."

The boy's breathing seemed to ease at the tone of his voice. Burl's words came out smooth and deep and mellow and evoked in the boy some dim memory of a time before memory. Burl drifted into a song he used to sing to the children in Carolina.

"Old Joseph was an old man, an old man was he - And he courted Virgin Mary, a maid of Galilee - And Joseph, he and Mary, were walking one fine day - 'Here are apples and some cherries, so pretty to behold.' - Then Mary said to Joseph, so meekly and so mild - 'Joseph pick me cherries, for now I am with child. - Then Joseph he got angry, in anger all he flew - 'Let the father of your baby pick cherries down for you.' Then the babe it spoke a few words, a few words to the tree - 'Let my mother have some cherries, bow down you cherry tree.' - The cherry tree it bowed down so low, bowed down onto the ground - And Mary she ate cherries, while Joseph stood around - Then Joseph he took Mary, he took her on his knee - 'Oh tell me of your baby, when will his birthday be?' - 'On the sixth of January.' - the babe said softly - 'On the sixth of January, my birthday will be.'"

The boy drifted and the Chickasaw tied the wound and leaned back and straightened himself as the other gently set the leg on the ground. Burl could hear a breeze drift through the upper branches of the oak trees and thought a moment on the sound of the wind at midnight, strange and impure, as it went from still to whispering and back to still again. The same stars sat rigid in the black sky and a thin cloud dimly lit drifted like a linen sheet in front of them. Burl looked at the Indian and said his first words to him since their rescue.

"Are we losing him?"

"Too much blood gone," the Indian said painfully.

"You couldn't get in before them killers was asleep."

The boy's chest began to heave and Burl could feel him fight for breath. He lifted the boy and held him tighter and rested his cheek against his face again. He wanted to make an end for the boy that was somehow separate from the horror he had last seen. He wanted to reach into his head and anchor his thoughts somewhere apart from the image of Little Harpe drunk and pain-nourished grinning at him. He drifted into the last line of the song again.

"*'On the sixth of January.' - the babe said softly – 'On the sixth of January, my birthday will be.*" Rhapsodically again, "*'On the sixth of January, my birthday will be.'*"

He felt the boy's lungs fill and empty and he pulled him tighter as the body took on weight and settled against him in death. He felt a surge of something in him. It worked at his inner crust and twisted like a copperhead, snapping at his inner carriage and mauling him. He looked down at the boy's face. Craig stared directly at Burl with a stark and empty nothing in the milk white of his eyes. In the center they were brown in the daylight but in the dimness of midnight were coal black and sharp reflecting thin pricks of starlight. His mouth stood half open and Burl ran his hand along the boy's forehead and downward closing his eyes. He was older than Little Charlie but still young and blemished and Burl couldn't keep his own people from his mind. It was the finality that struck him. He understood the Harpes' desire to kill, to call up death and watch it shape out circumstance in answer to their perverse artistry. He felt an utter hate for them in knowing them, and as he set the boy down, as he watched his inanimate form settle into the soft grass, he wanted nothing more than to see the two men dead, cold dead and bloody, dissembled and drawn apart to nothing.

They kept clear of the Trace and traveled the thin trails in the woods that took them north of Nashville and arrived at Cheek Stand long after dark the next day. The boy was on a gurney. Burl thought to bury him where he died but the Chickasaws knew his father would want him no matter his condition. Blood had seeped from the wound and dried onto the cut branches of the rough bed that held him. The trail widened toward the stand and became moist and slippery as they came into a clearing bordered by bald cypress and sycamore draped in dried moss. Fires glowed around the tavern, some close enough to sear the siding and some strewn into the makeshift street. A few of them burned remote from their makers but around others huddled figures sat still, retreating from a world that against their will they occupied. The flames blocked out the stars and made a blank dome of the sky as the clearing formed an insular cell of being.

Burl followed behind the gurney as it passed one of the huddled figures and looking he caught sight of a man's face from underneath a hat brim. His lips curled inward creasing around a protruding eye-tooth. He looked down with a cold expression and Burl saw that his face was deeply marked from smallpox with spots and lines cut from below his eye down his face to his chin. There was nothing strange in his look, but what caught Burl's glance was the deep gash from the back of his ear to below his collar. From the shape of the scar Burl knew it came from a serrated knife blade useless for everything but fighting. Burl had seen these knives before usually among people like the Harpes but also in the hands of those who felt the need to make themselves known. The man turned his head. The ligaments and sinew had been cut and his movements were marked by the wound. There was none of the fluid motion of normal flesh. The man lifted his collar over his neck and began stoking the fire with a thick burned branch.

The Chickasaws pulled the boy past other fires as Burl followed them toward the tavern. Around the side Burl could see the white and soiled thigh of a woman lifted high in the air. She leaned against the wall of the building and a dark form leaned in and thrust against her. As Burl came close he caught the edge of her face and the head of the man lifted upward as they saw him. The woman's lips rose to a smile and the man began thrusting harder and groaning and the woman opened her mouth and let loose a sound from some absent darkness within her. There was no pleasure in either of them. Burl slowed his pace and against his will looked on. His loins were far from his thoughts until now and his mind stood outside as a misplaced urge swept through him. The man pulled away from the woman and roughly spun her around and for a moment her long dress dropped down to her ankles. But she bent over and placed her palms against the building and the man lifted her dress again revealing her thighs and haunches now clear and white in the firelight. The man thrust again and to Burl the woman seemed magnetic and alive. He moved past them toward the tavern. He heard the woman's groans almost painful now merging with the man's as they moved out of sight.

They stopped in front of the tavern, which rose high and black against a jagged cliffside with tall windows staring yellow outward and past him to the trail. The plank siding was stained black from age and the boards curved outward in twisted ovals and splintered edges. The smoke from incessant fires left streaks and stains across the front and the steps to the flat porch were thick but jagged. The Chickasaws set the gurney down and stood silent and unsure of how they would be greeted. Burl reached in his pocket and handed one of them a bill.

"They'll take to anybody with money," he said.

The three of them stepped up the stairs toward the door. It was solid and hard and leaning slightly as Burl turned the knob and opened it. They came into the large floor of the bottom tavern crowded and flat except for tables and chairs scattered around the room. A pile of wooden crates was stacked uneven against the wall and in them Burl could see bottles and gourds and loose straw. The Chickasaws both seemed uneasy and moved toward a darkened corner by the door. Burl stepped into the center of the room near a table with men clustered around it drinking from three gourds. They were all dead drunk and beyond laughing, half sick, with rough chuckles rolling out of them in answer to nothing as they glared babbling and eyeless under the whiskey. One man leaned against the wall sleeping with his chin to his chest and a thick layer of vomit fanning down the front of his shirt. The room was enclosed and airless and smelled of stale breath and sulfur and bile. Burl knew the visceral ugliness of the territories and he had traveled them many times before, but coming from the outside with the fires and the darkness and the man and woman rutting took away his breath and made his gut rise. In the far corner of the room he could make out the bare chest of a trapper, his hair creasing around the soiled lapel of his shirt. At first Burl saw only his chest rise but he looked down to the man's waist and saw the back of a woman's head moving. He could hear the sound of her spit moistening the man who reached down and grabbed her by the hair. Burl looked at his face and saw nothing but a telling blankness. The woman seemed a void. She was there only to do something other than sleep or die.

Burl walked past the tables and toward the back of the room. He forgot why he was there, although he knew it was too dark to travel onto the poorly marked trail beyond the stand. He had lost his hunger and he wasn't cold and he moved forward dreamlike and senseless. He walked to a darkened corner underneath the stairwell and in the shadows he saw a table and behind in the darkness a figure in silhouette sitting in a chair. He could make out the dim outlines of the man's hair thin and parted in the middle pouring in wisps down to his collar. Without speaking Burl sat down. The man looked at him as he lit a pipe and roughly slid a whiskey bottle across the table. The flame of the match lit the man's face only for a moment and Burl could make out the sharp angular curve of his jaw and his thin reptilian lips. As the tobacco burned it reflected red into the man's eyes and through the pale flames Burl thought he saw a dim reflection. But as the embers in the pipe died down the image darkened again to a thin trace.

"Who the hell are you?" Burl said.

"Nobody."

Burl paused and studied what he could make of him. The figure moved only slightly and threw his hair back with a quick movement of his head. Burl looked past him relieved that he couldn't see his eyes.

"You like my tavern?" the man said.

"You'd be Cheek?"

"No, I'm some other som' bitch," he said scornfully. "You like my tavern?"

"It's a foul place."

"Well now, there's an honest man. Are you an honest man?"

Burl shifted in his seat but found an odd comfort in facing the dim image of the man and placed his feet squarely on the floor. Cheek noticed him and seemed to know him and Burl thought he could make out a thin smile through the embers of the pipe.

"You could get the hell on out of here, then," Cheek said.

"Yeah, I could. But I'm tired."

"I don't think you're tired of traveling," said Cheek. "But you're tired."

"Ain't you a riddling son-of-a-bitch."

"You want a riddle?" he said. "About six inches long and a mighty pretty size; not a lady in the country but what will take it between her thighs."

"What?"

"What do you think?"

"I don't know."

"You think you know."

"Fuck you."

"The left-hand horn on a lady's sidesaddle."

As Burl stared across at him a woman walked through the front door and stumbled toward the crates near the wall. Her dress was long but tight around the waist and her blouse was a thin faded white. Her breasts were high and firm and protruded from her shirt and she walked the room knowing their effect on the men there. Her eyes scanned as she walked a circling path near a table of drunken trappers. Burl's eyes fixed on her form as Cheek looked across the table.

"Who is she?" Burl said.

"Some cunt."

"You know her?"

"What do you mean, know her?"

"Who is she?"

"My wife."

Burl looked across at him. The woman's body aroused him against his will but the image of Cheek drifting formless in the shadows drew him out and hardened his anger and wariness. He thought on the Harpes and Sam Mason and the ugly women they traveled with and the children they would spawn and hate and the killing they would do before they ended. He thought on his own sick rage that breached the distance between them.

"You want to hump her?" Cheek said.

Burl felt the hair on his head rise and a haze cover his reason as he looked across at Cheek who like the Harpes and

Mason had become the outer shape of something pervasive and omnipresent. Cheek looked back at him and across at the woman, who stopped and playfully straddled a man at a table.

"The cunt has a set of teats on her, don't she?" said Cheek.

"You're a sick bastard."

"You can't decide what to do first, kill me or fuck my wife."

From his own depths he felt his hand move toward the knife in his belt. Cheek sat immovable drawing on the pipe with his eyes lighting and fading in the smoke. The woman screamed and from across the room Burl could see her flailing as the drunken man lifted her onto the table and raised her dress above her thighs. He quickly removed his belt and lowering his pants moved her undergarments aside. Burl could hear Cheek begin to chuckle but as the woman appeared to struggle his voice rose to laughter and his white face emerged like a half moon from the shadows. Burl left the knife in its sheath and stood up toward the table. The woman was far from his mind now and he was aware only of the strength in his hands as he reached toward the drunken man. He felt a fire in his limbs and a tingling in his palms and he seemed almost outside himself. Burl took the man by the collar and lifted him and stared into his face as if it were a pane of glass. It changed before his eyes as the lust and laughter left and he awoke from his stupor and stared down wide-eyed and scared. The woman screamed again.

"Let him loose!" she yelled, looking across at Cheek. "Who is this son-of-a-bitch?"

"Just a traveling fella," Cheek said, leaning back into the darkness.

She looked across at Burl with curiosity and anger as he let loose of the man and dropped him to the floor.

"Mind your own affairs, mister," she said.

Burl's mind let go and he looked toward the door. He shook his head and felt at once himself again. The Chickasaws were huddled in the corner of the room but as Burl straightened they moved into the light. Cheek's form was enveloped again in darkness but Burl could hear his low chuckle. He straightened his belt and turned away and walked toward the door and stepped outside with the Chickasaws behind him. The fires were gone and the trees were motionless as the constellations faded into the dim light of sunrise.

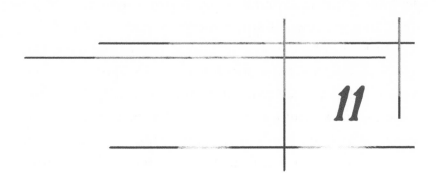

11

*T*he wagon limped across the wheel ruts in the hardened
mud toward the base of a knoll that rose from a grass
meadow. The team moved steady and slow as Sam walked
ahead of them, head held down, his face hidden under the
rough edges of his broad-brimmed hat. The new axle was
solid. They had cut it in less than a day and set the bad wheel
secure. He lifted his eyes and saw a thick mist roll over the
steep hillsides and hollows. The mountains in Tennessee
were tall and rough and dense with color and the trails were
tentative and angular and searching. Thin ridges not ten
feet wide rose above the tree lines and disappeared, yielding
to sheer cliffs and valleys thick with trees. Dense stands of
maple stood among the spruce and beech and hemlock, and
the colors were changing as the leaves burst forth in fluid
rushes of crimson and yellow. They would be bare in a matter
of weeks, but he knew that the woods would remain thick
and impenetrable and the gray sky would press down and
blanket them in mystery. The wagon edged along a ridge and
downward along the trail that curved into a virgin forest of

red spruce. Giant patriarch trees rose out of the underbrush and tall ferns and wet rotting logs draped in moss covered the ground and sometimes hugged the edges of the trail. He could see among them the low-growing galax, its green leaves turning bronze. The underbrush was speckled in red as the wild strawberries now beginning to fade in color began to drop from their stems and roll randomly across the black soil. As he walked he became acutely aware of his own materiality, his own identity as a breathing thing captured in sight and sound. At times he found himself wondering what worlds were eclipsed by seeing. Even though his eyes were primary he didn't even look for the swallows but knew they were there, noisy and hungry as they picked at the bugs on the logs and tree branches. He glanced downward and saw a small creek as it flowed out of the woods and found low elevation along the side of the trail. Near a rock shrouded in thick grass three lungless red salamanders breathing through their skins sat entwined in a chaotic tapestry of color.

He passed out of the tall spruce forest, the wagon moving steadily along the flat of the trail, and in a clearing White's Fort stood in front of them ragged and humble against the thick trees. The flag was in the center of the fort's enclosure but seemed to sit to the left of the closest structure. Eve Mary and the little ones were in the wagon and Lucetta drove the team. She had insisted she stay there. She had yet to reach her limits and feared them more than the cliffs and rivers and mountains they had crossed or anything that lurked silent in their future. Elisha and Little Charlie were at the rear, both keeping an eye on the wheels as they slipped into the ruts and rolled out clumsy but steady in motion.

"You think Uncle Burley's here yet?" Little Charlie said.

"Maybe," Elisha said. "There ain't no reason for him to be in any hurry, though."

"Things will be a bit livelier when he gets here. Pa's more somber than usual."

"Your pa's thinking about what could have happened up on the pass."

The fort was a shabby group of attached shelters, a smattering of log buildings scored to square and daubed heavy in gray clay. The rooflines were uneven and hung at angles and the roofs themselves were covered in thick and rough-cut shingles. Each one-room cabin-like thing had a stone chimney that rose high enough so the sparks and embers wouldn't fly free. The buildings were linked by thin walls of cut logs some scored to square and some still round with the bark peeling away from the points. To the side of the cabins were pens for cattle and livestock and in front of the closest structure a stump for woodcutting and a small shack for axes and blades and implements. Sam looked up from his hat and took hold of the harness on one of the oxen near the yoke to lead it. As they moved forward past a line of trees they opened into a cut field and on the other side of the stock pens he could see the wagons and the tents and the lean-tos of the settlers who would leave with them down Avery's Trace. He couldn't easily figure their number and many of the single camps held more than one family. But he guessed from the streams of rising smoke that there were more than a hundred fires burning, and he could smell the game cooking and hear the hum of voices and the sound of a dulcimer.

"To your left, Lucetta!" he shouted back. "There's a line of tracks. I think there's some flat ground back behind all these folks."

Lucetta moved the reins and the team ambled off the main trail onto a thin set of tracks newly made. Ewan crawled from the wagon and sat next to his mother and Elisha and Little Charlie ran from the rear of the wagon toward Sam. When they arrived he kept looking forward and Little Charlie looked at him and then scanned the rough line of tents and spindly leaning structures.

"Damn, Pa," he said. "There's a lot of folks here. Do you think most of them's going to the French territories?"

"I don't know," Sam said. "Some maybe. Most of them's probably headed into other parts of Tennessee or Kentucky."

"Those would be the ones that ain't crazy like us," Elisha said.

Sam looked forward up the trail and ran his eyes along the rough horizon of ridges and tree lines. The mist from which the mountains took their name drifted between the hollows and long-leaf pine and downward to the maple and elm that hugged the edge of the clearing. The wagon moved and Sam saw a flat piece of ground with grass near one of the camps that opened into a larger open space. He motioned toward it looking at Lucetta and she steered the wagon as they circled a small knoll. It looked to Sam like as good a spot as any and at least it was flat and high enough to stay dry. Lucetta knew where to go and Sam walked ahead of Elisha and Little Charlie and standing on the knoll he could see across the settlers' camp. It was not yet dusk and still light and there was a bustle among the twisted shelters as women stood over fires and ovens and men stood in circles holding pipes and jars of whiskey or kneeled over wagon wheels and scattered piles of wood. From his view on the hill he saw a panorama of movement and he knew he was a part of something large and limitless and beyond him. The emptiness of the territories and the expanse and sweep of open spaces pulled at him but up until this moment he had felt alone. Now as he gazed into the settlers' camps and past them to the fort with its tattered flag it seemed he was being carried by something inanimate and indifferent to his own small and pathetic hope. There were canvas tents and branches draped in skins for storage but most of the structures were lean-tos of roughly cut logs covered in cloth and skin and thatching with mud to seal the open spots. Toward the center of the camp he saw an old woman walking alone, her profile to his side, a gray bonnet hanging around her face with tie straps uneven and dangling. His eyes fixed upon her. She walked slowly with a hunch and a limp and at the base of her knee-length hems he could see her thin legs like cut branches dissimilar in length. He looked at her. She carried something close to her chest. He tried to see it but could only make out that it wasn't food but was some kind of garment. As she walked past a group of children and ignored them one small boy picked up a pinecone and threw it at her hitting her in the shoulder. As she turned toward the child Sam could see the outline of her features. Her jaws were high and her cheeks sunken and her eyes deep and small. Her expression betrayed her as she tried to muster an anger no longer in her and her face showed no hint of surprise. She kept walking as the children laughed and the parents stood to the side working and saying nothing. She passed between two tents and Sam lost sight of her.

Lucetta arrived at the center of the clearing with the wagon and pulled back slightly on the reins as the team ambled and stood. Ewan jumped down and ran to Elisha and Little Charlie. Sam turned from where he stood on the knoll and walked down to the wagon. Lucetta climbed down slowly and from her movements Sam could see she was weary. He looked at her for a moment and she caught his glance.

"I'm all right," she said.

He kept his eyes on her for a moment and watched her as she walked toward the back of the wagon. Eve Mary handed Raymond to her and jumped out and looked across the clearing to her brother.

"Ewan!" Eve Mary yelled. "Get on back here and help me get the ovens and them victuals out the back!"

"Let him run, Evie," Lucetta said. Sam touched her and looking around saw Charlie standing with Elisha as he unhitched the team.

"Come help your sister set up for supper,"

"Damn, Pa."

"Get on over here," Sam said.

Charlie walked with shoulders hunched and head down and with an agility Sam noticed he jumped lightly into the back of the wagon. Eve Mary stepped down and took what Charlie handed her, first the Dutch oven and then the iron braces that would hold it over the fire and then a bag of parched corn and a handful of potatoes. Sam saw when they were finished.

"Guess it's taters and corn tonight," he said, pointing toward the camp closest to them. "Eve Mary, you ask them folks where the water is, and Charlie you go cut us some thin logs for a shelter."

Charlie picked up the flintlock and he and Eve Mary went out, one toward a dense stand of spruce and the other toward the fort into the center of the settlers' camps. Lucetta had walked back from the woods and looked tired but more calm now and sat down and leaned against the wagon wheel, placing her head between her legs. Elisha looked at Sam who set his eyes on Lucetta.

"We're here, Sam," Elisha said. "We made it."

"I know it," Sam said in a breathless tone, knowing the message implicit in his brother's words.

"There's a few more weeks of fall left," Elisha said. "You think we ought to hunt tomorrow?"

"Reckon so," Sam said. "Unless we figure to eat taters and clabber all winter."

"I wonder what the game's like here."

"With all these settlers, we'll have to range out further south into them mountains," Sam said, pointing. "I'm sure there's bear and deer, but I don't know about hogs. I expect they're probably hunted down."

"There won't be many hogs the further out we range."

Lucetta looked up and met Sam with her eyes. Elisha stopped speaking.

"Send Little Charlie and Elisha," she said. Sam just looked at her and Elisha nodded almost imperceptibly, his lips pursed in a thin smile. She lifted her hands upward and placed them on the spokes of the wheel and Elisha moved to help her to stand. Sam picked up the Dutch oven and the iron braces and walked over to a flat piece of ground and began setting it up. Lucetta came to help him and Elisha unhitched the team and stored the tack. Then he followed Little Charlie into the woods. Lucetta stood over Sam as he pressed the iron into the hard ground. She lifted her eyes and saw the mist as it rolled out of the woods over the settler's camps. She had noticed the mist was more alive in these mountains, prone to movement and active at the setting sun. The settlers' voices were palpable and alive but their figures faded to outlines as the poles of their humble structures rose out of the haze and their fires burned dimly. She stared at the flames and out of the mist she saw two silhouetted forms walking toward them. Before long she recognized one of them as Eve Mary. The other she couldn't quite place but seemed somehow familiar. As they came closer, she saw him.

"Burley!" she yelled, as Sam rose up. Burl came toward them with Eve Mary standing still.

Sam rose to standing as Burl came out of the mist, his hunched form leaning toward them as he stopped in front of his nephew. He looked Sam in the face and Sam stared back blankly, bobbing at the shoulders, unsure of what to do. Lucetta ran past her husband and wrapped her arms around the old man who lifted her and spun her around. She was warm against him and he took in the smell of her and the memory and the flood of associations and images of home and a life long lived and buried. He set her down and she leaned back and looked at him. Her face was round and full, and he saw her eyes and knew from years of seeing the look that she was with child. She took in his expression with a smile and leaned forward and kissed him. Eve Mary walked up slow and Sam stood back as Burl stared past Lucetta at him.

"Get your skinny ass over here, boy!" he said laughing and stepping toward him took him by the shoulders and hugged him. Sam's tight posture released as he took hold of his uncle. As Burl stepped away, he looked at each of them with calm, as if a door had closed on the chill of twilight and he saw something he knew and this time understood.

"Where's the rest of the bunch?" he asked. Lucetta looked off in the distance and Sam looked straight at him.

"Elisha and Little Charlie are over there in them woods," Sam said, as Burl stared back at him with a look of confusion that flashed only briefly on its way to recognition.

"Your Pa?" he said. Sam just looked down and dug his toes into the ground.

"Uncle Burley?" Lucetta said moving toward him. He lifted his hand to her to tenderly warn her off as he walked away, up toward the knoll that looked over the settlers' camps.

Sam walked over to the wagon and pulled out a clay jar from underneath a tarp of woven burlap. He walked back to Lucetta who was standing still looking upward at their uncle. She put her arm around his waist.

"He and Pa was thick in friendship, brothers but more than brothers," Sam said. "You know Burl courted Ma before Pa did?"

"Course I did," said Lucetta. "Your ma would always chide your pa about it and then get mad because she couldn't rile him."

"Pa weren't easy to rile."

"She missed that about Burl once he left."

"She was Pa's wife."

"Yes, she was."

Sam lifted the jar to his lips and handed it to Lucetta who took a light swig and rolled the bitter liquid around in her mouth. Eve Mary walked up next to her and seeing Lucetta took her by the hand.

"I guess it's good he heard it from us straight up instead of in some letter," Sam said.

"Yeah, but it waters down the reunion," Lucetta said.

"Burl won't grieve long. He'll just remember long."

"I guess he'll be laughing about some damn thing your pa and he did before supper's over."

Elisha and Little Charlie came walking from the edge of the woods. Elisha's arms were full of thin-cut spruce branches and Charlie carried the big carcass of a male raccoon. As they stepped up to the wagon Burl walked down the hill and met them.

"Hope you two boys don't mean to eat that creature without me helping you!"

"Ha!" Elisha yelled, laughing. "You old fart smeller. You don't look like you need no food."

"That's true enough," Burl said, pressing his hand against his gut and pushing it out making it larger than it was. "I got me plenty of pretty girls along the line to keep me round."

Elisha took hold of his uncle by the shoulders and hugged him tight. Little Charlie stood by them shyly, the dead animal at his side. Burl stepped aside and looked long at the boy.

"My God, son," he said. "You're taller than a damn cane stalk and almost as skinny!"

"I growed up."

"Well, almost," Burl said. "Give old Uncle Burley a hug."

Charlie dropped the coon and grabbed a hold of Burl with nothing self-conscious in him yet and just a hint of shyness at meeting the uncle he hadn't seen in a long time but who loomed large in the family's sense of itself.

"Burley, you hear about Pa?" Elisha said, cautiously.

"I did, son," Burl said, turning away toward Lucetta and the wagon. He looked over his shoulder at Little Charlie.

"You going to skin out that coon?"

"I am," said Charlie.

Charlie picked up the coon anxious to show his efficiency with the knife. Burl sat down and crossed his legs as Elisha and Sam and Lucetta settled around him. Charlie had already cut the jugular vein and bled the animal just after killing it to keep the meat fresh. He took the knife firm in his hand and rung the legs at the foot joint. He split the pelt from the rings and the hind legs downward to the crotch and did the same with the front legs to the animal's chest. He placed the point of the knife into the soft folds between the hind legs and sliced the pelt upward to the chest and then to the jaw. He was swift with the knife and Burl noticed and smiled at him and he was happy about it. Little Charlie cut around the underside of the tail and connected the split and skinned out the legs. He sliced between the bone and the tendon and inserted the gambling stick and hung the coon from the canvas between the opening of the wagon. It swung pathetically with its front legs pointing downward and its body twisting in comic gesticulation. Lucetta lay back on the moist grass and Sam handed the bottle to Burl who looked wistful across at the settlers' camps. Charlie took two small sticks and placed them together with the tail of the animal between them. He pulled evenly and carefully with the sticks held tight as the tail slid off the tailbone. He worked the pelt off the front legs occasionally slicing at the mesentery between the muscle and the skin. He pulled the pelt free and skinned out the front legs and sliced under the forearms and cut around and removed the pear-shaped musk glands that would sour the meat. He skinned around the neck and cut free the ears and around the eyes leaving the eyeballs staring odd and ridiculous at the grass beneath them. He dug the knife surgically into the animal and split the carcass in the middle and pulled free the organs and intestines and dropped them to the ground at his feet.

"Little Charlie, pick them guts up and carry them outside of camp," Lucetta said.

She stood up and walked over to him and reaching into the wagon pulled out a wooden bucket.

"Ewan, go on down to the creek and fill this up so we can soak that coon."

Charlie picked up the guts and walking a few paces from the wagon dropped to his knees and dug a hole into the moist ground. He set the guts into the hole and rolled the soil on top of them. He picked up the knife from where he had dropped it and cut off the head and feet. Burl leaned against the wagon wheel and Elisha sat next to him as Sam stood by them.

"Ain't it odd to watch these young ones grow up," Burl said. "First they're just a dream and then they're squalling and sucking on the tit, and before you can blink they're talking and thinking and arguing and skinning out a coon like they been here forever."

"You ever thought of being a preacher or some other kind of sermonizer?" Elisha said, laughing. If you weren't so rawboned and ugly I'd confuse you with one of them black-gowned English missionaries."

Lucetta looked at Burl and smiled, knowing he had been talking as much about her as about Charlie.

"Don't you pick on Uncle Burley," she said playfully. "I've missed his dreamy talking."

"I considered being a missionary," Burl said. "But frolicking with married women ain't exactly what I like doing with my free time."

"Burley," Lucetta said in playful anguish as Elisha and Sam laughed.

Ewan returned with a bucket of water and handed it to Eve Mary who poured the water into a pot and hung it from the iron braces. Charlie set some kindling between the cut logs and pinecones and dry bark. He lit them with a flint and nursed the sparks gently as the flames grew slow and fed themselves on the dead wood. Lucetta lifted the coon from the ground and set it into the pot of water. Eve Mary went to the wagon and returned with a handful of salt, two pods of red pepper and a sprinkle of black pepper. She dropped them into the pot and reached in to stir with her hand. Sam looked across at his daughter and Lucetta caught something in his eyes that she thought perhaps she understood but couldn't frame in words. She walked to the wagon and removed a handful of lard and walked back to the fire. After greasing the oven she looked down at the headless body of the coon as it spun in the water and started to boil. She could see the flesh and make out the outlines of bones and sinew and the thin oozing of blood. Set free from its skin it looked almost human. But as she glanced back at the men near the wagon she sensed something more in them, something essential that lifted them out of the carcasses they embodied. She spun the coon with a stick and the water boiled as Eve Mary dropped in some broken spice-wood twigs to mute the wildness. She added three small onions and a handful of sliced potatoes. Sam sat down next to Elisha and Charlie with Ewan crouched at their feet. Ray was stirring mildly in the wagon as Burl pulled a pipe from the pocket of his overshirt and took from another a small pouch of dried leaf. He filled the pipe and lifted it to his mouth and lit it taking an even draw. Then he handed it to Sam.

"What finally set you on coming west?" Burl asked.

"Ma and Pa was dead," Sam said. "I want some land for these kids."

"That all?" Burl said, turning to Sam and looking at him gently. Sam drew on the pipe and looked forward.

"I don't know," he said. "The same thing as the rest of these folks, I guess."

"I wish we knew more about where we was going," Elisha said.

"It's fine country. There ain't much out here that ain't fine if you're talking about the land itself."

"What about the people?" Elisha said.

"People's people, ain't they?"

"They got to be different if the living is different," Sam said. "If it ain't as hard to get by and you got freedom and can respect yourself."

"I been out here some time, and folks seem the same to me," Burl said. "Maybe I ain't looking close enough."

"All I care is that there's people like there was at home," Elisha said.

"Mostly I just want some of the freedom they kept ranting about during the war," Sam said. "I don't care what it says in no papers. There ain't no freedom without you got land and money."

Burl looked at him more intently, knowingly.

"I figure you're out here for more than land and money," he said.

Sam rested back on the wagon wheel and looking at his uncle for a moment turned and gazed out over the silhouetted tree lines and the pin-like stars above them. Eve Mary went to the wagon and took out a handful of flour. Lucetta lifted the coon out of the pot and placed it on a flat rock near the fire. Eve Mary came back and Lucetta rolled the animal in the flour and added salt and pepper and placed it in the Dutch oven. Then removing the boiling pot from the flame she hung the oven from the iron braces. Sam took another long draw on the pipe and handed it to Elisha who traded him for the clay jar. The fine jagged ridgeline was black now and cleanly drawn against the sky. There was a half moon bright enough to obscure the starlight around it but high in the sky the constellations sat fixed and timeless. Sam could hear Burl's breathing and Elisha began to hum a tune that harmonized the stillness. He first remembered it as a song he had heard his mother sing late at night after the children had turned in, but he couldn't place its meaning. As he looked upward he set his eyes on the sky and saw for a moment its depth next to the flat black of the mountains. He recognized Elisha's song as a hymn drawn from the Book of Psalms.

12

The spruce logs of the shelter froze solid before they were dry. Sam stood outside with Little Charlie tapping gently on one of the front support poles. Autumn had passed to winter now since they arrived and the poles were bound in ice and Sam knew they were secure. Lucetta and Eve Mary and the children were still inside sleeping and Charlie stood next to him, his shoulders hunched, rubbing his bare hands against his legs. He had placed the dried kindling into the last night's coals and waited for his uncles to return with the wood. Sam stepped away from the shelter and together they looked down the knoll toward the fort wall where Elisha was placing logs on a stump as Burl split them. Sam looked at them and tuned his thoughts to the music of their movements, Elisha setting the log and Burl splitting with a broad axe, Elisha taking up a piece of split wood and Burl coming down again, their motions evenly timed and rhythmic and effortless. The trees were bare now and the sky was gray and pressed down like a leaden weight onto the ridges. Cliffs and broken rocks stood out in hard relief against the bleak and barren woodlands. Busted layers of stone embedded together for millennia jutted out of the cliffs like the tips of dull knives. Sam looked along one flat cliff. The land seemed tortured in winter, the absence of green revealing the twisted tectonics and making clear the chill brutality of time, its inexorable passing and the granite reality of its omnipotence. He stepped toward the fire and took in thin remnants of warmth as Burl and Elisha returned to camp with the wood. After they dropped it on a pile Elisha took up two logs and set them into the center of the pit and Charlie leaned over with the flint and stones to light it. The air was crisp and the wood was dry as the kindling quickly took to flame. Within minutes a fire blazed forth and they sat in a circle around the warmth.

"Any of you boys hungry yet?" Sam asked.

"I can wait till the women get up," said Charlie.

Burl and Elisha stood silent, both staring at the moving flames, watching the fluid motion as they curled and wrapped the thinning logs.

"Feels fine to be setting at a fire with someone besides myself," Burl said.

"I expect it does," said Sam.

"Long walk from Natchez," Elisha added.

"Lots of time to think. Lots of quiet," Sam said.

"There's such a thing as too much quiet," said Burl.

"Not for old Sam," Elisha said. "The quieter and lonelier for him the better. He likes to set around and think about what's going to happen two or ten year from now."

"Someone's got to think about the future," said Sam. "Or it'll pass you by and leave you hungry."

"Truth is, the future matters," Burl said. "But in the end you can't do much to change it. We can't change ourselves much, neither."

"That don't make no sense," Sam said. "If you can't change things, why try?"

"Because we ain't got no choice."

"Burley, you need to spend more time in towns," Elisha said, smiling. "There's people in them that will pull you down when you start floating."

"What do I need them folks for when I got you, boy?" Burl said, elbowing his nephew and grinning.

Charlie hadn't listened and after a time he lifted his hands up to the fire and pressed them forward until he hit the spot where the radiating heat seared his flesh and warned him away. Then he looked over at Elisha.

"Did I tell y'all about the barring out yesterday?" he said.

"There's a schoolhouse here?" Burl said.

"Small one over at the fort," said Sam.

"The barring out got wild," Charlie continued. "The master was boarding at the fort with some mean fellers from somewhere where they don't bar out the teachers at Christmas time. They heard what was being planned from one of the boys, and the master didn't know they heard it. I was over there, and I seen the boys come to the schoolhouse early. They was sneaking in real quiet, and since it was near Christmas I figured I knew what they was doing, so I stayed and watched them. After a bunch of them got in, they closed the door and I went to the window. I seen them barring the door with benches and wood and all sorts of heavy things. Soon the feller the master was boarding with and three of his grown sons come up and looked at me funny and asked me what I was there for. I told him nothing, and he tried to open the door. They was laughing inside and hooting at him to keep trying. He yelled at them to open up now so he could hit them upside the head with the master's switch. The old man bantered long enough until one of the bigger boys got mad and come out and set on the old man. When his sons come at the boy the rest of the boys set on the whole bunch, and they was quite a ruckus. Master come up to see the whole crowd fighting and tried to stop them but it was too late. They fought away till they was tired and the master was confounded that the men he was boarding with had never heard of a barring out."

"I wonder where they was from," Sam said.

"I think I heard they was from Prussia."

Burl listened only slightly as he warmed his hands in the soft folds of deerskin beneath his arms. He let out breath and watched it merge with the smoke from the fire and twist and disappear into balletic patterns of flying embers. He looked across at Sam just as Eve Mary stepped out of the wagon. She was wrapped in a worn folded quilt that she held over her ears and her eyes were full of sleep but when she saw him she opened them to acknowledge him shyly. She walked toward them, her legs not quite conscious of the ground as she sat at Burl's feet and lay against his leg. He leaned himself into her and she rested her head on his knee. Sam saw her and smiled as Elisha and Charlie sat smoking.

"Your mama still sleeping?" Elisha said.

"No, she's stirring."

"Y'all sleep all right?" said Burl.

"Ma slept hard, she didn't talk none," Eve Mary said. "But I had a funny dream."

"Bad dream?" said Charlie.

"No, not really," she said. "I was setting high up in a tree, twenty feet up or so, and the only thing under the tree was hard ground. No grass or mud or nothing. For some reason I had to get down right away and there was nobody to help me. So I just dropped on out of the tree and landed flat on my side. An old granny woman come up, and I don't know how she could tell, but she said I broke my neck and some of my ribs and my collar bone. It didn't hurt none, and I could move my legs but she told me to lie still. She told me I'd be fine so long as I lay still for a while. So I just laid there all night resting till just now when I woke up."

She reached out from under the quilt and warmed her hands against the fire. Burl moved his leg around and she leaned back on him and he rested his chin on top of her head. Charlie took a long draw from his pipe and handed it to Sam, and Elisha began whistling long notes between his teeth, mournful and low and gentle, audible but not alien to the silence.

"That ain't a hard dream to figure, honey," Burl said.

"What's it about?"

"Look at how it came out," he said. "Was you ever worried or scared?"

"No. Not even when I was up in the tree."

"And you wasn't in no pain?"

"No."

"And the granny woman told you to rest and you did?"

"Yep."

"Well, there you are. It's been a long trip."

Lucetta stepped out of the wagon and leaned back stretching her back and yawning. Sam looked up at her and their eyes met and she smiled. He glanced past the wagon down the knoll and looked across the settlers' camps and beyond them to a leafless stand of dogwood. The trees were uniform in color, a muddy brown, and the trunks seemed thickly woven and misdirected, the underbrush dense and dead and frozen into the mud. Lucetta walked past them as they sat at the fire toward the stone oven they had built just at the edge of the camp. Eve Mary began to rise but her mother motioned her to stay sitting and rest. Lucetta was farther along now and more herself. Her limbs obeyed and she felt a deeper well of fortitude within that she knew and always counted on. Her vision was more acute as she looked at them near the fire, and though she knew the coffee would still make her sick and that too much fat in the food would stunt her energy, the stale taste of her own tongue had faded and she was more often ravenous than ill. These were signs she had become used to and remembered, and she wondered sadly at what it must be like for young women with child for the first time, girls who had no older women to talk to. She lifted the skin tarp off the cut logs and took two and smacked them together until the dry bark dropped to the ground. She set the logs against the gray stones at the base of the oven and lifted up the bark and set it inside. She picked up a stone and a flint from near the oven door and struck them together. The sparks were weak in the cold and she kept at her movements.

"Charlie, bring me some straw," she said.

Charlie stood up and when he handed her the straw she set it tightly beneath the bark chips. She struck the flint to the stone again as the strands took fire and the bark set as well. As the kindling flamed she set the first log ablaze and seeing the fire she stood up straight and stretched again. Eve Mary saw the fire and stood and walked to the shelter. She stepped inside and went to the back. Ewan was still deep asleep. She looked at him lying on his back and she tilted her head to take in his face. His eyes were closed with no hint of movement behind them and his mouth was half open and a thin wisp of hair twisted in a curl down his forehead. Ray was next to him and stirred only slightly, lifting a leg onto his older brother who felt nothing and slept on in blissful delirium. She wondered for a moment at how they could sleep so hard and envied them. She pulled out a sack of flour and yeast and six potatoes along with a small sack of sugar. She tied the tops of the sacks together and carried them outside and returned to where Sam and the rest of the men were sitting. As she sat at Burl's feet again Lucetta handed her the Dutch oven and smiled at her knowingly as if they shared a secret. Elisha looked down at the potatoes and his eyes brightened and Burl let out a pleasant chuckle. Sam just drew on his pipe.

"Light bread," Elisha said. "Damn, I love light bread."

"Taters is getting scarce," Sam said, looking at Lucetta. "Should we use them up like that?"

"It's Christmas time," she said.

Eve Mary dissolved the yeast into the water in the oven and Elisha took his knife from its sheath and began skinning the potatoes. He peeled them making sure that none of the meat was lost. Eve Mary dropped in the sugar and when Elisha was finished she began smashing the potatoes with her hands and dropping them into the oven along with the flour. She kneaded the mixture as Elisha leaned back. Burl reached out and ran his rough palm across the length of her long hair as Sam watched them and Charlie sat smoking, the dense odor of the tobacco filling the camp and mixing with the smell of burning maple and the light scent of frost in the dead and broken leaves of grass.

Sam stood up and walked over to the stone oven and placing his hands on the top to warm them he looked inside. The maple logs burned slowly as the bark darkened to white coals and dropped down beneath them. He felt the warmth of the flames and the warmth of the people near the open fire and he was sure again for the moment that the current was with them. He had sensed the discontinuity at other times between his own want and the desires of his heart and the oblique and liquid presence of something wholly other that was the truth and final architect of things. Now he felt that everything was right and they were where they should be for the right reasons. Elisha seemed lost to it. He had spent much of his time drunk, and he cavorted too much with the girls down near the fort. He never left off his work and Sam couldn't complain. Burl seemed amused and Lucetta understood and even smiled a bit when Charlie went down with Elisha one night and didn't return till near sunup. Sam needed his brother and he knew he could rely on him, but he struggled to figure how much joy Elisha could take in so little, how much pleasure he could derive from things so simple. He turned and walked back to the fire as Eve Mary lifted the light bread loaf into the Dutch oven and set it aside. She wiped her hands on her breeches.

"I was over at the fort the other day, and I heard some folks complaining that folks from the mountains was unclean," she said.

"Who was they?" said Charlie.

"I don't know," she said. "But they wasn't from Carolina."

"Some folks are persnickety," Burl said. "I seen all kinds in the territories, especially down in New Orleans. When you hear them talking you walk on up to them and tell them that back home you seen a black-gowned preacher come up one day to your house and asked about why the hogs rested under your porch."

"Hogs under the porch?"

"Tell them the black-gown asked if hogs under the porch wasn't unhealthy. Then tell them you said, ''taint one of them hogs died yet.' That ought to set them damned old bats talking."

They all laughed as Sam sat down and Lucetta returned with a handful of dried ashcakes and some slices of cured hog. She passed them out as Charlie snuffed his pipe and they all began eating. Sam passed a jar of water and Burl took a short sip of whiskey and passed the jar to Eve Mary. Sam took a bite of ashcake and chewed it slowly and felt the sharp taste of salt and corn on his tongue. It felt good in his mouth but dry so he washed it down with water. He glanced over at Elisha who ripped at a piece of meat with his teeth and sat back as he chewed and looked at the fire. Lucetta sat down with them and took a sip from the whiskey jar and ate a palm-sized ashcake in one bite. Sam noticed and looked at her satisfied and Burl smiled.

"Looks to me like you're hungry enough," Burl said.

"I can't get enough in me these days."

Sam's mind drifted elsewhere for a moment and the talking kept on without him until he awkwardly came in with a question.

"Burley, how much rain and mud can we expect if we leave here in early April?"

"We don't need to leave that early," Burl said.

"But can we?"

"We can," Burl said. "Some will, I guess. There may be some rain and mud and the rivers may not be thawed yet."

"It'll bring us to Nashville before the rest of these folks," said Sam. "This many of them makes me nervous."

"About what?"

"He's thinking all the land will be grabbed up," Elisha said.

"There's a lot of folks after it," Sam said irritably.

"True enough," said Burl. "The Gilchrists of this world seem to get places before the rest of us wake up."

"Still, there ain't no use worrying about it or getting stuck in the mud," Elisha said.

"That's true enough too," said Burl.

"So we can leave then?" Sam said.

"We can. If you want to."

Lucetta and Eve Mary stood and gathered the scraps of food and began cleaning the camp. Sam and Burl stretched themselves against the chill and Elisha still sat staring into the flames. Then he looked over at Little Charlie.

"What you figuring to do with yourself this Christmas day?"

"Play shinny and help get the bonfires ready."

"I'm going to find me a tree and sleep through the afternoon so I can stay up all night," Elisha said. "With this many folks here, it'll be quite a party."

Burl looked down at them remembering many an Old Christmas at home when he was young, but he had felt the impulse to anecdote in recent days and held back from talking because it made him feel old. He stood looking at Charlie with a tortured smile. Sam looked down at his son as well.

"You don't figure there's something you can do around here, boy?" Sam said.

"Let the boy range a bit," Burl said.

"It's Christmas," Lucetta said. "Folks will all be there to watch the boys play."

Sam looked at her with a cold stare and she saw but ignored it as Charlie stood up and walked to the shelter. Elisha draped a thick coat around his shoulders and began toward the fort.

"Damned early for him to be cavorting," Sam said, looking at Burl.

"It ain't never too early," said Burl. "I'm always randier in the morning."

"Me too, I guess," Sam said, fighting back a smile.

"At least he's got someone to use it on. Instead of wasting it against a tree."

"He's got more than one, I expect," said Lucetta, walking up to them with two cups of water. "Hope he's careful, or else we'll lose him to some family headed for Kentucky or somewhere."

Charlie came out of the shelter and standing cinched his belt and began walking toward the fort. The sun was breaking dimly through the trees and the smoke from fires around the wall drifted upward and the sound of voices could be heard along with the distant thud of an axe against frozen wood. The path was hard but flat and he worked to keep his footing on the slope as he moved around the sidewall to where a group of young men were gathering. As he walked up one of them handed him a hand-sized block of tobacco and he took a bite and handed it back. There were six boys there all bored at camp life and ready to leave. One of them looked at Charlie with something like admiration. He was small but thick-set and strong with straight blonde hair and as Charlie stood there he kept his eyes fixed on him.

"Your uncle sure gets himself a lot of tail, don't he?"

"Always has," Charlie said.

"How's he do it?"

"He tries hard, and he keeps trying, mostly. Women like him more than most, I guess."

"You boys ready for the game?" another boy asked.

"Yep," said Charlie.

There were tall flat sticks made of ox bone leaning against the wall and they all took one and moved to a flat spot at the crest of a hill in clear sight of the fort. Two sets of rough-cut poles were set in the ground at each end of the field and the winter grass was dormant and pressed clean to the ground by footsteps. They arrived at the top and another group of boys appeared. The gates of the fort had opened and people walked toward them with blankets and burlap sacks and woven baskets and jars. Charlie could see Lucetta coming up the thin trail with Eve Mary behind her holding Ray and Ewan running ahead with his mouth yelling something beyond hearing. Sam and Burl followed them walking together, both carrying walking sticks and jars. The air was filled with traces of laughter and thin wisps of music and as they arrived he could hear the tuning of strings and the hum of voices in fragmented pieces of song. The tall trees in the clearing that held the fort were soon filled with seasonal joviality and anticipation. The people began to sit along the edges of the field and the boys formed two lines facing each other, and between them was a hand-sized and oblong sphere of dried leaves stuffed into thick woven cowhide. The shinny game began with a count, as one of the boys took the stick to the hide and began toward the goal. Charlie worked hard to get to the hide and was mad when he failed. He took the punishment of elbows and knees but always struggled to get his share and felt the need to keep it as long as he could. He didn't want to pass off and looked to the goal and let go only when another boy called him and had a clear shot. The game was a ritual way to plume their tail feathers but it seemed to him a false one because the skills it took were not his own and really not needed outside the game. Still he knew that people were watching and young women too and the games would continue until he was old enough to say no. Sticks smacked together in search of the hide and he felt an elbow against the side of his eye. His head spun and he could see the top branches of a tree as he fell to the ground. The nerves burned in his nostrils and he could feel the wetness of blood loosening from his nose as he rose to his feet again unsteady now and rushed to catch them and slammed his way into the crowd. In a moment he found himself in control of the hide. He worked it back and forth along the base of the stick toward his goal with another boy behind begging him to pass off. He held it and seeing a tall boy in the clear slapped the sphere with his stick and the other boy took it and cleared the passage through the poles. There was a roar from the crowd mixed with laughter and a congenial shriek from an old woman sitting spread-legged in the center.

The games kept on into the afternoon with groups of boys alternating. As time passed and the sun dimmed into evening men began setting logs together for bonfires. As the light faded the clearing was scattered with piles and before long they were ablaze and laughing men ran wildly in between them and the smell of cooking flesh was everywhere and whiskey and singing and laughter sifted through the camp. From behind the fort the sharp crack of fireworks rang out and the whistle of rockets as they lit the sky sliced through the tree lines. Lucetta and Eve Mary and Sam sat with Burl and the kids a safe distance from one of the fires, but Charlie and Elisha were among the laughing men yelling "Old Christmas!" while running in circles. The fires blazed high into the night sky and after a time the logs began to settle and fall. The revelers kept clear of them knowing the danger even under the liquor. Lucetta leaned against Sam's knee and took hold of Burl's hand.

"You hear our boys out there?" she said.

"Can't say I do, can you?" said Sam.

"I do," Eve Mary said. "I hear Little Charlie. Listen close. His voice starts off low and gets high pitched at the end."

"I hear it," Lucetta said.

They could see three men near the wall of the fort setting a tall pole deep into the ground. One man stood on the wall and sunk it with a hitting beetle as the other two held it steady.

"I ain't seen a stanging since back home," Burl said.

Soon a crowd appeared near the pole silhouetted against a fire holding a man tightly. He was struggling and kicking. They set him roughly against the pole and held him as two men tied his hands and tossed the rope upward along the wall. They hoisted him onto the pole and lashed him to the top with his legs and arms behind and his chest pressed outward in forced defiance. He yelled out curses and the men on the ground yelled back.

"What'll you give?" one man said with others echoing him.

"Nothing, you bastard!" the captured man returned.

Burl and Sam looked on with a smile, and Lucetta shook her head indifferently.

"What'll you give?" shouted a voice that sounded like Elisha.

"A dollar."

The crowd of men roared and the man began to weaken.

"My arms is hurting," he yelled out. "Let me loose."

"What'll you give? another voice yelled.

"Five dollar," he answered back. "Let me loose."

The crowd roared again in approval and the man on the wall began lowering him. There would be no money exchanged only words and when he was lowered to the ground two men set their mock victim against the wall and one of them kneeled down and handed him a jar of whiskey. He took a long swig and stood up.

"That's quick barter," Burl said looking on.

"Hurts up there," said Sam. "I got caught a few year ago."

The crowd dispersed and the fires burned brightly for a while and the fireworks cracked and the missiles lit the sky until the moon rose and the people slowly drifted staggering back to their camps and waited for sunrise.

13

*B*url bridled the mule and took in the sweetness of the air and the palpable scent of ash. He had bought the animal for a dollar. They would use it to range south into the highlands for large game. Sam stepped quietly from the shelter and stretched himself as Burl looked on at him. He saw just a glimmer of the boy's father in his face and a hint of something he knew but couldn't place. Burl lifted the reins over the animal's head and cinched the girth tighter as Sam walked to the wagon and returned to him with the flintlock and powder.

"We're early enough to make Sinking Creek by nightfall, I expect," Burl said.

"How far is it?"

"About ten mile. But it's a hard trip."

"You figure there's more deer there than here?"

"I know there is," Burl said. "These folks is smart not to take to them mountains."

Sam handed him a sack of small woven burlap that held some hardened ashcakes and flatbread and another with parched corn. Burl set it on the animal's neck and tucked the hide straps under the blankets on the mule's back. Sam walked ahead and Burl took the reins under the mule's mouth and led him forward. Dawn was only dimly there between the sharp creases along the ridgelines, but they could begin to see the mist as it moved in ghostly procession up the slopes and between the tops of jack pines and barren cedars and out creeping dogwood branches. As he walked ahead Sam wondered at the bleak duality of these dogwood trees. In spring they would bloom out white like the risen Lord but now they were death incarnate. The mist hung ghost-like to them in a horror more chilling for its familiarity. He had witnessed this annual spectacle since he was a child, and it seemed to him a scripture weighty in portent but cryptic and beyond reading. He had learned some time ago to keep to himself on it. But when he looked at Burl he knew he wasn't alone in his quiet fright and reverence.

They passed by the tall main wall of the fort with its sharp log spires carved white and frozen and its jagged bark broken in pieces and hanging like tattered cloth. At the fort's end they entered a flat space broken by the stumps of cleared trees that were cut at the base and smooth on top and sheathed in ice. They once were maple and alder and dogwood with long-leaf pine among them and the roots reached out along the surface of the ground like thin fingers in relief against the black soil. The settlers at the fort had begun the girdling, having burned many of the stumps deep into the earth and cut free the roots and burned them too until the ground itself was veined in black. Sam settled his pace and Burl steadied the mule with his hand at the bit as they walked side by side into the woodlands. The trail was wide enough for the mule and both of them but no wider as it sloped upward along a steep ridgeline, canopied in low-growth and maple. The trail was slippery with sharp rocks slicing out of the hardened mud. The mule stumbled and Burl lifted its head but the animal soon steadied itself to the terrain and plodded slow-paced upward toward a sharp bend in the trail. Sam held the flintlock in the crease of his arm and looked ahead at the rocks well conscious of his footing.

"These is tougher mountains that you're used to east," Burl said.

"I reckon. They're higher and thicker in trees."

Burl was quiet. He didn't know how to breach the silence that divided them since he arrived. But he wanted to and knew he needed to. It was always there when he had been gone a while.

"Was your pap figuring to come with you before he passed on?" Burl said.

"You know he weren't."

"That old boy could make honey out of mule shit just by talking to it," Burl mused. "I always marveled at his steady soul."

"He was a lucky man in that."

"He was lucky in most things."

"There was a lot about Pa that was lost on me."

"Yeah," Burl said knowingly. "Bless the man but he lived in a fool's paradise. The more I live the more I envy him."

"He never spent much time at it, but I can't stop thinking. My mind races through things, over and into things, all the time."

"Mine too, I guess."

They both looked ahead and took in the silence as the trail moved southwest through canyons and hollows beside rock-strewn creeks with falls that dropped down in sharp angles from the black cliffsides. They kept to the trail always careful and steady in their pace. There were shoots of young maple on the slopes and a carpet of dried crushed leaves and wet pine needles and rocks covered in wet black moss. Burl walked with skill but Sam kept his eyes on each footfall, knowing the blank cruelty of circumstance that hovered near every step. By midday the path trailed downward to the southwest and flattened and opened into a meadow of young pine and tall fescue. The mule moved more smoothly as they rested from concern. They kept on into the evening through the dense woodlands along steep ridges down trails into the gorge cut by Sinking Creek. They entered a flat grove of mixed trees and Burl stopped the mule in a clearing bathed in cold haze.

He dropped the reins and the mule stood still and Sam leaned his musket against the trunk of a tall cedar. Burl walked into the underbrush that lined the clearing and began gathering twigs and Sam took the axette from beneath the blanket on the mule's back and grasping the handle at the end ran his forefinger gently across the edge of the blade. He stepped behind the cedar tall and mature and dense with bare branches and kicked his feet into the underbrush to warn off anything hiding and looked for dry wood. Finding a dead maple log he took the axette to the branches and hewed it clean and carried it to the clearing. He dropped it and rested on his knees and began to cut the log in two. He began breathing hard lacking the leverage of the broad axe and was amused in thinking that some time past someone had thought to lengthen the handle. It was experience that led to things like axe handles but maybe they didn't just grow out of need but from grim will and the desire to think unceasingly and to know. He managed to cut the log in two and moved into a clearing under the open sky away from the tree branches. The breeze was light so he entered the underbrush again and kicked free some stones and removed them to the clearing and circled them. Burl came out of the brush with an arm full of dried kindling and dropped them to the ground. He kneeled and set the thin branches carefully and took a rock and flint from his pocket. Sam stood behind him with a log in his hand, and as the kindling took flame and settled to coals he gently placed it into them. Burl took a pipe from his breeches, stuffed it and ignited a piece of bark. He lit the pipe and took a long draw and handed it to Sam. The night was moonless and the starlight broke out brilliantly. Sam stepped from the fire and seeing him Burl followed. The pricks in the sky did nothing to light the landscape and neither man could make out even the tops of the trees. The stars were cold white, alive and incandescent in the still lunar absence, and they looked on them with a rare contemplative ease incongruous with daylight and the demands it levied. The silence broke only for a moment under the cry of a nightingale. Then they moved into the firelight.

When he was done smoking Burl went to the mule that was feeding on the thick leaf strands of fescue and pulled two pieces of flatbread and a slice of dried pork from the pouches that hung from its side. He took hold of the skin bag that held the liquor and returned to Sam and handed him the food and they both sat and began eating. After a while Burl looked at Sam.

"It's good to see you, boy," Burl said. "It's been too long."

"It has," Sam said. "The older I get the faster time goes, though. There was a time when I was younger, I'd look at the old folks and think that if sickness didn't get me I had a long time to live."

"Not no more though, huh?"

"No," he said. "Judging from Pa, I got more time behind me than ahead of me. And too much to do."

"What you figure you got to do?"

"I got to raise my kids and make sure they're settled."

"That'll happen soon enough," Burl said. "What else?"

"I don't know. Seems like there's something."

"I know you, boy. You and me both I know because we're the same most ways," Burl reflected. He kicked his feet against the stone ring around the fire and as the rocks bumped the log he watched the sparks spin into darkness.

"The same how?" Sam said.

"If I had to peg you, son, I'd say you want more than most."

"I want to get to the French territories and get settled there, that's sure."

"I wanted to see the Mississippi," Burl said. "And travel the Ohio and see the ocean in the east and travel west on the Missouri up to the Platt. I still do." He sat for a moment staring into the flames. "It's painful to want things and get them and watch them sift through your hand and still want more." He paused. "There's something peculiar in the way some men think, boy. They want things that don't measure up to what they thought they wanted, at least not when they get them. It ain't the things themselves neither. They don't care nothing about the things themselves."

Burl stared past the fire, and his eyes fixed on nothing and his face took on an enigmatic expression.

"I can't see no other way to be," Sam said.

"For you, there ain't," Burl said. "Don't get to thinking you're too uncommon, neither. The territory's full of men like you. And there's less and less frontier for them to range in. There's times I'm glad I'm old."

Sam picked up a thin branch and stoked the fire and Burl lifted the whiskey pouch to his lips and handed it over. He stood up and pulled the blankets from the mule's back and laid them onto the bed of grass next to the fire. The two men leaned back and took in the heat and the starlight and the blissful quiet. In the chill with the insects silent and the barren tree branches lifting into the blackness, Sam remembered lying under the open air when he was a boy. He recalled only dimly the wonder he felt at night and how when he was alone he could chant quietly and rest his mind in the still remove of immutability. He would take a bow to God and speak away his senses. If there were no God there'd be no stars. If there were no God there'd be no moon. If there were no God there'd be no trees. If there were no God there'd be no hills. If there were no God there'd be no time. Out of the absence his soul would stand out pure and consequential. The miracle of his own breathing was a wonder and everything made sense without thinking and it seemed like maybe death wasn't an end to things. These moments were gone now, eroded by living in the world too long. He closed his eyes and drifted off to sleep.

He awoke to the crack of a log in flames, with Burl standing and briskly rubbing his shoulders.

"It got colder last night than I thought it would," Burl said. "Your teeth was chattering."

Sam was stiff and thankful he was weary enough to sleep through the pain. He sat up. The trees held the frost with no sign of thaw and the fire sent thin wisps of smoke into the air. Sam moved closer to the flame and set his frozen boots on a warm stone and wrapped his arms around his knees. The heat sifted through him and he awoke more fully as his mind cleared and he remembered the reason they were there. Burl came to the fire with some ashcakes and another handful of jerked pork and Sam took them from him listlessly.

"Let's hope we get us a deer," Burl said, reading his nephew's face. "Then tonight we can put this fire to work on something worth eating."

They finished the food out of duty and stood up and killed the fire. Sam checked the musket for frost rubbing his sleeve along the flint to make sure it was dry. He picked out a branch on a distant maple and sighted along the barrel. He knew it was pointless to check the sight without firing but did it out of habit more than anything and more to orient himself to the weapon again after sleeping away from it all night. Burl tightened the blanket around the mule and leveled the halter and cinched it tight and began along a trail that moved flat and even through the tall grass between a stand of jack pine. The ground was moist with puddles and patches of frozen black moss and there was deer track all over and horning bushes and an occasional pile of droppings. Together they looked for a quiet place to set up a stand and when they found one they would move the mule a quarter mile downwind into the trees and come back and wait. Sam walked behind and Burl turned to him and pointed up a slope that looked down over the broad sweep of the trail. There were two old pines fallen crossways and covered in thin branches. Burl lifted his nose to the wind and led the mule away and Sam made his way to the fallen trees and set down the musket. They formed a natural cavern with just enough height for them to sit uncomfortably but snugly. He began gathering scraps of branches and glanced over at a man-sized stump of a tree broken by lightning. On it was a thick sheet of moss draped like a blanket hanging to the ground. Sam lifted the wet branches that held it to the stump and carefully moved it, trying not to tear it too much as he spread it onto the ground. Once it was flat he gently rolled and lifted it onto his shoulders. He brought the moss back to the fallen trees and hung it over the opening and reached into his breeches and pulled out a knife. He cut three openings for their eyes and the musket. Burl returned from hobbling the mule and stood in front of the stand.

"That's the strangest looking piece a moss I ever seen," he said.

"It is, ain't it?" Sam said. "I was damned surprised when it didn't just crumble up on me."

"I'll hold the powder and the balls."

Sam handed him the pouches and Burl took a ball and opened the powder and Sam held the musket as Burl loaded. Then they both entered the stand and sat down cross-legged and gazed through the eye slits. After a silence Burl leaned back and began whispering.

"Your pa and me set a whole day with your grandpa in a deer stand along a slope near Cradle Gap when we was boys," he mused. "That old man was single-minded when it come to hunting deer. He was loud and talked all the time except when he was hunting. Then he was serious. He'd set there looking through the eye slits for hours and shush us if we got to whispering. He'd wait and wait, and when a deer come up it were as if he knowed it were coming before he saw it. He'd pick up the musket like it were a baby and set it gentle onto his shoulder and sight down the muzzle."

"Did he mostly kill them clean?" Sam asked with reverence.

"Hell, no. The old son-of-a-bitch was blind as hell and didn't know a trigger from his dick." Burl smiled big and laughed without voice.

"You old bastard," Sam said shaking his head.

"Sorry was the deer that old boy plugged," Burl continued. "He usually hit them in the ass or the back leg, and me and your pa would run off after him with the old man screaming and trying to load the musket while he was running and the poor animal bellowing."

"I guess it were a good thing you had stock."

"If he didn't your pa and me would have gone hungry."

They sat talking in whispers with Sam looking through the eye slits when the herd of young doe appeared. At first two stepped from behind a stand of maple into a grass clearing spotted with puddles. They were tentative and unsure with their ears pointing upward. The first took a step and looked toward them and then away, ears bobbing and tail spinning and waving. They were too small to amount to much meat and Sam waited to see what else would arrive. More doe came into sight until a small herd filled the clearing and began grazing on the wet grass and drinking from the puddles. Sam thought on whether to pick one but Burl touched his shoulder to get his attention and shook his head. They both looked through the eye slits again until a mature doe of good size entered the clearing. The others moved around as she came between them, and she surveyed the scene with her eyes and ears and in a moment began eating. Sam kept her in his sight and slid the musket through the slit and quietly rose to his knees. He sighted along the barrel and focused on the center of her chest and slowly pulled back the hammer and eased onto the trigger. The shot rang free and the musket sizzled at the stock and the big doe raised her head toward them, her eyes full of fear and anger as the ball hit her in the shoulder. Dust flew from her and the blood came as the other doe scattered and the wounded animal bounded through the underbrush.

"Shit!" Sam yelled as he pushed aside the blind and stood up to chase her.

"Damned if your grandpa didn't teach you how to hunt deer before he died," Burl yelled out.

Sam kneeled to reload and Burl let loose with a laugh. When Sam finished they started after the deer through the brush. She had broken the branches cleanly and wasn't hard to follow as she cut her way into a box canyon thickly wooded down toward a creek. They kept after her with Sam yelling, "Shit" every time a branch hit him and Burl following and laughing. The deer took them nearly two miles into the canyon down a slope near the water but the underbrush was fallen and thick on the bank and the deer had leaped through it with her last bit of spirit and stood in the middle of the stream, eyeing them in anger as they came into her view, her chest rising and falling. Sam sighted again and she stared him down without moving as he sent another ball into her chest. Her mouth opened wide and her neck stretched upward as she fell into the shallows. Sam and Burl worked their way through the brush and waded the stream where she lay. The blood flowed freely into the water but she was still alive, her eyes wide and her chest heaving and her head too weak to rise. Sam stood above her and lifting his leg he slammed his boot heel onto her chest. She bellowed once and heaved. The breath left her as her eyes glazed over in death.

Burl came up just as Sam began lifting her hind legs and dragging her onto the bank of the stream. He pulled her over near a maple with a strong branch growing outward and dropped her flat on the ground. He took his long knife from his breeches and lifting her hind leg sliced cleanly through the skin below the knee and worked around the scent glands, cutting them free and throwing them into the brush. Burl took his knife and severed the jugular vein as the blood fell freely onto the ground. Sam took a strand of thin hemp and tossed it over the branch and tied the hind legs together and Burl began lifting as Sam saw her black eyes looking through him. The stare of a dead animal never failed to mystify him.

They cleaned her out and the water flowed and the stream was soon clear as the woods shocked silent by the gunfire began to sound out again in quiet rhythm.

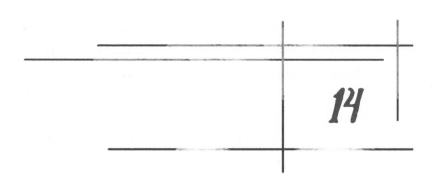

14

*T*he Clinch River was shallow but the ferrymen were busy.
Burl knew the toll would be high since the travelers were
so many, most of them standing silent and wonderstruck at
the sweep of the landscape west of the Blue Ridge. He walked
toward the man at the ferry stand and saw the riverbank
beaten and muddied with the hooves of oxen lashed to
Conestoga wagons heavy with children and household goods.
Farm wagons were drawn on crude sledges with rough-cut
runners of hickory or oak and they pressed against the bank
flattening the mud to a palate of dull gray. Lucetta sat on
the seat holding the team and Sam stood with Elisha looking
down to the river at Burl.

"I didn't figure there'd be this many folks traveling west,"
Elisha said.

"Me neither," Sam said uncomfortably. "I guess we
shouldn't be surprised though."

Sam looked at the crowd. When he was alone and pushing his family forward he could believe in the intensity of his
own will and its power to carve a roughhewn symmetry out

of circumstance. Leaving for the territory it seemed possible he might shape something essential out of the immensity of the continent and hold it for his children and find himself a home, but it didn't seem so now, not with the wagons here in such numbers and the people waiting and the animals milling near the ferry stand. Now he was one small seed blowing on the wind and he felt suspended in time, like a single blade of tall fescue in an uncut meadow. He leaned his shoulder against the wagon and fixed his eyes below him and looked at two farmers who stood rawboned and weathered against a wagon, one with a young girl on his back, the other with a skin sack holding some meager clothing and food and skins to trade. The men were together but both stood wide-eyed and muddled, stunned at the density of the teeming life along the banks and unsure how to speak their way clear and back to the purposes that brought them where they stood. They crystalized the moment in being there and Sam felt removed from them only because of the experience and protection of his uncle. Elisha saw and understood his brother's stare and looking at him leaned an elbow on his shoulder.

"Burley will get us across soon, Sam," Elisha said. "One way or another."

"I know he will," said Sam. "It's just that all these folks make me uneasy. I can't say why."

"I guess we wasn't the only folks with the bright idea to leave home and travel into the wilderness to get kilt by Indians or starve," Elisha said, patting his brother gently on the back.

"Guess not," Sam said, smiling wryly.

Burl worked his way through a team of unhitched oxen and arrived at the ferry stand near the bank. It was a solid structure with logs driven deep into the mud and rough-hewed planks nailed to them and ropes wrapped to poles and a moveable ramp slanting from the ground onto the upper structure. Burl stepped up onto the stand and the ferryman motioned him backwards.

"The boat ain't here yet," he yelled down. "You got to wait."

Burl ignored him and stepped up onto the planks and stood there.

"What's the toll," Burl said.

"Two dollar," the ferryman said, visibly irritated at being ignored.

"Too damn high, friend."

"That's the toll," the man said, looking at him and seeing his skin leggings and worn chapeau and realizing he wasn't a settler.

"You best lift your cap up over your ears, fella," Burl said, his face firm and his eyes set inward and his jaw tight and hard. "I said two dollars is too high."

"How you figure to get across, otherwise?"

"I figure I'll use your boat."

"A dollar," the man said.

"I'll ask you one more time, mister. This ain't the first time I've crossed this river."

The ferryman looked at Burl's stout form and knew from his rough-hewn breeches and the set of his eyes that he was of a sort unpredictable and adapted to the place more than the people and families he had been cheating.

"Fifty cents."

"All right. That'll be for everybody on this trip."

The man nodded slightly and turned away and Burl looked back and motioned Sam forward. He could hear a low grumble among the people between them on the bank and he stepped down from the stand and began to help a few of them on board. As the boat pulled up to the stand he took hold of the yoke of an ox team hitched to a Conestoga that was heavy laden with kitchen goods and implements. The settler who owned it obeyed him without speaking and as the wheels moved up the ramp he stared at Burl with the eyes of a supplicant. Burl scanned the banks for another wagon as Lucetta eased the team through the crowd. Edging in between them were two mules packed with skins and two men, bearded and sun worn, wearing wide-brimmed leather hats made of cowhide and weathered breeches and faded leather boots. One of them stepped forward toward Burl.

"Hey, old man," he said, with sarcasm. "Who said you was to head up this ferry stand?"

Burl looked up at him calmly with no surprise in his face and looked away again and motioned a second wagon onto the ramp.

"This river ain't deep, son," Burl said. "These boats is for families with wagons and children and goods to carry."

"I figure they're for whoever gets here first. And me and my partner was first."

"If what I said don't make sense, you best take a while to think about it."

"We're getting on now, you hear?"

Burl turned toward Lucetta and the wagon as they slid down the mud toward the ramp. He kept his eyes away from the man and lifted his left arm toward Lucetta and called her forward but in fluid motion snapped his right fist at the man's neck. The man fell back gagging and coughing and gasping for breath and his partner ran forward looking at Burl in dismay and dragged the choking man to his mules. Lucetta guided the team onto the planks and the wheels lifted upward as the wagon rolled smoothly over the stand onto the boat. Sam and Elisha stepped aboard and Burl followed them and the ferryman at the bank motioned to the pilot who checked the rope. The men standing with Sam and Burl and Elisha among them all gathered and took hold of the hemp and began hauling the boat into the current.

Sam pulled along the rope with Elisha in front of him. He saw his brother's back heaving and he tuned his motions to him and looked across at the driftwood along the shore and the rough cliffsides rising upward from the water. The land to the west of the river was rocky and uneven as shale walls sheathed in black lined the banks and were covered in low growth. Rising from them were elm and maple and jack pine with leaves budding out and creasing the tops of the tree lines with green mist. In a month the dull brown of branches would disappear under broad leaves, but now they reminded him of the cold and the frost and the void of winter, the boredom at the fort and the fear in stillness that left him only when they were moving. The wind was light and cooled them as they worked and soon they could see the ferry stand on the other side and the ferryman waiting. Eve Mary was with the children under the canvas and Lucetta held the team steady and Sam could hear her turn back and warn Ewan to stay inside. He could begin to hear the current as they approached the shore and the lap of waves along the banks as the pilot lifted his hand to his partner on shore to signal what he had onboard. They all began pulling more slowly and Burl stopped altogether and moved toward the front of the boat to work the gate. As the pulling slowed the current took them and the rope heaved and arched as they moved toward the shore.

"Keep pulling, you bastards!" the boatmen yelled. "We'll hit the stand crossways!"

The men all began hauling again and tightened the slack as the boat eased up to the stand and the ferryman took hold of the line. Burl lifted the rope from the gate and dropped it down and eased the gate inward setting it against the plank siding. He laid the plank ramp and began directing the wagons over the stand onto the shore.

The mud was thick on the bank but the wagon road was solid above it and Lucetta pushed the team through the mud quickly and the wagon slipped to the side as the animals lifted it onto the hard ground. The road was clear and empty with a single wagon visible in the distance as the maple branches canopied the trail and brushed and scratched against the canvas. Burl moved ahead of the rest and Sam and Elisha and Little Charlie walked just to the side of the team. Sam took the musket and Elisha the flintlock pistol and Charlie carried only a rough-cut walking stick. Sam looked back at Lucetta who held the team steady. She reassured him with a glance that everything was fine as the wagon bounced hard on the embedded rocks in the road.

"Ma's doing much better than before we wintered," Charlie said.

"Your ma's got more in her for hardship than any of us," said Sam.

He looked back again at his wife who sat straight and lashed the team. The years before he married her seemed real in the details but dreamlike, like a long sleep separated him from another life. It saddened him to think about her because of all she did to sustain them and all he needed from her in labor and love. It seemed to him her work meant more to them than his, though she would never say it, and maybe it was always that way with women, whenever they marry and bear children and nurse them and bury them. He kept looking at her for a moment and quietly turned his head.

"Uncle Burley's been silent the last two days," Little Charlie said.

"It ain't like him," said Elisha.

Sam looked forward on the trail at Burl who walked with his eyes in the distance and his ears attentive.

"He's worried about Indians," Sam said. "He told me the other night."

"What Indians?" said Elisha.

"Cherokee. We're in their territory."

"I thought we had treaties with them?"

"We do. But the terms say the treaty line is just west of Standing Stone, and we got to ask permission and pay a fee," Sam said. "Burley says the army's been cutting this road since eighty-seven without clearing it with the Indians or renegotiating."

"That'll rile them, I guess," said Little Charlie.

"Burley says they raid along here pretty regular," Sam continued. "We'll pull up in that clearing and wait. He'll gather some of the wagons coming behind us and we'll travel together, at least to Johnson's Stand."

"It'll feel safer with more of us but I ain't sure it is," said Elisha.

"He says detachments from the army come through here pretty often heading up to guard them boys cutting the road," Sam said, ignoring Elisha's comment. "Burl said they will slow up to escort wagons if they see them. Otherwise, we're on our own."

The trail twisted into a clearing and Burl turned to them and raised his arm at Sam who motioned to Lucetta to move the team off the road and wait. The wagons that were on the ferry with them followed and Burl returned to them walking up to Sam.

"Let's hope them ferryman bastards let some wagons on the next boat instead of them trapping and trading sons-of-bitches," he said.

"Whoever's onboard should be coming up the road within an hour," said Elisha.

"Are we just going to wait?" Sam said, impatient, looking at Burl.

"Yep, son. We will if we ain't foolish."

The meadow rose to a crest and the wagons rested on the dry grass. The tall fescue drifted in the breeze and Sam stepped forward ahead of the wagons to follow the road with his eyes into the next stand of trees. He came to the top of a knoll and looked down the field and was stunned in wonder in seeing the rhododendrons in bloom, sweeping in a purple shroud across the flatland between the groves. He looked down at his feet and he could see a single flower, its petals woven neatly around the stem and finely laced with dim yellow and inlaid with altered tones of blue, as if someone had sat alone and envisioned it and calmly painted it onto the landscape then left it to move to currents alien to itself. Taken together in his eyes as he looked down the meadow the individual blossoms were a lake of color and blended with the grasses and rose to a stand of mature dogwood with branches lifting upward and sideways with broad blossoms covering them in white. One rose above the rest and to Sam it seemed like an archangel presiding. He sensed there was something alive and breathing there that was more than the leaves and the grasses and the buds in bloom, something in contradiction to sight that evoked in him a fear akin to wonder and alien to repose. Burl walked up to him and looked down the meadow as well and Elisha arrived with Little Charlie behind him.

"I ain't never seen the flowers bloom out like this," Sam said, looking at his uncle.

"The land gets flatter the further west," Burl said. "Except for a goodly rise we'll get to later near Winter's Gap. There's meadows like this across to Nashville and even upward to where we're going."

"That's about the prettiest thing I ever seen," Elisha said.

"Somebody will plow it under before long, damn them," said Burl. He was sorry when the words came out and looked at Sam, who caught his eye and smiled as if to say he understood the sentiment, though he had always lived against it.

"This land looks more like home than it did where we wintered," Charlie said, looking at Burl.

"This don't look too much different than around Ste. Genevieve where we're going. But west of there, it flattens out even more."

"How far west of there you been?" said Charlie.

"Not far yet, but I figure to get there soon, before they plant me."

Burl looked down the field and across the tree lines and Charlie followed him with his eyes and looked at him and tried to penetrate his stare but lost himself in it. The four men stood a while and Sam broke the quiet, turning back to the wagon.

"Let's make sure the guns is loaded," he said. "Charlie, you take the pistol, and stand on top the wagon and make sure them kids stay nearby. Don't let them more than a few feet away."

"Unhitch the team and let them graze, son," Burl said. "Keep them yoked though."

Charlie walked to the wagon and Sam followed with Burl and Elisha as well and before they arrived with the others they could see the horns of a pair of oxen break through the trees behind them on the trail. They were pulling a flat farm wagon with implements aboard and a tall gaunt man beside it with a woman at the reins. As it entered the clearing another appeared and then another and Burl saw them and was relieved they were farmers. He walked down onto the trail so they could see him and motioned them to slow up and wait. Settlers on these trails were obedient to anyone who appeared to know the territory and Burl was used to their deference as they stopped and stood when he made his way toward them. Sam and Elisha could see him talking and the tall farmer nodding and when they were finished Burl motioned for Charlie to leave the team hitched so they could move. Lucetta had worked her way to the back of the wagon to slice some dried pork for a meal and stepping out from under the canvas she gave a handful down to Sam and took hold of the reins.

"These beasts is hungry," she said, looking at the team.

"There'll be plenty for them tonight," he said. "Burl wants to try to make Winter's Gap by dark. There's a road crew and probably regular army there."

Burl walked back and passing waved for them to move and Lucetta snapped the reins and the team lurched forward onto the road as the other wagons followed. Burl walked ahead of the wagon but kept closer than usual with his eyes straight and his head sometimes drifting sideways. The wagons rolled down the knoll into the meadow and slowly into the woods again. Sam and Charlie walked along one side and Elisha along the other and Lucetta held firmly to the reins, her right leg lifted and her foot set high on the planking above the seat. Her belly pressed against her clothing but not enough yet to restrict her movements and the team moved slowly with shoulders rising under the yoke as the trail rose sharply along a ridge. Sam watched the reins and saw as the wagon turned that the straps were caught around the buckle of the harness. He stepped over and unhooked them yelling over at Elisha.

"Elisha, watch them reins."

Elisha heard him as the wagon lifted roughly onto the rocks and the trail angled upward along a ridgeline into the hills again. The woods became dense with low growth and

young pine, and the elms and maples draped over the trail
and darkened the road as the wet air clung to the leather
of the harnesses and moistened the dirt-spattered hides of
the oxen and drifted into the rest of them mercifully. The
hills were rough again, though Burl told them that once
they passed Winter's Gap, their pathway would ease into
flatter more rolling country. Lucetta held tight to the reins
and remembered the mishap on the Blue Ridge before the
fort and kept her eyes on the shoulder of the oxen. Sam
looked up at her and noticed her tension and slowed his
steps, walking next to her near the wagon. He motioned
to Little Charlie to stay ahead a bit, and as Sam walked
alongside Lucetta she could see him and her face eased and
her shoulders dropped visibly. She looked upward along the
rock walls that lined the trail as they jetted out in blades of
busted black shale. Sam followed her eyes.

"It's hard to believe they could cut a road through all
this rock, ain't it?" he said.

"I can't see how they can do it."

"Slow, I guess. With a lot of men breaking their backs
on it. Burl told me there's been men working at it for near
fifteen year, between Knoxville and Nashville."

"They're done with it?"

"He said they finished cutting it last year," he said. "But
now they got to keep it up. There's crews all along here.
There's one clearing the gap just a few mile away."

The road began to level and straighten as Burl stayed
ahead of the team and Lucetta steered them and Elisha and
Charlie kept their eyes firmly on the harnesses. Sam held
them all for a moment in his eyes and saw in them a harmony

palpable and reassuring. The panorama of movement they formed and their expression as well appeared before him as the argument for their leaving, since they deserved more than the team of stupid beasts that pulled the wagon and more even than the French territories could give them. Lucetta held tightly to the reins as the wagon eased into a thin notch in the trail with shale walls rising above it and Elisha placed his arm up to steady the yoke and guide the oxen and seeing him Charlie did the same. The road straightened and flattened and they rose up the crest of the ridgeline and they could begin to hear the ringing of tools and the dim hum of voices that signaled they had reached Winter's Gap. Burl ran ahead and as they moved forward they could see the men working the cliffsides with pickaxes. Some of them were regular army with military breeches barely visible under the mud and some were hired men and a few were Indians. They worked both sides of the trail in disordered groups of three and four. Sam could see that Burl found the leader and stood talking to him. They passed a man tied to a post with his arms lashed around back and his chest thrust out and his face raised in a grimace of anguish and anger. He was a young Indian with hybrid clothing, a pair of leather boots and a cotton shirt with a leather drape around his neck and earrings and a cloth tunic of colored fabric around his head. Burl walked back and joined them, motioning for them to keep moving past the work team and down to a narrow meadow where they could make camp.

"They caught him stealing," Burl said. "That captain there figures displaying him like that'll warn the rest of them. I told him I knew these Indians well enough, and it would likely provoke the opposite, but these regular army bastards ain't got no sense."

"You couldn't convince him?" said Sam.

"No. He was stubborn about it. And it don't help our situation none," Burl said, looking forward on the trail as it drifted along the ridgeline that led downward through the woodlands toward Johnson's Stand and Nashville.

15

*I*t was early spring and Lucetta was just beginning to ease
from the aching fear that one of the children might take
sick when Ewan began to cough. She heard his voice lower
and his chest rise and soon he couldn't breathe and lay sweltering on a straw mattress in the corner of the wagon. She
sat with him and at midnight told Eve Mary to take Raymond
outside with the men so they could all rest and keep clear of
the sickness. In the early morning Ewan's fever rose higher
and he was still breathing hard but his coughing stopped and
he slept. Lucetta stepped outside and restoked the fire and
taking a jar of whiskey and a pinch of sugar from the wagon
she mixed them together in a small pan. She placed it neatly
above the fire and in the quiet she set herself hard against the
fear, knowing that most of all she mustn't lose herself. Ewan
filled her mind above all the others and sharp images flayed
her memory. She recalled him at four years using a stick as a
saber playing a character in one of Burley's stories from the
war. She remembered his lusty hunger at the table and his
tongue licking the clabber from the edges of his mouth. For

a moment she let herself think on his curiosity for common things, his boy's mind taking hold of a life he deserved and expected, not knowing the death that was ever present in a spoon or a kiss or a wisp of wind. She felt her stomach rise and a wave sweep upward in her chest and she cleared her mind of thought and placed her focus on her hands. The whiskey and sugar rose to a simmer and she poured it into a wooden cup and walking back to the wagon blew away the steam. Stepping up the planks she looked at the rest of them under the wagon, and she saw Sam twisting restlessly under a bearskin. He probably wasn't sleeping and she remembered his silence when the other boy died and his absence when he was with her afterward and she knew she nearly lost him. She crawled to the back where Ewan lay under the blanket rolling his head fitfully, his body wracked in fever, and she lifted his neck and poured thin droplets of the mixture into his mouth. He took the liquid still sleeping.

Sam lifted the bearskin from him and rolled from under the wagon and stood up into the chill. He stepped into his leggings and lifted the straps above his shoulders and pulled his thin shirt over his head wrapping the skin around him. He walked to the fire as Eve Mary awoke. On any other morning they would break camp and start, hoping to make the better part of a day's distance by early afternoon. Sam knew that with Ewan sick it might be better to stop altogether and let him rest, but there was a lot to do when they arrived and if they were too late to plant they would be ruined. If they stopped for Ewan the other wagons would leave them with the threat of Indians and they would have to stop when anyone took sick, which would leave them nowhere and with nothing. The rolling of the wagon would be uncomfortable but wouldn't hurt the boy, and his mother would have to stay with him. A blank and empty stillness beyond knowing would tend him in a void of silence and inevitability.

Eve Mary stood up and walked to the wagon without speaking and all she could hear was the whispered breath of Ewan's delirium as she lifted a bucket of whey and another of sour milk and handed them out of the back of the wagon to Sam. She took them and stepped outside and walked to the fire. She poured the milk and the whey into the oven and hung it above the flames, which were burning high and sending waves of sweet gray mist through the camp. Burl and Elisha awoke and Charlie did as well, lifting Raymond to his chest and wrapping him tighter in the blankets and setting him down again sleeping. They all stood near the fire in the warmth waiting for Eve Mary to finish the clabber.

"How much sleep did Ewan get?" Burl said, looking at Eve Mary.

"Some in the morning," she said. "But it was fitful."

Elisha and Charlie listened without speaking and Sam kneeled near the fire to warm his hands. The flames lifted high above the logs and creased the edge of the oven as Eve Mary stirred.

"Where will we make it to by nightfall?" Sam asked Burl.

"Are we traveling today?" Elisha said.

"Yeah," said Sam, still looking at his uncle.

"Johnson's Stand. I hope." Burl said.

"How far is it? What kind of country?" said Sam.

"About five mile out of these hills. Then about ten mile of rolling country."

Sam stood up as Eve Mary began dishing the clabber into a bowl. She tried to give it to him but he refused so she handed it to Elisha. Then she filled two more and gave them to Burl and Charlie.

"You need to eat, boy," Burl said.

"I ain't hungry," said Sam, kicking his foot lightly against a stone near the fire. "How's the road to Johnson's Stand?"

"Last time I was here it was smooth," Burl said. "It all depends upon the rains and whether them army boys have been keeping that part of it clear and passable. I expect they have. They mostly stick to the stretch between Winter's Gap and Nashville."

"I hope it's easy."

Lucetta lay with her head down half-sleeping and her arm over Ewan's leg and her hand near his chest. His voice rose and woke her, "She ain't yours, she's mine," he said, his face turning sideways with beads of sweat gathering on the soft folds of his neck, "I done found her and taught her how to sit." She pulled the soiled sheet from his body and opened his shirt and moistened a cloth in a bowl of cool water. She bathed him gently, watching the soft skin of his chest as he struggled to take in breath. His head rolled as he kept rambling and she fixed her eyes on him. His hair was wet with sweat and his eyes absent but his cheeks were full and alive as she placed the rag on his forehead and touched him softly, running the palm of her hand down the length of his brow. She focused on him and tried to sift what was material in him from what perhaps was essential and beyond even death. It was harder now when dying threatened and he wasn't awake to speak to her, because it was speech and thought and the visible journeys of his mind that seemed the true emanations of his soul.

They broke camp when they were finished with the meal and Elisha hitched the team as Charlie climbed up to take the reins. Lucetta told Eve Mary to hold Raymond and ride in front to keep him away from Ewan. The other wagons were readying themselves and Burl walked forward to talk to them and Sam looked at him and knew what he was going to tell them. One of our people is sick with fever. We're ready to go but later if he worsens we may have to stop. The road is clear enough and you can make it to Johnson's Stand without us but it would be safer if we all stayed together. You can make up your minds when the time comes. He walked back after a few words with each of them and stood for a moment next to Sam.

"None of them said nothing," Burl said. "I hope they're smart and ain't over-anxious to move fast."

"If we got to stop later I guess I can't blame them for going on," said Sam. "They may get skittish about the fever. They ain't our people."

"No, they ain't," Burl said. "But folks ought to help."

Sam went to the wagon and took the musket from under a blanket behind the wheel and cinched the pouches to his leggings. Elisha finished with the team and joined them and Charlie tossed down the flintlock to him and he blew the moisture from the hammer and wedged the pistol tightly into his rope belt.

"You boys stay up close and I'll stay with you, right up next to the team," Burl said. "The road's clear, so we don't need no one to guide the way. We should stay together, just in case."

Charlie started the team and the wagon eased forward on the trail with the other wagons following and Burl walking on one side as they rolled down from Winter's Gap into steep passes that led to the flatlands and meadows and thick wooded forests of middle Tennessee. They moved steadily between the hills as thin branches with new-grown maple leaves hung above them, making the time of day impossible to trace and leaving them feeling separate and removed from the rest of the breathing world. Sometime late morning they passed into a valley thick with tall grasses and groves of red oak and a stream that was bounded by a stand of spruce just budding and wedged to the creek-side. Lucetta could see the trees from a random cut in the canvas, and she looked at them dazed for a moment by the green. Ewan's fever had risen higher but there was no reason to tell the others and she bathed him as the sweat blended with cool water and beaded onto the straw mattress. His head twisted back and forth and his ramblings became more senseless but she took them as a sign of his struggle. As the trail became smooth and added less to his movement she noticed his hand. It began twitching and jerking and twisting and his arm did the same and soon his whole body was contorted and shaking and his voice ceased and the spit gathered in a pool in his mouth. She knew the fever was sending him into convulsions and that she must stop him from swallowing his tongue, so she grabbed a wooden spoon and wedged it down hard in his mouth. She yelled sharply and Charlie heard her and pulled the team to standing.

Sam climbed into the back of the wagon and catching Lucetta's look saw Ewan writhing. He took hold of the boy and lifted him against his chest and could feel the searing fever though his clothing. Lucetta stepped from the wagon and Sam handed him down to her and pointed toward the stream. They both began running and Burl stopped them.

"Sam, you get them down there safe and get back here quick as you can," he said. "I don't like this meadow. It's too open. Lucetta, when you get the boy into the water find a deep pool that's got some thick cover."

He pushed them on as they ran through the waist-high grasses into the spruce that lined the banks. Sam ran ahead pulling fallen branches aside to clear a pathway. They were heavy but he couldn't feel their weight, only the fire in the veins behind his neck as he took in breath and lifted and tossed and moved forward. Another boy dying seemed to signal a vortex of loss that might waste him and he feared it more than any threat he could see and fight openly. Lucetta was just behind as he continued through the clearing and he could feel her press against him, and as they neared the stream he jumped knee deep and turned to her. She handed Ewan down and lurched forward and falling into the water she felt the sandy bottom against her face. Water dripping from her she took the boy from Sam. He saw her face, blank and solitary, and both of them knew he must leave her and return to the rest of them.

As Sam took hold of a broken root and pulled himself onto the bank Lucetta held Ewan to her chest and lowered him into the stream. The water chilled her skin but soon she was numb as she took water in her palm and bathed the boy's chest. His cheeks were flushed and red with fever and his eyes sunken and his hair streaked in oil from the sweat.

His voice was nearly still and he used only scattered words and Lucetta listened for them in between the groaning. She rocked him backwards and remembering Burl she scanned the bank. Across the stream only a wagon's length away was a cliffside of dark soil with low growth above and a patch of three clustered dogwoods sending roots through the ground into the water. There were branches and leaves from trees hanging down entwining themselves with the roots and soaked deadwood in the water forming a cavern. She worked her way across careful not to lose her footing and arriving she ducked inside keeping Ewan submerged to his neck. He was no longer convulsing but she could feel the heat of him even in the chill of the water. She set her eyes on his face and held him to her chest and began to mumble a prayer. And just as she finished she heard Charlie scream.

The natives had waited behind the tree lines until they saw the wagons break free and then they moved taking each of them in separate bands. Charlie leaned over one of the oxen checking a harness when he felt the searing heat of a musket ball slice through him. He felt only the impact and not the pain until he realized and fell to his knees. Hearing his voice from the back of the wagon Burl rolled forward under the wheel and crawled to him and taking his arms pulled him under the hooves of the team and behind the wagon. Knowing the direction from which the first musket discharged he moved to where the wagon wheel would protect them, hoping they wouldn't attack from both sides. He had a flintlock with three balls and a long knife. Sam and Elisha heard the musket's report and Charlie's cry and without speaking they sheltered under the front of the wagon near the back of the team.

"Give me the powder, Sam," Elisha said.

Sam dropped the pouch of powder between them so that each could use it and leaned shoulder to shoulder looking in the direction of the trees. They were only a few feet away from Burl and Charlie.

"Where's he hit?" Sam yelled over, trying to steady his voice.

"In the meat of the thigh above his knee," Burl yelled back. "He didn't get hit nowhere vital."

Sam stared forward and saw the natives as they began to appear from the trees, some of them running and yelling with voices pitched high and others on horses of Spanish breeding and others on mules and one small native sitting odd and ridiculous on the shoulders of another sweeping his hands in comic gesticulation. As they came closer Sam could see their hybrid clothing, one of them astride a dust-gray mare his head shaved clean and red with a long strand of black hair dropping to his shoulders and a plumed raven's feather rising from behind. His eyes were on the top of the wagon and he wore a gray cotton shirt buttoned to the neck with a tight chain wrapped around him with Spanish doubloons of dim gold attached and shimmering and glistening in the sunlight. Creased around his upper sleeves were two iron bands stolen or traded away or taken by another in some distant battle with the French infantry and as he rode a red cloak sailed behind him sending a crimson bloody wave across the grasses. He seemed to lead the others or at least he had in the beginning but now they all followed their own lights and took to the wagons enraged at the sight of them between the trees.

Sam's weapon was already loaded and Elisha took the powder from the ground and began to load the barrel as Sam placed the musket to his shoulder and scanned across the meadow. He knew the time it took to reload and was afraid to miss and he looked across the crest of the hill where the natives were descending and spreading into thin ranks and hitting the four wagons together with the leader taking to the settlers near them. He saw in front of him a native riding a stolen mule with its back still marked with the settler's pack swinging an antiquated long barrel of French making taken from the wars in the north. Sam held him in his sights and saw that his eyes were deep and black and he was draped in a thick deerskin coat with lapels of fur and a belt of woven hemp. He wore a shirt of spun cotton as well held at the neck with the tie of a French nobleman and a red turban with a teased plume lifted above it tossing in the breeze. Elisha struggled to load as the native lifted the musket at the wagon and Sam set the barrel between the broad sweep of the native's back. He squeezed slowly on the trigger as the hammer released and the powder lit and sizzled in his ears. The ball took to the air almost visibly and creased the top of the native's shoulder and sliced a piece of hide and spun itself into the grass.

"Shit!" Sam said, turning to Elisha who had finished loading and slowly set the musket to his shoulder. Sam wanted to take it from him and try again but held himself back seeing the resolve in his brother's face. Elisha sighted down the barrel and let the hammer down and sent a ball square into the native's chest dropping him ten yards away. They took the powder and loaded again and saw that the band had made their way to the other side. Without speaking they leaned back to back against each other. Sam took aim and hit his target this time and in both men the panic ebbed and they were moved only by instinct. Elisha reloaded and Sam missed again but wasn't shaken and reloaded as Burl yelled over to them.

"Them other boys in the other wagons is all right!" he said. "I can see them from here! There's only about fifteen of them Indians!"

Charlie rolled to his belly and rested the loaded pistol between the spokes of the wagon and looked across the grasses but couldn't see to take aim. Burl saw another coming but Elisha hit him in the shoulder and dropped him from his horse. Burl knew that scaring them was their best hope but that settlers in wagons evoked no menace so he rolled from underneath the wagon and unsheathed his knife. In the thin sweep of a moment there were no natives within musket range but most were among the grasses and could see him as the wounded man struggled to stand. Burl ran at him and rammed a shoulder into his chest leveling him to the ground. In an instant he cut his throat and removed his scalp and with his chest spattered and his skin leggings sheathed in blood he raised the scalp above his head and stood in front of the wagon inviting them to come on.

They stood still on the crest of a knoll in scattered groups looking at him, the hooves of their horses dancing as they pulled at the reins. Sam could see the red-plumed leader with his shoulders forward and his face vexed and indecisive and he could see too a desperation stone-carved and per-petual. The men at the wagons kept loading muskets and pistols but stopped firing when they saw the band gathering out of range. Burl stepped forward again holding his knife in the air and the bloody scalp above his head.

"They could all come down on him and he'd be dead," Elisha said.

"I think he figures they won't," said Sam.

"Does he figure they're scared, you think?"

"My guess is they thought we was defenseless settlers and they weren't worried about getting kilt," Sam said. "If they come on him, they know they can get him, but not without him taking at least one of them along. He thinks he can convince them not to gamble on who it's going to be."

"That's a risk."

"He's figuring it's our best chance," Sam said, and in an instant remembered Eve Mary and Raymond above them in the wagon. "Eve Mary, you all right?"

"We're fine Pa," she said. "We're on the floor. We can't see nothing."

"You stay there, you hear?"

"Yeah," she said. "Pa, they shot a hole in the water barrel. It ran out all over the back of the wagon."

"Just stay down."

Sam and Elisha looked upward toward the knoll where the natives stood looking at Burl standing like a monument. It was a moment of interminable length before the band began to disperse into the trees. Burl stayed there until they were gone and then dropped the scalp onto the grass and turning he motioned toward the creek. Sam knew Lucetta was there and likely safe since the attack came from elsewhere and he was worried about the foodstuffs and supplies.

"Elisha, get down to the creek after Lucetta," Sam said. "I got to see after the water so it don't ruin the food."

"I'll check the provisions. You go."

"For once don't argue with me."

Burl walked back to them his face normal again as Elisha crawled from under the wagon and Sam stepped up into the canvas. Elisha began running down through the grasses toward the creek and was chilled by the silence in the trees but he followed the visible path they had made before toward the water.

Lucetta sat sheltered and silent among the branches holding Ewan under the water and listening to the musket fire and the yelling and the distant cries from the children in the wagons. She heard a spent ball reach the end of its range and skip slowly into the stream and she knew she was safe as long as they held out and she stayed hidden. Ewan slept in her arms and the cool water seemed to soothe him and his fits stopped as his chest heaved steadily. She scanned his soft face and she saw her husband's features and wanted him and worried suddenly for his safety. She moved her lips to a psalm as the sound of footsteps came from the bushes. Her heart rose in her chest and the pounding of the blood in her ears seemed almost to betray her when she heard Elisha's voice.

"Lucy, it's me," he called. "Where are you?"

She stepped from under the branches and saw him as he waded knee-deep across the stream. Fear gave way to sadness.

"Where's Sam?"

"He's tending to the wagon," Elisha said, seeing her expression but trying to divert her. "Everybody's fine. Charlie got hit in the leg but the ball went through. It didn't hit no bone."

She was swept away in weariness and her legs began to falter. Elisha took the boy from her arms and felt his body against him and in a moment they looked at his face as Lucetta ran her palm across his forehead. He was calm now and sleeping.

16

*E*wan's fever broke near midnight, and Lucetta leaned against the canvas and felt his even breathing and the cool sweat lifting from the side of his face. They slept into the morning even after the wagon began to move. Sam walked with his hand resting on the yoke and as they crested a rise west of Johnson's Stand he stopped the team. Standing Stone rose like a sphinx in front of them with its face staring westward along ridgelines that lifted into the sky and drifted downward to the Cumberland River. The ground near the monolith was flat and grassy and the trees were absent and the sandstone figure filled the air with sanctity. To Sam the people that carved it were nothing more than shards of broken pottery preserved there in attic mystery, and he gazed upward with his eyes set on the stone and sensed he had been there before, would always be there, silent at the base of the monument as the stars stand fixed and the red oak live and die and the ground-swell heaves beneath them. Burl saw him looking at the monolith.

"Indians worship here," Burl said.

"Who built it?"

"No one knows."

They reached to the crest of the hill and rolled into a deep valley that was newly cleared for planting and near the trail the logs of white pine and spruce and chestnut were piled high in stacks and branches were wrapped in rough-woven hemp. The wagon moved slowly with Elisha at the reins and Lucetta and Eve Mary inside tending to Charlie and Ewan. The boy slept deeply and silently but his chest rose in rhythm as Lucetta stayed near to keep the blanket from slipping from his chest. She was relieved he was safe but she was wasted from the ordeal and vexed by the dark purposes that could send the Cherokee on them at such a time. Since her fall into the river there was a dull ache in her belly and some light spotting but she was too tired to worry. She wasn't angry with Sam for staying with the wagon but she felt the lack of him and it hurt her since when she wanted him he was elsewhere among other concerns. He saw her pain and she knew she punished him with her silence. She looked down at Ewan as the wagon rolled and the canvas tarp buckled above her in the breeze.

Sam walked next to Burl and looked at the meadows as they passed them and the cleared fields with implements resting and the small log houses nestled near the trees. The ground was red and rich and ready for planting. He worked himself over and tried to push away the haunting resonant fear that they were losing time. Burl read his face.

"These fields been cleared three year now," Burl said. "They won't plant a crop for two months."

"Hope nothing slows us up no more."

"We're free of Indians now that we're west of Standing Stone. Nothing to worry about now but weather."

"That's enough, I guess."

"Don't concern yourself so much, boy. Any weather we get will slow up everybody. We'll get there in time for you to plant. Nashville's just a few days out, over them hills."

They traveled for three days and on the third they moved slowly into a dense dogwood thicket with broad branches reaching toward them. The woods were deep and rich with color, and the sun broke through only dimly but the leaves and the flowers took hold and altered the light sending material streams of color among the trunks of trees and through the low-growing ferns and galax. Clearing the woodlands they could see the smoke rise in wisps from small fires as Nashville appeared to them in the distance.

It was early evening and the sun was melting into the hills when they arrived at the edge of town and rolled past the first of the buildings standing square and even on modest and equal plots of land. They were built of rough-hewn chestnut and oak and were daubed in red clay but the logs were trimmed with an excess of care and the clay was shaved smooth and sculpted for appearance as much as use. They passed into town through the mud streets toward the square, and Sam saw an empty space strewn with shards of burned planking.

"Who owned that old place, I wonder?" he said, looking at Burl.

"That's what's left of Captain Williams' and Black's Store," said Burl. "It burnt down three year ago. Nobody's figured to clean up and rebuild yet."

"How come these houses all look the same?"

"The town planners decreed it," Burl said. "They're all on lots one acre each, and all the houses are sixteen feet square and eight feet clear in the pitch. Till now salt's been hard to come by so all the salt springs is public property."

"When I was a kid, I always heard it called Nashborough."

"The County Court of Davidson changed the name in eighty-four because they was riled at the British. They was probably taking a bow to the French."

They passed into the public square and Elisha slowed the team and stopped as they stood looking across the street at the courthouse and the prison that framed the pillory. There was a whipping post stained in drying blood and a tall sycamore that rose blank and horrid into the sky. From its outer branches hung a thick strand of hemp and at the end a single man swung lifeless and Sam walked ahead and could see his matted hair and chestnut skin and cold black and forward-looking eyes staring dead and wasted into nothing. He turned and looked across the square near the courthouse at an erected platform where four naked slaves stood chained and hunched with eyes pitched down. A tall man in a dusty waistcoat yelled prices and others dressed with equal care looked blank and curious and indecisive at the merchandise. Locked in the pillory was a white man alive but delirious with legs writhing and fists clutching as he exchanged the pain of standing with the pain of hanging. Sam walked back to Burl and the wagon.

"Wonder what the nigger done to get hung?" he said.

"Could be anything."

They passed by the stone facing of the Methodist Meeting House on the southeast corner through the square where people stood milling. Some were local women with silk finery draped about them and some were local men officious in their carriage and some were travelers and trappers and farmers from the river valley trading for supplies. But most were settlers leaving for regions north and west, and they were resting from the trail and relishing in the bustle and the movement and the sound of voices. Elisha worked the team with care and Sam and Burl walked ahead as Eve Mary came from the back of the wagon and climbing to the front looked out across the street.

"I ain't never seen a town with this many people," she said. "Look at the wig on that woman. She's powdered down to the shoulders."

"She's pretty," said Elisha, looking only briefly at the woman walking with a group of well-dressed ladies then turning his attention to the team.

"She ain't as pretty as Ma."

"No, she ain't, honey," he said, smiling. "She ain't as pretty as you."

Sam and Burl came to a crossing in the public square near a sign that said *Market Street*. They paused at a plank building stained black with moss and marked with whitewashed letters saying *Nashville Inn*. Wagons lined the storefronts and near the inn women and children gathered in huddled groups under the eaves as men stood smoking and talking near the doorways. Sam worked through the crowd onto the loose-nailed and uneven porch planking and saw an ad from a newspaper hanging on the wall.

NEW STORE
WILLIAM CASSIDY & CO
Have just opened, in the STORE HOUSE lately occupied by Mr.
Robert Talbott, next door to the Post Office & the Nashville Inn,
A Large & Elegant Assortment of Dry Goods, Hard-Ware &
Groceries. Among which are the following.
Superfine Cloths & Cashmeres
Bearskins, assorted
Negro Cottons
Rose Point & Striped Blankets
White, Red & Yellow Flannels
White & Colour'ed Marseilles, assorted
Laced Cambric Muslins
A handsome assortment of Chintzes and Calicoes
Silk & Muslin Shawls
Ladies Fashionable Head-Dresses
Hosiery, assorted
Fine Hats
Books & Stationery
Queen's Glass, & Japan'd Ware
Kid & Morocco Slippers
Men's fine & coarse Shoes
Saddles & Bridles
Nails, assorted
Madeira
Sherry
Lisbon
Jamaica Spirits
Cognac Brandy
Imperial

Aoung Hyson
Souchong
Congo
Coffee & Chocolate
Loaf & Brown Sugar
Pepper
Ginger
Allspice
Allum & Copperas
A small Invoice of Medicine, With a number of other Articles too
tedious to mention - All of which will be sold on the most reason-
able terms, for cash, Cotton, or to punctual men.

Sam walked through the door with Burl following him. The store was newly stocked and disordered. There were folded garments in stacks against the wall and open crates with books and bottles and kitchen implements and other dry goods and linen sacks of grain and cornmeal and sugar. Next to the crates in strewn piles were a hatchet and a hayfork and a striking maul, and near them was a winnowing tray used to store a hammer and a mortising axe. There were reaping hooks leaning against the wall and pegs newly driven to hang them and a flat table covered in goods. A gaunt man in a white shirt with a worn black vest stood behind arranging them. There were men and women idling in the makeshift aisle and others waiting to ask questions and Sam worked his way forward, unmindful of them toward the table.

"I need some cornmeal and---" Sam said.

"Hello to you too, mister," the man interrupted.

"Sorry, I didn't mean to be short. I just got people waiting outside."

"What do you need?"

"Cornmeal, blankets, some cheap whiskey and a sack of sugar."

"Sugar's costly these days."

Sam turned to Burl with a look of mild distress and his lips thinning with concern and indecision.

"Lucetta asked for sugar straight out," he said.

"You got to decide."

Sam looked back to the gaunt man, "We'll hold off on the sugar for now."

"How many blankets?" the storekeeper said.

"Make it four."

The man walked from behind the table and gathered the goods, and lifting them onto the table he took breath and Sam noticed he was worn and wasted from the crowd.

"Are you Cassidy?" said Burl.

"I am," the man said, arranging the goods and looking at them and counting with his lips. "That'll be two and a quarter."

Sam reached into his pocket and pulled out his purse and took the coins and handed them over.

"Where are most of these folks headed?" Sam said.

"All over. Some of them's local or near local. They're heading across the Cumberland River to the bottomlands. Some of them are bound for Kentucky and further west."

"How many further west?"

"I don't know. A few at least."

"What's the weather like here in springtime?"

"Fair, rainy, usually passable," he said, sensing Sam's worry as another man stepped in wanting to be served.

Sam and Burl picked up the dry goods and walked out into the sunlight and saw the wagon resting against the railing. Elisha leaned smoking and Little Charlie crawled from the wagon and stood nearby with his leg wrapped cleanly scanning the square in blank wonder. Eve Mary was still in the wagon and Lucetta returned from across the street where a group of women gathered talking. She walked up to Sam, and seeing her Elisha joined them.

"Them ladies told me there was a meeting in a glade west of here starting soon," she said, looking at Sam.

"A big one?" Burl said.

"It sounds like it," she said. "There's more than fifteen churches gathered. The Ironsides among them call themselves the Cumberland Association."

"We ought to camp near the trail and get some rest," said Sam.

"The kind of rest I need I'll get at that meeting."

"We need to get out early."

"I want to go," Lucetta said firmly looking at the supplies they held in their arms.

"I don't see no sugar here," she said. "Did you get the sugar?"

"It was more than we could afford."

"I asked you for some sugar," she said to him as she coldly turned away. They could see the dime-sized spots of blood on her dress.

"Lucetta, you're bleeding," said Elisha.

"I know it," she answered back. "I'm just tired. I want to go to that meeting and I wanted some goddamned sugar."

"We need to stop a few days or a week and let her rest," Elisha said, looking at Sam.

"We got to keep on," said Sam. "I've seen this before. She'll be fine and if there's something wrong stopping won't change anything."

Elisha looked at him perplexed and expressionless and walked back to the wagon and climbing up took the reins. Sam looked at his brother's hands and saw them shaking. They loaded the supplies and he moved the team west to the glade where the association was gathering. The sun was setting and near the crest of a clearing two oak trees rose tall and cold against the sky and between them stood a plankboard structure. Sam saw that there were trails from all directions entering the clearing and people gathering near the trees. Lucetta walked ahead of the wagon and Little Charlie climbed onto one of the oxen as Elisha led the team into the open near the edge of the glade with Eve Mary looking out from under the canvas. Burl stood next to him. Elisha eased the wagon to a stop near a red maple and stepped down clumsily waiting for Sam and Burl.

"I'm seeing more and more of these meetings the last few years," Burl said.

"They do bring the crowds," said Sam. "Who runs them?"

"Shouting Methodists mostly," Burl said. "But there's a circuit-riding Presbyterian named McGready that's got himself quite a reputation for preaching a lively sermon. There's all kinds here probably."

Sam scanned his eyes across the field to a tree and on it hung a thin sheet of paper. Sam nudged Burl on the shoulder and pointed.

An abstract of Principles Held by the Baptist in general agreeable to the Confession of faith Adopted by upwards of one hundred congregations in England and published in philadelphia – 1742- which is a Standard for the Baptist.

1st We believe that the Scriptures of the old and new testament are three Persons in the god head the father the son & the holy ghost

2nd We believe that the scriptures of the old and new testament are the word of god and the only Rule of faith and Practise

3rd We believe in the doctrine of Eternal and Particular Election

4th We believe in the doctrine of Original Sin

5th We believe in man's Impotency to Recover himself from the fallen State he is in by nachure by his own free will ability

6th We believe that Sinners are justified in the Sight of God only by the imputed Righteousness of Christ

7h We believe that god's Elect shall be called converted Regenerated and Sanctified by the holy Spirit

8th We believe that the Saints shall persever in grace and never fall finally away

9h We believe that Baptism and the lord's Supper are ordinences of Jesus Christ and that trew believers are the subjects of these ordinences and we believe that the trew mode of baptism is by immersion

10th We believe in the Resurrection of the dead and the general Judgement

11th We believe that the Punishment of the Wicked will be Everlasting and the joys of the Righteous will be Eternal

12th We believe that no minister have a Right to the administration of the ordinences only such as are Regularly cald and come under imposition of hands by the Presbytery & C.

Sam walked around the tree and looked down an embankment to a creek. It was bordered in short grass with shallow clear pools near the banks and a sturdy rope bridge traversed it and a dry path led from the banks into the woods. He looked down near the bridge and saw three young women. One of them was knee deep in the water with her breeches held high up her legs washing her feet with her hands as the others sat drying theirs' and putting on their stockings and shoes. Burl and Little Charlie came up from behind.

"They walked a bit, I expect?" Sam said, looking at the girls.

"Most probably," said Burl. "There's flatlands all around here, south of the Cumberland especially, and there's farms and small villages and little churches everywhere these days."

"Most folks will go some distance for a meeting."

"Ma would," Charlie said.

"Sometimes," said Sam. "When she's of a mind."

People of all kinds walked across the bridge and through the trees into the clearing. They were mostly farmers from the regions around Nashville. But there were also merchants in modest formality and shopkeepers in rolled sleeves with vests and town leaders in tall hats and frock coats and ladies in imported silk finery, all of them carrying plates of food covered in stained muslin and jars of liquor already half empty. Some of them were more prosperous with slaves behind them carrying chairs and poles and canvas netting for shelter and others had dogs and children trailing them. They all walked with anticipation and excitement humming in their voices. One young man with eyes wide and smiling struggled to carry a melodeon, and as it slipped from his arms Elisha came between the man and his instrument and slid down the banks and crossing the stream he helped him across and into the grove. Sam turned and Burl and Charlie followed as the crowd was beginning to settle and the sun drifted into the Cumberlands and the men took to the logs and set the bonfires blazing. Lucetta stood midway between the preacher's stand and the trees and they all returned to her and stood looking. The first preacher stepped out onto the planks and looked out over the crowd holding the Bible in his thin fingers. He scanned the crowd and they remained comfortable when his eyes were moving. But when he fixed on someone a hush went through them and the whole crowd stood transfixed.

"I bet that's Will McGee. He's a Methodist," Burl said. "He's a part of most of these meetings here and up in Kentucky. Him and some other fellas named MacKendree, Whatcoat, and Asbury managed to get the Baptists and the Presbyterians to join them, at least out here in the open."

"How do you know about them? You old river-dwelling heathen" Sam asked, smiling.

"You can't spend more than a week in Nashville or around here these days without you hear about them."

McGee kept scanning the crowd and pausing and orchestrating a response as they waited for him to speak. Then fixing his eyes on the center he raised the hand that held the Bible high in the air and began, his voice melodious and strong and lyrical.

"And my sheep will know my voice, ah, and when I call, they will come, ah. And a stranger's voice they know not;

therefore, they won't come, ah. Now brethren," he continued, "my sheep is likened unto a little goat named Cato, that my daddy had in North Carolina, ah, that come up missing one day, ah, and the thunder and lightning and the wind was coming on a mighty rate, ah, and we children went out and called Cato, ah, and no Cato answered we children, ah. But Daddy just poked his head out of the window, ah, and he called Cato one time, ah, and poor Cato he done bleated, ah. So you see, my brethren, ah, poor Cato knowed Daddy's voice, ah, and as soon as he called he answered, ah. Just so it will be with us in the great day of judgment, ah. When the master shall call his sheeps, ah, they will answer; and a heap of them will answer, ah, that he did not call, ah; and a heap of them will have on wolves' skins, ah, and pretend they are sheep, ah, but the Great Shepherd will know which one of them wears the wool, ah. So Daddy called poor Cato, ah, and he done bleated, ah."

Lucetta stood still and closed her eyes and began to raise them upward as she lifted her hands above her head and held her palms toward the sky with her fingers spread wide. Sam could hear the light hum of her voice and he looked across at the base of the stand as a young woman began thrusting her neck backwards sharply in quick awkward jerks yelling, "Yeouk!" As her voice lifted repeatedly her movements became more pronounced and her neck twisted as her head flew in all directions and her hair snapped around like a bullwhip. Soon her shoulders and torso were shaking as well and she fell to the ground contorted and writhing.

"What the hell is that?" Sam said. "I been to plenty of these meetings but I ain't never seen any of that."

"The jerks," Burl said. "I been hearing about this the last few year but this is the first time I seen it. It started here in Tennessee at some meeting, and now there's people jerking all through the territories. Mostly women. The spirit working, I guess."

"Her yelping curdles my blood," Sam said.

The preacher kept preaching as a young man worked his way through the crowd toward the woman, his face fearful and apprehensive as he lifted the woman trying to get her to the edge of the clearing. She struggled against him and at the feel of her body he flew back against the crowd twisting and jerking and yelping.

"Yes my brethren," McGee continued. "When Gabriel shall stand with one foot on the ground and the other foot in the water, ah, and blow that long trumpet, ah, that will wake up the dead, ah, and the living will start running, ah, and calling, ah, to be saved from the blue blazes of hell, ah. And when Daddy called poor Cato, ah, he done bleated, ah."

"We are told, my brethren, that we must not put new wine into old bottles, ah, nor old wine into new bottles, ah; and it becometh us to fulfill all righteousness, ah, and not to backbite our neighbors, ah, nor our neighbor's ass, ah, nor anything that is his, ah, and the Bible says, ah, wives do good to your husbands, ah, and husbands do good to your wives, ah, and children obey your father and mother, ah. Now, I want to know tonight, ah, how many of you ain't done these things, ah. And Daddy called poor Cato, ah, and he done bleated, ah."

The crowd around the preacher's stand was thick but a few people near the edge of the crowd began to disappear into the woods. Burl and Charlie were still there but Elisha was gone and at the center of the field a circle began to form and in the middle two men stood with black Bibles in the palms of their hands. Coiled on top of the bibles and around their wrists were two rattlesnakes thick in girth hissing and spitting and thrusting their necks at the people near the circle's edge. Sam glanced at them for a minute and turned to Lucetta who was still staring forward at the preacher. He looked long at her from behind and sensed that he had entered her mind and he waited as she dropped her hands to her side and leaned quietly and calmly against him.

"Now, in conclusion, I want to say to you, my brethren, ah, that if any of you get to heaven, ah, before the rest of us, ah, just keep yourselves ready to meet us, for we are coming too, ah.

"And while I have been preaching this night, ah, some of my sheep have gone to sleep, ah, or have gone out into the dark to sin in the dark, ah."

"And my sheep will know my voice, ah, and when I call, they will come, ah, and a stranger's voice they won't know, ah, neither do they come, ah. And Daddy called poor Cato, ah, and he done bleated, ah."

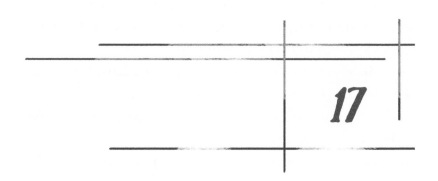

17

*T*hey passed into Kentucky near the West Fork Red through dense groves of mixed trees and low growth across wide streams and creeks high with runoff and as spring came the air was thick and rich with the smell of green. Ewan was stirring and beginning to complain of boredom and Eve Mary stayed with him and tended to Raymond. Lucetta drove the wagon again and held her attention steady trying not to think about the weight and size and growing tightness below her chest. Nature and circumstance gave no rest to women carrying children and she knew she was built to withstand work and weariness but the feeling in her belly was nothing like what she had known before. Her mind stood captive and she worried about the depths that would take her if something went wrong. She rested her eyes on the men and watched their backs. They stood straight and as their heads turned she heard thin wisps of words and phrases and laughter. She held them in sight and figured them as one thing purely and knew somehow that nothing would divide them from each other save dying. Working the wagon to the

STEVEN FRYE

center of the trail she rested her eyes on the team and held them steady on the shallow mud and on the animal tracks and the well-worn ruts carved by wagon wheels. Looking sideways she called back to Eve Mary.

"Evie, make sure Ray don't lean out the back," she said. She recalled that in the last week he had begun to test his legs by standing and walking with his hands across the gate of the wagon looking outward, trying his voice with strange and shapeless utterings. One of them stuck in her mind. As she lay half asleep against the gate he stood on her thigh and looked out over the field and pointed outward yelling, "Na nay nit!" It was clear from his face that he knew what he meant and thought others did as well.

"He's still sleeping," Eve Mary said.

"I want out of here, Ma," Ewan said. "I ain't sick no more."

"You keep yourself bundled, you little shit!" Lucetta answered in playful anger. "If you rest up enough today, I may let you range out with the boys tomorrow."

"But I ain't tired."

"You argue with me, you'll be setting in there till we get to Ste. Genevieve."

The men walked abreast with Little Charlie kicking his feet through the knee-high grasses. The road was flat and moist but passable and Burl was quiet masking his concern for Lucetta with silence. Sam looked over at Elisha and remembered seeing him disappear into the woods at the meeting with a little wisp of a girl they had seen in town among the settlers' wagons.

"You'd find yourself a woman where there ain't none," Sam said, half-smiling.

"There's a gift to it I guess."

"That old preacher had a few words to say about you in his sermon. He knowed where you were."

"I'm sure that sermon weren't the only seed he planted that night," said Elisha wryly. "Them hard-shell preachers get more tail than anybody. They got more to repent on too."

"Cavorting at a camp meeting, though. There's something downright sinful in that."

"There's got to be sin in anything that comes so easy," Elisha said. "Camp meetings is the best places for getting laid. Them sermonizers get the women all excited and you don't even have to convince them. Just stand there and wait along the edge of the crowd and they find you. They're like fish jumping out of the creek. You don't even need no bait."

"Never worked that way for me, brother," Sam mused.

"You was married before you was married," Elisha said. "Lucetta was always there, even when she weren't."

Burl walked with them silently and listened as the wagon moved behind them and a Cooper's hawk screamed and the moisture from the thick air gathered on the ferns along the side of the trail. His leg nearly healed Charlie drifted away from them holding the flintlock pistol and followed a thin game path along the edge of the woods. He limped only slightly. Elisha was quiet for a moment then he looked at Sam.

"Why don't we stop and rest, Sam? Lucetta's tired."

"We're all tired."

"Yeah, but we ain't carrying no child."

"Carrying a child inside is hard on women anyway. Lucetta's tougher than most."

"Sam, she don't need to be tough. There ain't no reason we shouldn't stop."

"Yes, there is," Sam looked at him directly. "You got eyes like the rest of us. There's folks everywhere on these roads and all of them heading west. The ones that push on will be the ones that get the best land and can make a go of it."

"You worry too much," Elisha said. "If you tend to your people everything else will fall together."

Sam felt the blood quicken in his veins and his temples begin to pound and the thoughts spun in his mind too quickly to frame into words. He could see Elisha's wry smile in the dim light of the bonfires as he flirted and bantered with the small woman, and he remembered the easy lightness of his movements as he followed her into the trees. He loved his brother but love didn't bridge the distances of spirit and temperament that knew their origins in mystery, in some chasm-like place beyond reaching. For him, to gain the moment was to lose himself, and to live for a joke and a clay jar and a piece of any woman's flesh was to forget what was genuine and fine in the one woman he had given all for. In his children lay the argument and the synthesis. They made the future absolute and the pursuit of it necessary and the commitment to it holy. He looked at Elisha angrily.

"Don't talk about my people. Don't you never do that again," Sam said. "I've got to drive us hard because I'm the one with the wife and the children. You don't know nothing about that, you hear?"

Elisha looked at him wide-eyed and shocked and he stopped and stood silent. Burl quit walking and Sam turned to face him. Lucetta saw them in the distance and slowed the wagon but wasn't near enough to hear their words. Tears welled up in Elisha's eyes but he gathered himself.

"I don't know why I ain't married," he said, with his voice shaking. "And I don't have no children because I ain't got no wife. Your children are my children, else I wouldn't be here. I'd be home in Carolina where I belong."

Sam stood looking at Elisha and couldn't think of anything to say but regretted his words and the flush of anger that fired them. Elisha saw and turning walked to the other side of the trail near the grass where Little Charlie was hunting for small game. Burl stayed with Sam.

"You be careful boy," Burl said. "You and your brother ain't exactly alike but you've always been cinched tighter than most. Watch you don't do nothing to change that."

Sam looked at his uncle and took his warning and the old man knew he heard as he slowly turned toward the trail. Lucetta moved the team and the wagon began to roll again and Little Charlie disappeared into the trees. Sam walked ahead and looking upward saw a pair of Cooper's hawks spinning and tumbling above the tree lines. They seemed to be mating but then he saw between them silhouetted against the sky a black snake rolling in the air. The smallest of the birds was flying higher and taking the serpent by the neck and arching upward into the sun then dropping it. The snake twisted and reached out in comic desperation for the earth as the other swooped down and caught it and snapping its neck sliced its talons backwards. He heard the sharp call of the highest bird as the other lifted upward on the currents until both of them drifted out of sight. He fixed his eyes on the tree lines and backwards to the trail and sensed the impotence of choice and the cost of inaction and he knew that indecision wasn't sin but lay next to it like a new wife. Sin was a thing that to the preachers was like an uncut meadow or an outfield lying fallow. With some little fortitude they could clear and burn it. To him it was no simple matter to know sin from sanctity. *All have sinned and are in need of salvation. All have sinned. All are lost and shall be found in his Grace.* What remained then with Elisha pressing him and Lucetta fading and the land they needed out there ahead of them? The voice that spoke out the answer was like foxfire, yielding to the world in a form wholly other, spending itself like a spark into the dim outlines of the maple branches.

The trail eased toward the northwest through a grove of white oak with thick low growth and as they entered they heard the report of the flintlock Charlie carried and they knew he had found some game. In a moment he came from the trees smiling wide and carrying a turkey, its wings spread out and dragging and his large head swinging lame.

"Here's supper for at least two days," he said to Sam.

Sam stepped to the side of the trail and turning waved the wagon past him with Elisha and Burl alongside it.

"Y'all keep on," he said. "I'll stay here with Charlie while he plucks out this bird."

Eve Mary tossed a cloth sack from the back as the wagon rolled through the trees and into another grass meadow. Charlie sat down cross-legged and began pulling the black feathers in clumps and tossing them into the grass, and when he was finished he took his knife and cut off the head and the feet at the joints and severed the backbone at the base and pulled free the entrails and dropped them a clean distance away. Sam held the bag and watched him in silence remembering the impulse now gone to guide and correct the boy and he noticed also his son performing even the smallest things differently. There was change barely there in the way he gripped the feathers and held the knife. He took the gizzard and liver and heart and placed them into the bag and began to stand, and Sam kept watching and then looked up at the trees. As they turned they heard Lucetta's voice.

They could see Elisha climb on the wagon seat and take hold of the reins and Burl near him with his body over Lucetta and they ran ahead with Sam in front breathing hard, his heart throbbing and his gut rising. As he came to the front he saw her leaning against Burl with her legs loose and lifeless and a thick swath of dark blood dripping from her dress and flowing into a pool onto the seat and the flooring planks. Burl's face was blank and his eyes were fixed and he lifted her to Sam and as he took her she screamed again piercing the trees and sending a flock of redwing blackbirds skyward.

"Set her down gentle on that plot of grass over there," Burl said, pointing. "Charlie, help your uncle with the wagon and stay with him and watch them kids. Send Eve Mary back here with some water and blankets."

Sam held Lucetta against his chest and walked with his knees bent to absorb the shock and settled her against the ground. Her eyes were wide and white and rolling in her head and she kept screaming and the blood flowed from her in streams.

"Lift up her dress and let me look," Burl said.

He could see the child's head pressing outward from the inside as her belly heaved and contracted and with each movement the blood flowed in crimson sheets onto the grass.

"I can't tell where it's coming from," Burl said. "If it's from the child or her. She may be bleeding from the inside. If she is, we can't stop it."

Sam held onto her and she grasped his arm with each heaving of her muscles and he looked forward at his uncle who stared down blankly doing nothing yet but waiting to see what she would do on her own. Sam's limbs were on fire as he held her against him. For a moment he cared little about the child only Lucetta, knowing the time had passed when they were bound and that death could take them together or separately. He felt his chest rise and the panic well and his legs weaken beneath him, and as his eyes began to roll he heard Burl's voice.

"Firm up, boy!" Burl snapped, reaching down to Lucetta's belly. Sam couldn't see what was happening at first but then he saw his uncle working the baby's body from the outside. Lucetta screamed again as he reached inside her.

"I can feel it but it's twisted up wrong," Burl said. "It ain't moving. I got to turn it."

Sam saw his uncle's face with his eyes intent and inward-looking and he saw the movement of his shoulders and his muscles and the tightening of his jaw. He found himself wishing he could cry at least so he could take in air again, and he gasped and held her close to him feeling her breath and her warmth and her heaving chest. He took them as bleak signs that she was still with them.

"I got it turned," Burl said, reaching in with both hands and pulling the child hard by the shoulders with his fingers under the arms as it entered silent and still into the open air. Eve Mary stood with a blanket and took the child. The blood still flowed from Lucetta but less freely now. As her screaming stopped she lay heavy and white against Sam's chest. Burl looked at Eve Mary who sat shocked and crying with the blanket in her arms.

"Stillborn," he said, in a whisper. "She's blue," looking at Eve Mary. "Take her back to the wagon and wrap her up tight in a clean blanket."

Sam sat silent in the grass with his eyes backward and sunken holding Lucetta against him. She was white and breathing weakly and Sam's jaw was set in a grimace of weak fortitude as if the legions it held back were thickening at the gates.

"Come to, son," Burl said in a quiet and even tone. "Let's carry her gentle back to the wagon. We got to get her where it's warm and dry."

They stood her up and Sam held her by the shoulders and felt her cold face fall against his own. Burl took her under the knee and Sam looked at him and saw his eyes wet and red and his face swollen and his lips pursed as if to hold something inside them. Elisha stood at the edge of the clearing leaning backwards and to Sam it seemed he would fall but he caught himself clumsily, his face lifting upward and the tears streaming and his mouth open and hanging. They arrived at the wagon and lifted her to Charlie. As Sam let her go she seemed not to know him as her head fell limp against her son's chest. They placed her on the straw mattress near the canvas and Sam stepped in and Eve Mary followed. They covered her in the bearskin and Sam stayed with her, his mind lost and dislocated. For a moment he didn't know where they were. Eve Mary moistened a towel and placed it on her mother's face and Sam rested his head on her shoulder but she was sleeping and didn't feel him. He looked down to her waist and spoke out weakly.

"Eve Mary, check and see if she's still bleeding."

Eve Mary lifted her soiled dress and spread aside the torn underskirt and looked.

"There's some blood coming out, but it don't look like much. I don't know, Pa."

"Get Burley."

Burl heard him from outside the wagon. He stood up from where he was sitting near the wheel and entered the wagon and worked his way to the mattress and lifted her dress again.

"She's closed up inside. "She ain't bleeding no more. She ought to be fine unless she gets the fever. Eve Mary, you keep her cool. Son, you best come outside for now. We got us a baby to tend to."

Sam stood up and felt his legs weaken as he traversed the length of the wagon taking hold of the arched wood bands that held the canvas. He followed Burl outside. Elisha was sitting in the grass and seeing them he stood again as they walked toward him. Little Charlie followed with the bundle.

They gathered together in the waist-high grasses and Sam took the child from Charlie and walked to the edge of the trees. Elisha followed him unsteady in his footing with

Burl behind. Charlie took Raymond from Ewan, and as they came to the base of a tall poplar Sam placed the child onto the ground and began to dig into the moist earth with his hands. He lifted the earth high and the deep roots of the grass ripped free until the hole was deep enough for the bundle to rest well covered.

"You got to name her," Burl said.

"I can't."

"You got to," Burl insisted. "She's old enough to name."

"Elizabeth," Elisha said weakly, his voice more breath than sound and his eyes glazed and trancelike.

"Elizabeth," Burl said.

"Elizabeth Ann," Sam said finally.

Sam set the bundle into the ground but paused and rested his eyes on the red earth piled beside the makeshift grave. Burl touched Elisha's arm and motioned him to follow as they walked down the slope toward the wagon. Sam kept staring at the soil. His private hate more often harbored in silence gathered itself. He reached down and took a handful of dirt and pressed it in his palm until it turned solid in his grasp. He threw it hard against the tree and began taking handfuls and throwing them and when the pile was gone he reached his fingernails into the earth and began pulling tufts and holding them to his face and heaving them away. Elisha saw and began to move further away but Burl held him, and they heard a low moan rise from Sam's throat as he kept up digging as if he would dig out another grave, sweeping his arms from side to side and slamming his palms against the tree until he weakened and leaned against it.

Burl stared at Eve Mary and reached for Raymond and then looked down at Ewan who stood shocked and unknowing at his father.

"Elisha, you and Eve Mary go on up there and get your brother."

"I can't."

"You got to find it in yourself, boy."

"He don't want nobody now."

"He didn't a minute ago, but he does now. You get on up there."

Eve Mary walked ahead. Elisha trailed her, turning back to Burl as he stumbled in the grass. Burl's face sent him forward into the trees.

18

The plankboards on the ferry from Kaskaskia were smooth and worn and slick with waste and Sam held tight to the harnesses to keep his footing and fixed his eyes on the dark water spinning in eddies from the bow point. The river was vast and wide like nothing he had seen with *bateaux* and pirogues traversing its breadth, the islands thick in dead trees and branches bare of leaves reaching skyward and thin mists skirting them ghost-like and treacherous. The plateau of the *Grand Champ* south of Nouvelle Ste. Genevieve and Nouvelle Bourbon seemed his inner condition, blank and barren and thin of life, the desire that brought him here now gone, its absence keen and hard felt in the infinite hollow of his chest.

Burl and Elisha stood together near the back of the boat leaning against the split-board railing with their shoulders nearly touching but their thoughts floating rudderless. Lucetta lay sleeping in the wagon. She was able to stand and talk but instead drifted in and out of things, her eyes staring black and piercing through the narrow opening in the canvas. Sam knew her mind would answer only inward and he felt the impulse to worry but couldn't. He looked to the shoreline as they neared the ferry stand that marked the French Creole country at the opening of Gabouri Creek. The *Grand Champ* rose from the banks of the big river and even rows of tilled land slanted toward the hills into stands of black oak and chestnut in meadows newly carved with grasses rising. As they drifted closer the dim lights of Nouvelle Ste. Genevieve appeared against the twilight. The air held a late chill and the ferryman still wore his winter clothing, his pants of loose blue canvas draped in a hooded deerskin coat, the lapels wide and loose with a thick crimson sash binding it, his hands in thick gloves directing the pilot. As they touched the edge of the stand he took hold of the rope and bound it firmly, reaching to bring the stern around.

"Il y en a encore?" he said to the pilot.

"Deux charrettes. Mais elles attendront jusqu'à demain."

The pilot lifted the locks on the railing and the oxen sensed his movements and began to pull against the yokes. Little Charlie held the reins and waited for the signal and Sam moved as Burl and Elisha jumped the railing onto the stand. Sam caught his brother's eyes, wide and blank as he looked down the creek toward the town. His face was sullen and his movements stunted and strained, the anxiety and disorientation palpable even in the careful steps that carried him onto the shoreline. Burl stood next to him speaking low and Sam couldn't make out the words as he followed the wheels across the planking onto the soft mud of the road. He looked up at the ferryman.

"Pluie de printemps," the ferryman said.

Sam nodded like he understood as Burl walked up to them. Elisha stood back, his head drifting at once to the town then back across the river again.

"We're going to walk ahead," Burl said. "I'll see if I can spy out the land office and a place where we can make camp. I think it's best I get your brother into a town."

"Can you talk to these people?"

"Yeah."

"You speak their language?"

"Some."

Charlie led the team up the slope as the wagon slid sideways in the mud and Sam worked his way to the back and held tight near the wheel guiding it onto the flat ground. *La Grande Rue* ran along the edge of Gabouri Creek and on the crest of a hill Sam could make out the untrimmed logs of the abandoned fort overlooking New Town. The road was thick in mud but flat, and the wagon drifted as Charlie held the team. Sam walked just ahead near the creek and looked down the banks into the broken hedges and pathways toward the rocks as sounds began to rise above the moving water, dim wisps of music only half known, the clang of a hammer against an anvil and the hum of voices patterned and strange. As the town rose beside him he strained to take in the shape of the buildings, tall and high with rooflines pitched in angles, first slight then steep, with logs rising skyward and chimneys placed evenly in the center. One was a private home with log-spike fencing and a porch circling the whole of it. Sam sensed the town to the left.

"Turn up here, boy."

As they turned the corner on *Rue à l'Englise* he could see a free-standing kitchen in the back of the house built of uneven brick and sheathed in clay, its shingled roofline rising steep into a spired point with a chimney cradled along the side. The mud on the road began to thin out and the wagon moved straight and Charlie's eyes darted, taking in the town and the buildings and the lights along the quay just ahead of him. Sam saw him and waited for the wagon.

"These houses is all different," Charlie said.

"It's a different country."

"Them rooflines is funny. How come they set them logs up and down?"

"I guess that's how they done it where they come from."

"Are we going to build one like that?"

"Maybe. If there's a need to."

Sam looked at his son and saw a sharp divide between the boy and Elisha. The strangeness of the French territory pulled at him and his eyes grew large and intense and searching, with a native hunger in them Sam had seen in others along the way. Charlie's wonder wasn't courage really and Elisha was anything but a coward, but as both men stepped from the ferry they saw between the lights and the hills either the outer image of hope or its darker self in mystery, one man pulled forward into spaces beyond knowing and the other drawn to home. Looking at Charlie Sam felt uneasy.

"They're just houses, boy."

Charlie kept moving his eyes from place to place and a bustle could be heard in the wagon.

"You hear your ma at all?" Sam said.

"She's stirring a bit. I heard Evie talking to her."

"How are the kids?" Sam continued, struggling to speak now, and unable for a moment to find words. "How did your ma sound?"

"They're fine. Ma ain't changed."

Sam walked forward again as the wagon rolled down *Rue à l'Englise* toward the square. Dusk gave way and the stars rose but were dimmed by lanterns hanging from the eves and coal fires burning in the street. The town was trim and neat and full of order. The buildings were washed and the street smooth, with manure spread evenly and horses and wagons lining the quay. Even in their randomness there was precision. As they entered the square people milled about near the center, three slaves stepping in front of them pulling a two-wheeled charette, its thin poles rising from the side traversed by another and its heavy wheels like trusses digging hard into the mud. An old woman walked calmly on the planking that lined the road and seeing Sam and the wagon looked at him with a firm expression as if she'd met him before. Her eyes were wide set and brown and her nose long with thin lips drawn inward in dignity. Nothing about her said wealth or stature but Sam knew the manner. Her head was draped in a thin cotton shawl black in color and her dress was the same, falling dark and clean from her shoulders. She held a book in her hand, black and thick with a cloth binding, and she walked toward the square with a calm that both attracted and repelled him. There was a bustle of activity ahead in the square.

"What's bringing people up there this late in the day?" Sam asked her, signaling the direction with his head. She understood him only from his motions.

"Une vente aux enchères. Les affaires de ménage de notre ancien cure, l'Abbé Paul de St. Pierre," she said as she calmly walked on, not waiting for another question.

They entered the square lit by a circle of fires. The tall and shingled spire of the parish church rose in front of them, and near the front steps people gathered and milled about and talked in words and gestures strange and lost on him.

"Look at them round glass windows," Charlie said.

The church was wide at the base with a light sloping roof rising to a steeple and a belfry covered in trimmed and even-cut shingles. There were no eves along the roofline but the tall standing logs that made up the walls were cut square and white and set with care and bound with pegs and secured with clay. The planks holding the roof were dark in contrast and rose to the roofline evenly, angled and measured and cleanly placed. The door was tall and wide and above it a semicircle of colored glass decorated the face and near the roofline was a circle of the same. On the glass Sam saw strange flat figures of vivid hue draped in robes tied at the waist carrying objects he'd never seen though he could tell they were sacred. There in the dusk with the light falling on them strange and portentous, he knew these figures were deceptive. In spite of their colors they were shadows thin of substance but suggestive and full of meaning.

Charlie pulled the wagon next to a plankboard walkway and slowed to a standstill and hooking the reins on the footboard peg jumped down into the street. Sam walked forward toward the crowd and stepped between them toward the center. Neatly organized were sets of household goods, a French Creole chair with a split-hickory seat and another with a leather cushion, both with lathe-turned legs. A hutch of dark pine had been placed in front and behind it a modest armoire with little adornment, its tall sides rising without trimmings and two long doors planed evenly but rough on the face. A small table sat to the side and on it were kitchen implements, four pewter soup spoons gray and tarnished and three wooden bowls set in a row, a French clay pipe with an Indian woman on a chamber pot and a heavy cast-iron pan near three large wooden ladles. Sitting separate was another French Creole chair with legs oblong and bent, the split-hickory on the seat worn and broken in the corners. Behind them a small man with thinning red hair stood with his arms folded in front of him. He wore a long black robe with a collar reaching nearly to his cheekbones, the lapels wide, thinning only near the waist and bound with a leather belt. He stared at the crowd in tortured dignity, his green eyes forward and his chin firm, his lips tight and expressionless. Next to him stood another man dressed like the ferryman on the river with canvas leggings and hooded skin overcoat.

"I wonder who that man is in the robe," said Charlie.

"We're in front of a church," Sam said. "I'm guessing he's a Catholic preacher."

"Is he going to preach?"

"It don't look like it. Not with all these things here. Looks like an auction."

"What the hell is he doing at an auction?"

"I don't know. Maybe they're church goods."

The priest was silent and the hooded man began calling out. Sam and Charlie stood watching and couldn't make out the words but from the raised hands and answers it was clear the auction had begun. People in the crowd came to the center and took away what they had bought, first the chairs and the hutch, then piecemeal the kitchen goods and soup spoons and bowls. A tall young man with sloped shoulders took the clay pipe and finally the priest stood by as the hooded man began the bidding for the armoire. The voice of the old woman in black rose above the rest.

"J'aurai cette armoire, vous comprenez?" she said angrily. "C'est là où le Père béni gardait ses vêtements sacerdotaux."

"On prend des enchères, Madame Vallé."

"Vous n'accepterez aucune enchère, Phillipe Virault," she said firmly. "Où l'église sera votre seul soutien à Ste. Geneviève."

"Madame Vallé, le Père St. Pierre nous a quittés---"

"Ça suffit," she said. "Vous êtes un faux curé et un Irlandais. Je ne vous permettrez pas de gâcher davantage le souvenir du Père avec ce spectacle."

She turned to the crowd and holding her black book in front of her.

"Il était votre propre Père béni. Vous l'aimiez tous. Et vous voilà qui achetez ses affaires après qu'il a été chassé par des hommes mesquins et des accusations fausses. Rentrez chez vous!"

She stood staring at them as they dispersed with their eyes down and the goods in their hands. Sam could hear a hum of voices but little dissent and the hooded man stood near the priest shifting nervously with his eyes darting directionless. The father stood firm as the woman looked at him.

"Monsieur le Père Maxwell. Vous achèterez le terrain, et vous augmenterez votre influence, mais vous n'aurez jamais l'amour de ces gens."

She pulled the book to her chest and walked away. Sam stood looking and for a moment thought he caught the father's eye as he turned toward the church. Charlie leaned against the wagon and looked down the road toward the center of the square, the light piercing the window-glass sending a thin film of gold under the archways and across the quay. There were foreign voices pitched high and fiddle music and the faint sound of an accordion playing.

"Stay here with the wagon," Sam said. "I'm going to find Uncle Burley and Elisha."

"Can't I come?"

"We don't know this place, boy," said Sam. "You know you got to stay back? What's the matter with you?"

Charlie's shoulders sank and his chin dropped to his chest and Sam felt an animate tension rise and hover between them. The boy should know his place and do what was right and his sense of enchantment couldn't excuse him. The strength needed to rein him was greater now with the sights in front of him, everything new and curious and captivating, the foreign speech and the tall rooflines and the priests in vestments. As Sam walked toward the town center he saw along the plankboard walkways the teeming variety of the Creole town, the *cultivateurs* in worn farm clothing and *engagés* in dirty breeches and torn shirts and *journaliers* in much the same. What made Sam most nervous was the men of Burl's variety, the hunters, trappers, boatmen, the *voyageurs* in dress from places beyond a mind's reach that drew young men away and made a thin worn and prosaic memory of family and home.

Sam followed the voices to the tavern on the left. The light was bright through the windows and the door opened toward him sending a rush of light and sound outward to the road. The ceiling was high and the walls were lined in a rich imported paper, a rococo floral with leaves hanging loosely from long vases, water-stained in spots and discolored from the humid air. Thick oaken borders ran waist high along the sides and below them an altered pattern of dark green paper covered the surface to the floor. The walls were lined awkwardly with framed paintings and engravings of various sizes, some of them landscapes or interior social scenes or portraits, one with a female figure from myth standing near a draped canopy loosely dressed in linen and holding a vase. Sam had never seen its like before, the face staring at him but also inward at the vase as well, eerie in the movement created by the contours of its clothing and strangely alive in the setting of the eyes. Together with the others it enlarged the room and seemed almost a doorway beyond. Candles were placed around the room to light the tables, but on the far wall sitting high was a hanging candelabra. Two candlesticks stood in front and behind them was an oval frame baroque in design with a crown resting on the top and a lion's head within, its eyes set in anger and its teeth bared. The candle flame brought the eyes to life and as Sam walked across the room they followed him. He understood the illusion but was no less struck by its playful exterior, since it seemed to laugh at the thin limits of his senses. Above the bar hung a long portrait of Louis XVI with a black and windblown wig and thick rich garments waving, the face staring away with eyes open and a slight smile, oddly it seemed toward the lion's head.

The room was filled with tables evenly placed, each of them lit by standing candles, and behind the bar a tall man in a long modest coat of dull black poured cognac into three snifters and handed them to a hunched and well-dressed man. Burl and Elisha sat at a table across the room with wooden mugs in front of them, Burl playing a game of cards. The room was a mixture of types, trappers in thick worn skins and miners in loose canvas and boatmen in faded white linen. Among them were the town's elite, two of them sitting across a table with papers spread out and a pile of gold doubloons and Louis XV silver coins together with a silver plate and two silver inkwells. One of them leaned back with his fingers touching his chest while the other examined a folded document, his hands adjusting his spectacles. Both of them wore powdered white wigs tattered with age and import and long coats with wide sleeves and lapel buttons. Tucked beneath their chins were faded linen scarves, one wrapped tightly and the other hanging trim and straight. Sam walked past them to the back of the room and caught his brother's eyes. Elisha seemed at ease after a mug of tafia rum and looked up with a lazy smile. Burl was intent on the cards, holding and considering them calmly as two young boatmen waited. There were card games going at other tables and the barman poured as men sidled up to him behind the railing. The door opened again, and the Irish priest walked through and sat down at a table and tapping a deck waited for the cards to be dealt. Sam looked at Burl.

"What did you find out?" Sam said.

"Hang on a minute, son."

Burl dropped two cards on the table and picked up two more. One American boatman picked up another and the other took three.

"Five pesos," Burl said.

Burl set down his Spanish coins, still in use in the French territory, and the first boatman dropped in five and added three. The other followed reluctantly.

"Well," Burl said. "We got us some fellas that's easy with their money."

"What do you have, old man?" the first one said.

"Now hold on," Burl said smiling, dropping in three more coins. "There's the trouble with you young ones. Everything's got to happen fast. You got to learn to relax and wait."

"This ain't no schoolhouse, mister."

"Two more," Burl said, tossing the coins onto the table. The second man dropped his cards and the other matched Burl and waited. Burl set his cards down smiling.

"King high straight. Shit!" the young boatman said.

"That's enough for me, boys." Burl said. "My folks is here."

The first boatman looked up and with a firm expression challenged him to stay. But Burl took hold of the money and walked around toward Sam. Elisha stood up unsteadily.

"Did you find out anything?" Sam said again.

"Talked to them rich boys over there," Burl said. "There's plenty of Americans hereabouts but most of them is settled up on the *Bois Brûlé* some five mile from here. But the land you was told about is some forty mile west, near Mine la Motte."

He dropped the coins into his leather purse and picked at his tooth with a thumbnail.

"The land office here keeps the records and signs out the land. There's a new American settlement out there, called Dogwood Crossing."

19

*T*he road from Nouvelle Ste. Genevieve to Mine La Motte was well used and dry and Charlie leaned to the side making way for the two-wheeled charettes carrying lead ore to the smelting furnaces scattered in camps beside the road. Elisha listened less to Sam and walked ahead alone, sometimes stopping and talking to the slaves and the *engagés* pulling the carts. Sam and Burl walked behind and Sam looked forward at his brother.

"He worries me," Sam said.

"Some folks take to settling easier than others," said Burl.

"I can't talk to him. He don't hear me."

"He's hurting," Burl said. Seeing Sam's lost expression he knew he needed something more. "Not just about the child, son. It goes further back than that."

"I never thought much about what he wanted."

"Sure you did."

"I guess I didn't weigh him heavy enough."

"There's a lot of men come into these territories, some alone and some with family," Burl said. "A lot of them don't stay."

"Why?"

"It's a hard way to live."

Sam looked down at the ground and watched his own footsteps as the dust gathered heavy on the rise of his boots.

"I never figured it would be easy," he said. "I knew we'd have to work hard, but we'd own what we worked for. We'd be free of Gilchrist and his like."

"I ain't sure there is such a thing as freedom. You figure old Gilchrist was free?"

"He didn't answer to anyone."

"He answered to himself."

"That's freedom."

"Men are all slaves of a sort. They can't get outside their own skin and their own thinking."

"You got to have freedom to think like that."

"Maybe."

Sam turned and looked ahead. Elisha walked along the side of the trail moving into the grass and gazing at his own feet then staring to the side into the air as if he heard something.

"I'm tired of trying to make him understand."

"He is what he is, boy. We all are."

"Well, you're right about one thing. It ain't going to be easy. Hasn't been so far."

"I guess it ain't the work that makes it hard," Burl said. "Everything's different away from home. Folks get homesick and some stay that way. It don't matter how unhappy they was where they come from."

"Except for these pits, this country looks a lot like home."

"But it ain't," Burl said. "And your brother knows it. It's more than leaving Carolina that's eating at him though."

Burl adjusted the strap of the musket on his shoulder and Sam looked at him curiously and directly, thinking it strange to hear these sentiments from him of all people.

"The reason I done this is to make it better for us all," said Sam. "Families ought to stay together. Now even Charlie seems to be thinking of other things."

"He's young."

"That ain't it."

"No."

"It's these changes," Sam said, looking at a charette passing by with two *engagés* pulling it and jagged black rocks of rich ore piled high.

"I expect it is, son."

They both looked ahead as Elisha stepped from the road. Burl followed him and Sam worked his way to the front of the wagon. Ewan held Raymond and sat with Charlie. Eve Mary leaned out from under the canvas. Sam looked at her.

"Your ma?"

"Sleeping again."

"Keep to the road," Sam said, looking at Charlie. "We'll catch up with you."

Charlie looked at him and smacked angrily at the reins and the oxen lurched forward. As Charlie and Elisha drifted from his purposes Sam wondered at the emptiness in his gut, with his infant child buried over the river and Lucetta lost in silence. But he knew that beyond the ridgelines he owned six hundred arpens of land that would take from him more than labor. He walked from the road and caught up with Burl and together they met Elisha at the edge of an abandoned pit. It was vertical in shape and sunk twenty feet into the ground with shale walls bleeding with dark spring water, the tracks of the moisture black and yellow with streaks of gray. The floor was riddled with busted rock and stagnant pools and scattered bits of decaying wood. Elisha looked downward.

"This was the way they mined it some years ago," Burl said.

"The ore was right here under the ground?" asked Elisha.

"I heard that fifty year ago you could pick it up with your hands it was so thick," Burl said. "You didn't even need no pickaxe or shovel."

"So they started digging these shallow pits?"

"Surface mining. They still do it some places but it ain't as fruitful as it once was."

"How do they do it now?"

"When Moses Austin and Amable Partenay got here they started sinking deep vertical shafts in the ground and splicing them with long shafts to walk through," Burl said. "Most of the digging's done underground by niggers and Creole *engagés*."

"Cuts the hell out of the countryside," Sam said.

"No more than farming," said Burl.

"At least farming brings in a different kind of green," Sam said. "This looks like shit."

"Them rich fellas own a lot of this land?" said Elisha.

"They claim a lot of it. But there's disputes," Burl said. "A lot of the land claims here that come from a few years before ain't backed with paper titles like yours."

"How do they keep it, then?"

"They got claims in with the governor and other men got counterclaims. Meantime they take out the ore and turn it into money and men like Austin protect it with bad men and guns."

"Seems like easy money."

"Easier than before," Burl said. "They got new smelting furnaces that get more lead out of the ore, instead of using them old bonfires."

Burl looked beyond the pit across a grass meadow and followed the road into the woodlands. From a distance they appeared thick with underbrush and rising from it were tall stands of white oak and hickory mixed with red cedar and maple.

"You think the road's clear through them woods?" Sam said.

"I expect so," said Burl. "But that don't mean it's safe."

"What's the danger?" Sam said, his fear oddly muted now. Burl didn't answer but kept speaking.

"You and me best walk ahead and see what's there and how thick them trees is."

"Both of us?"

"Yeah. We'll take the muskets. Elisha, you and Charlie move slow and keep your eyes open."

Sam returned to the wagon and Burl moved ahead and Sam reached him just before they came to the forest. As they entered they were enveloped in gray mist, with syca-more trees blocking the light and tall white oaks rising like blemished angels beseeching and repentant lifting branches into the heights and obscuring the sun. Between them were thick red cedars covered with ice-blue berries and nearby bloomed the fragrant verbena, flowers bursting like purple fire out of long leaves and low grasses. Between two adult cedars stood an infant persimmon, its bark covered in a blanket of orange fungus and pale lichen. Sam lost himself in a chaos of color but looking longer he saw it was bound in with cause, the trees rising toward the light and the young shoots drawing water and the new leaves sending seed and pollen, the beauty of it palpable and full of purpose. Near the persimmon was a young dogwood green and full with white bloom, its thin-fingered branches once dead now resurrected and alive. The sound of his footfall sent a broad-headed skink into the underbrush and silenced the birdcalls and Burl walked ahead of him staying on the center of the road his head moving and his eyes searching into the shade. The road cleared the first stand and opened into a small glade lined in maple and covered in low grass and yellow tickseed blossoms. Beyond the trees Sam could see a ridgeline clear of trees and traversing it the narrow outlines of the road. Burl stopped ahead of him.

"Listen into them woods ahead," Burl said. "You hear anything?"

"No."

"No birdcalls or sound of any creatures in the underbrush?"

"No."

"There's something wrong."

They moved slowly into the next stand toward the sound of a rushing creek. Mixed with the water they could make out the sound of voices and among them a woman crying. As they came to the trees lining the banks Burl touched Sam and motioned him downward. They crawled silently toward the creek and hid themselves in the underbrush at the base of a tall white oak. Looking down toward the water they saw the Osage, all young men in ornate dress standing in front of a party of eight whites, naked and shivering knee deep in the stream. One of the natives wore a thick woven band around his head with a plumed black feather rising from it. Another was draped in a loose crimson overcoat lined in white silk, and a third wore a tight cotton shirt bound with a red sash. One held a knife and two held muskets. Among the whites there were three men standing and two women ministering to the woman crying. Two more women stood next to the men with arms covering themselves. Clothing lay in a pile behind the Osage, breeches and coats and dresses and undergarments. Sam looked at Burl who signaled him to stay still.

"We'll stay where we are," he whispered. "Until they show signs of hurting somebody."

"Think they're just after the goods?"

"That's my guess."

One of the Osage gathered the clothes and another stepped between the trees and up to the road to inspect the wagon. He returned with a few items and after a moment spoke to one of the white men with threat and emphasis in his tone, then walked away from the road down a game trail into the woods. The victims stood still as Sam and Burl came down the bank. The young woman kneeling screamed again and another held her mouth as the two women standing scrambled for the bushes. The three men turned and met them.

"Thank the Lord," one of them said.

"All they done was take your goods?" Burl said. "We just come through them woods."

"They took all the women's clothes and left us here without nothing," said the man.

"Where are you headed?" Sam said.

"This here's a wedding party," the man said. "Were headed for Ste. Genevieve to get married, me and my bride there." He pointed to the woman in tears. "Name's Henry Padgett."

"Why you going all the way to Ste. Genevieve to get married?" Sam said.

"There's no parish priest in Dogwood Crossing."

"Parish priest?"

"You must have just come cross the river," Padgett said. "The only legal marriage here's a Catholic marriage."

Sam looked on at the man and Burl turned his eyes away as the women made their way to the wagon.

"You got any more clothes?" said Burl.

"None they didn't take, I expect," Padgett said. "Them Osage was up at the wagon. You boys going to help us get them back?"

"Let's just take these folks with us," Sam said, looking at Burl. "We can get them to where they come from since that's where we're headed anyway."

"No, we got to go after these raiders, son."

"Why?"

"We don't, they'll do it again. They may even hit us down the road." Burl said. "At least from here we can track them and clear our own way to safety."

"I'm obliged to you," Padgett said. "I'd go with you if I weren't bare-ass naked."

Burl took off his coat and handed it to him.

"Wrap your young woman in this and head back down this road," said Burl. "The first wagon you come to will be ourn. Say what happened, and they'll take care of your women and get them some clothes. Tell them I said to stop. You and your men stay on and help guard the wagons. We'll be along."

They crossed the creek and cleared the boulders at the edge and climbed to the game trail heading into the woods. The passage was thin but worn and the moisture from spring rain made the tracks clear. Burl turned to Sam after sighting the first footprint.

"Check your musket," he said. "Follow me and keep low. Don't make no noise. Where's your knife?"

It was hooked in his belt and rested against his back. He slid it around in front.

"Keep it where you can get to it easy," he said. "They ain't far away. I expect they'll stop soon to see what they got."

Sam followed Burl noticing the change in his movements and posture. His footfalls were silent and his shoulders curled forward and his head ranged across a wide spectrum of sight. The trees were thicker than before and the underbrush high but the pathway was free of branches. The stand was deep and they walked for a mile until the light began to break through the trees. Burl slowed and turned and motioned for Sam to stay silent and as they approached the glade Burl dropped quietly to his knees. Sam followed and as they came to the tree line they could hear the sounds of young voices and laughter. The Osage were at the far end of the clearing sitting in a circle.

"They're just young bucks," Burl whispered. "Boys no older than Charlie."

"Old enough to strip five women naked and take their goods."

"They come up in hard times."

Burl pulled back from the glade into the trees and Sam followed him.

"From here we're out of musket range," Burl said. "If we show ourselves they'll either run away or run at us. We got to sneak around this clearing and get closer and take them by surprise."

They worked their way backwards keeping the light of the glade in sight and Sam tried to walk softly. It was harder now without the game trail. He followed Burl's movements as he rolled his steps from toe to heel slowly and quietly. They crossed into a stand of black willow to the left and came to the edge of the clearing resting themselves behind high grasses laced in bloodroot. They could hear the voices of the Osage clearly and Burl looked through the grass, motioning for Sam to keep low. One of the young men rifled through the garments and picking up a red-laced winter shawl wrapped it around his shoulders and stood up thrusting his head out and smiling. Another leaned against a rock drinking from a skin flask and the other sat cross-legged and silent. They were only about twenty yards away.

"See the one sitting without the flask?" Burl whispered.
Sam nodded.

"I'll take him. You stay behind me and keep an eye on the others. Keep your musket up and point it back and forth at them two."

Burl crept to standing and lifted his musket.

"You young fellas just stay right there!" he yelled. He didn't know if they spoke English but knew they understood him. They stood silent with their eyes wide until the one sitting reached slowly behind him. Burl pointed the musket directly at him and he stopped moving.

"We're here for them goods, boys. And I expect you'll need to see the commandant in Ste. Genevieve."

The boy wearing the shawl motioned toward the clothes as if to offer them back and Burl caught his eye. But a bird-call lifted from the trees and Sam looked to the woodlands and the Osage sitting rolled toward his musket. The other with the flask pulled a knife and lifted to throw it and Sam released the hammer and sent him flying backwards against the rock. Burl ran at the boy with the musket hitting him hard before he could rise and Sam pulled his knife from his belt just as he took a charge from the other. Sam tossed his knife from his right hand to his left and lifted his arm high to block the native's blade, feeling the searing of nerves as it cut through the sinew of his arm. The emptiness in his gut left him now and his body tightened as he wrapped his arm around the boy's shoulder blocking the knife again. The Osage grasped his wrist and they rolled into the waist-high grasses and Sam held him to the ground and saw for an instant the grief embedded in fossil form in the cold granite of his eyes.

"Let go and I won't kill you!" Sam yelled.

He could tell the young man caught his meaning but ignored him as he pushed back hard trying to roll and free his knife hand again. Sam pressed his weight down and felt the arm give way, and as his blade pierced the young man's chest he saw his eyes widen slowly and glaze to blankness.

Sam pulled the knife free and stood up dazed by the rush in his veins. Burl was covered in blood and kneeling. The last Osage lay flat on the ground. His throat was cut and his neck broken and his head twisted in comic configuration against the broken shale.

20

*D*ogwood Crossing was little more than a mining town and a settler's outpost that rested at the base of a grass knoll just off the road to Ste. Genevieve. Mine La Motte was close enough for walking but far enough away that the sound of pickaxe and charge could be heard only dimly. They rolled into town at midday with the men standing near the wagon and Little Charlie still driving. Padgett stayed close behind but drifted back as they entered a muddy main street lined in plank buildings and lean-to shelters. A general supply and dry goods stood in the center of town with its front rising into the branches of an overgrown white oak. The plankboards on the building were unpainted and bent with weather and stained in black moss and the letters marking it were obscured by moisture from the rains. There were scattered structures and a large barn and livery. Padgett stopped in front of the store. Burl turned back to meet him and Sam followed, signaling Charlie to stop up ahead without blocking the street.

"You live nearby?" Burl said.

"I got a farm about four mile from here, just over the crest of them hills," said Padgett, pointing to a passage through a set of ridges to the west. "But we ain't going back now. I got to hire me an escort to Ste. Genevieve."

"I guess you're anxious to get yourself married?"

"Take a look at that sweet one over there," Padgett pointed at the young girl sitting silent in the wagon, her long brown hair drifting in soft strands down her shoulders, her chest exposed slightly and her eyes uncomfortable in the immodesty of her borrowed clothing. "Wouldn't you be?"

"You're talking to the wrong man," Burl said smiling, as Sam pulled a folded map from his breeches.

"Padgett, can you tell me where we're headed?" Sam said. "We got us six hundred arpens somewhere near here."

He spread out the map taken from the land office that marked out the plot he paid for in survey money. Padgett inspected it, confused for a moment by the foreign markings and symbols but finding the town for orientation.

"That ain't but two mile or so from my place," he said. "Follow this here road about a mile then you'll come to a less traveled road to the west that takes you into them hills. Take it into that narrow pass about three mile and you'll see my place on the right. Head past it through a thin stand of trees and go on about two mile."

He pointed to the map. It marked out some natural topography. "You see these here hills? They're just past my place. You see these? They mark the beginning of yourn. There's a tall stand of red cedar hanging over the road. Them's your trees. Just beyond there's a grass meadow. You got yourself a good useable piece."

"Thanks."

"You ain't concerned about heading back to where them Osage was?" Burl said.

"I ain't got no choice. They're a nuisance but what happened between you boys and them ain't common," Padgett said. "The commandant in Ste. Genevieve is François Vallé. I best tell him what happened. He's from an old family with land, money, and mines. But he's a fair man. He won't give you no trouble."

"Good," said Burl. "Take care of yourself on the road."

"I'll see you folks when we get back."

They returned to the wagon and passed through the town as people traversed the elevated plankboard walkways. Sam noticed that the place was more like home. He heard more American voices and the Anglo settlers were buying and trading and tall men were milling near the livery with hats hanging loosely around their eyes. One young woman lifted a sack of grain into a wagon, her skirt reaching only to her knees and the brown skin of her shoulders shining immodestly through the sweat. There were more slaves than he had ever seen and the Creole *engagés* and *journaliers* who worked the mines carried themselves with superiority. As the wagon passed near the edge of town two slaves wheeled a charette and three *engagés* sitting near a tavern shouted loudly. One stepped down into the street and heaved a handful of mud toward the blacks as they passed. The wagon rolled into the hills and Charlie veered west and continued for miles through woodlands and glades and newly tilled pastures past shallow pits of busted rock and decaying logs and broken trusses from the mineshafts. Padgett's farm appeared in a clearing.

They passed without stopping and carried on for nearly two miles and Sam pulled out the map and soon saw a cluster of red cedar leaning over the road. He motioned to Charlie to slow the pace and Burl and Elisha looked at him as the wagon eased up the slope to a grove and beyond to the grass meadow Padgett had mentioned. The glade was covered in waist-high grasses with tickseed and verbena bursting in a violent play of yellow and purple bloom. Bloodroot was scattered in brushstrokes against the trees. Sam could see the extent of the land they owned, the fertile meadow rising in an easy slope to a thick stand of hickory and linden bordered in sycamore. The beauty held him. He felt a hand upon his shoulder and turned around to see Burl and Elisha standing next to him.

"There she is, boy," Burl said. "Lovely, ain't it?"

He turned to the wagon. Charlie had stopped behind him and stared out toward the far end of the meadow. Eve Mary climbed from under the canvas and Ewan jumped from the back. Sam stood a moment looking at them and saw Lucetta's face peering from the canvas past him into the trees. He looked at her but she didn't look at him. He felt her absence again and turned to Burl.

"Let's get this wagon settled and find us some level ground to camp," Sam said, as he began to turn away.

"Stop and take it in, son," Burl said, taking Sam's shoulder and making him pause. He looked at his nephew, his expression worn and knowing, "It's been a long time getting here."

21

*L*ucetta lifted the handle on the Dutch oven and hooked it on the peg above the fire. The flame was low so she raised it with hickory bark and dried cedar shavings then salted the water. She turned to a table in the middle of the room and began halving the potatoes. Her strength had been with her since Ste. Genevieve but only in recent days could she bring herself to speak and stand, words coming out of her now instead of forming in her brain and settling heavy in her chest. Indifference had kept her in bed, but now as her mind came back guilt at her own behavior began to prick at her bringing bitter pleasure rather than pain. Thoughts numb and frost-bitten rose slowly to life in moments of exquisite shame. It was a feeling that always came when her mood lifted again to where she knew it should be. But she could take in breath only sparsely and work only briefly. Eve Mary came through the door carrying a handful of bear's lettuce.

"You make sure to mark down what we borrow," Lucetta said. "Where's Ray?"

"He's out front," said Eve Mary. "He can't keep his eyes off Ewan and Pa setting them fence posts."

"Ewan's keeping up with your pa well enough."

"He may be, but I'm tired. We went from building this cabin to planting and now to the fencing."

"Your pa wants to get the land around the cabin marked off so everyone looking will know them fields planted nearby is ourn," Lucetta said quietly. "There's enough dispute over who owns what and enough arguments over how to use it."

"Them big miners worry him some, I guess."

"Enough to keep him busy," Lucetta said. "He worries more about Elisha, though."

"Uncle Elisha don't cut up and laugh like he used to."

"No, he ain't himself. I figured he wouldn't settle easy."

"He works his share around here."

"True enough. But he's gone as soon as it's done."

"Pa's wore out some too."

"I suppose."

Lucetta set the potatoes in a pile and began wiping her hands with a moist cloth and massaging her tired fingers.

"You going to Mr. Padgett's wedding?" Eve Mary said.

"He already got himself married in Ste. Genevieve."

"I guess he wants to do it his own way too. There'll be some doins."

"No, I'll stay to home."

"Can I go?" Eve Mary asked imploringly.

Lucetta lifted her eyes toward her daughter and saw her tender face and clean flowing hair and the new shape now budding underneath her dress.

"Yes darlin', you can go," Lucetta said. "But you keep close to the women. Nancy Chalmers seems nice. At least she did when she come by to greet us with them tomatoes and that bear's lettuce."

Lucetta settled herself onto a wood stool near the table and began cutting again. Eve Mary knew she had finished speaking and was surprised she had gone on this long. Lucetta had wanted to talk to her daughter but chose her words with care since words weren't thoughts exactly but sharpened the contours of thinking and might take hold of her in ways she couldn't control. She kept at the cutting and heard the water begin to boil and walked over to the fire and dropped in the potatoes and turnips and broken ears of corn. She stirred as flames lifted steam into the rafters and the warm salted air watered her eyes. Charlie had skinned the hare but left on the head, so setting the animal flat on the table and breaking the spine she removed it with the knife and set the carcass in the pot. Eve Mary turned to walk outside and picking up a Creole shawl Lucetta followed her.

Ray wandered in circles with unsteady legs on the grass near the cabin. Lucetta sat on a chair and leaned against the outer walls and placed the shawl across her legs. They had raised the house in three weeks with the help of Padgett and a few of the neighbors around Dogwood Crossing, the walls of rough-hewn oak cut square from the grove south of the field, daubed in red clay and set level with plankboard roofing sealed in pitch, chimneys of chipped stone rising from each end and windows placed like eyes, eight feet each side of the door. Sam placed the house so the sun would set early on the front into a tall stand of sycamore, leaving it comfortable and cool with enough light to work into the evening. He built a springhouse near the edge of the glade and a paddock for the livestock and a covered shed of young hickory logs for tools and implements. Eve Mary sat down at Lucetta's feet and motioned to Ray who saw her and turned away. Lucetta felt the thick moisture in the breeze and the warm but cooling air of evening and she looked down toward the field at Sam. They had set three posts near the springhouse and Sam placed a fourth into the hole as Ewan lifted the sledge. The boy struggled with the weight but Sam let him handle it and showed no concern as the hammer came down near his hands. Between strokes Sam adjusted the post and they stopped to pack the base with clay.

Sam stood up and looked out across the field at the fence posts and the vertical stringers they had placed across the field to keep out the foraging livestock. The fields were planted and beginning to sprout at the crest of the hill with wheat and tobacco and stands of corn. The year before had been a good one they had heard and this year looked promising. The land around Dogwood Crossing was less risky. The *Grand Champ* near Ste. Genevieve was rich and flat and needed little tending and most years harvests were abundant. But when the floods came they fed the soil but washed away the crops and the *habitants* waited and hoped each year they would make it. Away from the river there was more clearing to be done and more planting on the hills and more need to rotate crops and feed the soil. But the river never threatened. Sam still worried though because the owner of the dry goods in Dogwood Crossing had advanced him the cost of the grain with his deed as collateral. The old merchant would collect from the first harvest and wouldn't carry them any longer since the big miners told him not to. They waited for the farmers to fail so they could take over the land and put them to work in the mines. Sam set his palm on Ewan's shoulder and motioned for him to stop and climbed under the fence into the field. He understood Lucetta's need for order as he set his eyes on the thin furrows and green lines of budding plants and even fences that formed a stark line against the dark woodlands. The carved land brought system and structure to the surface of things and gave him a sense of ease that was soothing, though in moments of brutal clarity he wondered at its precision and symmetry and the illusory purpose that drifted like a thin fog between the fields and lush stands of color. He stepped between the furrows in the wheat field and Ewan followed him as he turned toward the cabin. Lucetta leaned against the house and Ray walked along the edge of the grass and Eve Mary sat cross-legged watching him. Burl and Charlie were hunting in the woods and Elisha had disappeared into town. The three of them had helped with the buildings and the planting but with little heart. Charlie followed Burl on every jaunt into the woods and Elisha spent his time among the Creole *engagés* and *journaliers* who worked the mines. Sam turned to Ewan.

"Rest up, boy," he said. "We'll be out late tonight."

"When are we going to set the rest of them fence posts?"

"We got time, son. Tomorrow and the next day we'll get them done."

"With Charlie and Uncle Elisha to help we could finish tomorrow," Ewan said. "Then we could go into to Ste.

Genevieve to look at some of them new harvest implements Padgett was talking on about."

"We can't buy none of them this year anyway," Sam said calmly, warmed by the boy's energy. "If we take in a good crop, maybe next year."

They heard a voice from the edge of the field near the woodlands to the west and Sam looked up to see Charlie coming through the fence line with Burl. Charlie had convinced Lucetta to let him cut a pair of skin breeches out of the deer hide they took from the panther and he wore them tight around his legs. He lifted two wild turkeys into the air as Burl walked behind carrying the musket on his shoulder.

"How far away from here was they?" Sam said, looking at the birds as Burl and the boy walked up to him through the furrows.

"About four mile," Charlie said. "Them woods get thicker and thicker. There ain't but a few fields and we seen bear and deer track all over."

"I expect I'll take Elisha out soon to see what we can take in for the winter," Sam said.

"I can show you where they was," said Charlie.

"We can find them," Sam said, his voice firm and tense. "You best pluck and clean them birds if you want to go into town."

Charlie's face withdrew as he walked toward the implement shed. Burl came up and set the butt of the musket into the dirt and leaned against it.

"There was Indian track too along them game trails," he said.

"Don't appear like any of these settlers is worried about them."

"I ain't too worried, neither. They're mainly just a nuisance. But we best keep these muskets loaded."

"I wish you wouldn't always be taking that boy away."

"That's something you'll need to talk to him about, son. I ain't around long enough to say no to anybody."

"Hell, what am I going tell him? He does his share around here. He just don't like it."

Sam reached up and rubbed his shoulder, tired from working the fence posts. Burl took off his chapeau and dusted it against his palm.

"Elisha in town?" Burl said.

"He left two hour ago half drunk already."

"He's been a bit more friendly with the jug since he got here, ain't he?"

"He's shakier when he ain't drunk. I want you and me to take him into them hills. We'll leave Charlie here."

"You think you can get him to go? He's awful attached to that poor excuse for a town."

"I'll tell him I need him."

Burl shouldered the musket and they walked through the furrows with Ewan following past the fence line toward the cabin. Lucetta looked past Sam at Burl pulling the shawl firmly around her waist. As they came up Burl smiled and she noticed a hint of shyness in his face.

"Well, I guess we need them turkeys as much as them fences," she said, mocking him.

"I see you got you some color," Burl said. "It's good to see you outside, honey."

"The breeze is cool."

"Cooler here than in the trees."

"Did Little Charlie shoot them birds?"

"He did. Both of them. He's got him a sharper eye than his daddy," Burl said, elbowing Sam who stood next to him expressionless. Lucetta turned to Sam.

"I told Evie she could go with y'all to that wedding."

"We don't know most of these folks too well."

"Just keep an eye on her then. She's worked too hard around here for us to deny her a bit of pleasure."

Burl handed her the musket and told her to keep it close by and turned to Ewan.

"Can I get you to stay here tonight with me and your ma?" Burl said. "Some of us men got to stay."

Ewan's face turned inward but Burl's look of need was enough to hold him.

"Sure, Uncle Burley."

The sound of hooves could be heard on the road from the west and the sharp whistle of a musket ball and voices yelling. The horses raced into the clearing in front of the cabin and circled and milled as the riders spun their muskets into the air and let loose charges of smoke and powder. One tall man with a strand of thin hemp spun a bottle of whiskey above his head and yelled out laughing as the others pulled at the reins to hold the horses back from rearing.

"You spill that whiskey, you're a dead man!" one of them yelled laughing.

"Ain't a drop of this bottle is yourn, anyway!" the tall man retorted.

Burl leaned against the fence and Sam lit his pipe and Lucetta sat quietly looking.

"Padgett's friends is a happy bunch, ain't they?" Burl said.

"Everybody's happy the night of a wedding," said Lucetta.

"Hope none of the bride's people felled any of our trees," Sam said. "I like them big maples along the road."

"They'll lay something across the road to tangle these boys up a while," said Burl.

The riders left the grove passing down the road into the woodlands toward Padgett's farm. Sam and Charlie and Eve Mary left the house, Sam with the pistol and Charlie carrying a clay jar and Eve Mary holding the meat pie Lucetta had made as a gift. They came to the woods near the house and passed the row of cedars and walked through them into a meadow of tall fescue with flowers faded and gone. One tree was felled by the bride's people, and past where the road was narrow, twisted grapevines and under-brush blocked the way and a broken plow rested in the center. The air was still and hot and the moisture clung to their skin with the bugs still active in the early evening hovering in thin clouds near the branches and above the tilting strands of green. They passed through the meadow toward Padgett's farm and could see the radiating light of a bonfire lifted above the crest of a hill. Voices and laughter rose above and they could hear the faint sound of a melodeon and the high whine of a fiddle. As the farm came into sight flames rose and Sam looked down and saw the silhouette of his brother dancing near the fire with his form twisted and unsteady and waiflike and his arms around a young woman Sam had seen him with before.

Their voices were clear among the rest and distinct from each other as well, Elisha's drunken and strange and the woman's carefree and ridiculous. The horsemen from both parties were circling the fire and yelling and Sam could see Padgett standing nearby with two men beside him. As Sam and Charlie walked through the circling horses Eve Mary headed toward the house through a group of young men sitting amongst the musicians. Sam could see their eyes on her and he could make out a smattering of banter as he sat down against a rock. Charlie scanned the scene to find Elisha again then walked toward the house. Most of the horsemen were dismounting and stumbling in laughter but two young men from opposing parties reined in their horses and faced west through a stand of trees looking into a glade. Sam could see at the base of a hill four men standing with one of them holding a bottle of whiskey wrapped in a purple ribbon waving and drifting in the thick air. The man with the bottle signaled with his hand, and the young horsemen kicked at the animals' sides and sped rough and clumsy into the meadow. They passed the fencing at the same time and rose up the hill into the grass taking opposite sides of a black rock that divided the clearing, one of them jumping a log placed purposefully and the other a pile of high brush. Sam kept looking at the rider to the left, who appeared to be gaining the advantage, and from the corner of his eye he saw the other stumble. The horse's tail rose high as the hooves found a mud hole and the rider's hand rose as he pitched forward, the horse falling over him with withers meeting the ground hard but leaving the animal unscathed. The horse rose again in animal panic and trotted high-necked toward the trees. The rider stood up and looked ahead as his opponent reached the man with the bottle.

A tall man came from the shadows and sat next to Sam and handed him a skin flask. Sam nodded and took a long draw staring up the slope as the young man with the bottle lifted it above his head and trotted down the hill. The rider who had fallen from the horse met him and together they came into the light of the bonfire. Padgett walked up to them, smiling as they handed him the prize. Padgett bowed unsteadily uncorking the bottle and taking the whiskey to his lips. Sam looked at him briefly and rested his mind into the warm calm of the liquor as he scanned his line of sight for Elisha. He saw Eve Mary on the porch standing next to Nancy Chalmers and figures moved in silhouette in front to the light but he couldn't make out anyone he knew. From among the voices he could hear traces of speech and laughter and he thought perhaps he heard his brother among them. He handed back the flask and stood up following the others toward the house. The room was large and wide with furniture scattered in disarray and people milling and laughing and the fiddle and a melodeon playing. He saw Elisha sitting with a group of four men near the back of the room with his eyes glazed and his head sagging and his mouth fixed in a drunken smile. Sam walked toward them and sat down.

"Where's the young woman?" Sam said.

"Who?" said Elisha, half-listening.

"The young woman you was with out by the fire?"

"I guess she's over with the rest of them."

Elisha wouldn't talk and Sam was used to this because his brother had walked away from nearly every shared word since they crossed the river. Their bond these days was threadbare and though he resisted them words seemed the only means of pulling Elisha from the edge of a precipice.

"You seen Charlie?" Sam said.

"No. You bring him?" said Elisha, not really wanting an answer.

Padgett's young bride came into the room followed closely by his friends with his best man holding her firmly by the arm. Padgett stood up facing her as a bridesmaid came close behind. The bride and groom wore gloves and she put her left hand behind her back. He did the same and in jovial ceremony the attendants took them off. A voice rose high and volleys flew outside and the melodeon started playing again as liquor passed from hand to hand. A young boy in the corner hammered a rough jig from the fiddle and figures danced from corner to corner sometimes stopping to kiss openly with others clapping and laughing and drinking. Two men pulled a table to the center of the room, pushing the dancers out of the way and women began entering with big plates of food. Sam looked at Elisha. His eyes were set inward in stupor. Sam hadn't taken the time to eat any of Charlie's rabbit and the hunger rose in him as they brought in the meat pies and piles of roasted corn and boiled potatoes and roast pig. The bridal party sat at the table and others gathered around while the volunteer servers with Eve Mary among them brought the dinner. Sam rose with the others and walked to the table and took a plate and began serving himself. Two young groomsmen snuck along the wall and

Sam smiled as he saw them slide under the table. The bride held her feet beneath her dress as one of them crawled toward her reaching for her shoe. Eve Mary saw him and signaled one of the male servers who dropped a plate of greens on the table and rolled underneath wrestling the young man away both of them buckling in laughter.

Sam lifted his plate to his chest and took in the rising steam. He sat down next to Elisha and saw Charlie enter and walk toward the table. Eve Mary had finished serving and was chatting with one of the bridesmaids. Elisha stared blankly toward the people, his eyes swollen and red.

"You all right there?" Sam said.

"Piss off," said Elisha, slurring.

"No need to get riled up," Sam said, not surprised. "You want some food?"

"If I want food I'll get it."

Elisha scanned the room darkly and under the whiskey his mood shifted from laughter to gloom. Standing he stumbled toward the center of the floor. A young woman leaned into a man and Sam knew her as the same woman Elisha was cavorting with outside. Elisha approached and took her arm and the other man saw him and Sam rose just as his brother took the man's blow. Sam came to him as the man moved to strike again and Sam braced Elisha and stepped between them.

"Enough!" Sam said, looking hard at the man. "I ain't drunk, mister."

He took Elisha outside into the warm air toward the trough. He set him down and filling his hands with water he washed his brother's face.

"I told you, I ain't hungry," Elisha said, still stunned and delirious.

"Stay here," Sam said. "I'll fetch Eve Mary and Little Charlie. We're going home."

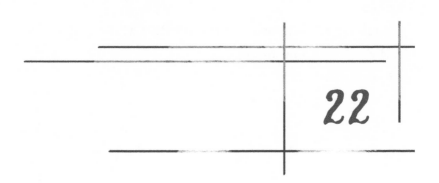

22

*B*url stepped from the trees and Sam could make out only part of him as he traversed the waist-high grasses. Elisha stood complacent kicking the tip of his boot into the moist dirt near the side of the trail. Taum Sauk Mountain rose behind them with mist gathering around the summit and together they looked forward at the flatland stretching for miles with the crests of the southern ranges making a rough edge of the sky. Sam saw nothing in Burl that bothered him and he knew they didn't need to go any further for game. But there was plenty of time before the harvest and Lucetta and the children were fine with Charlie there and Padgett nearby. The calm of the woodlands and a break from the town might free his brother from the snare that held him.

"Hot and misty, ain't it?" Sam said.

"I guess," Elisha said, half listening. "When are we going to set up camp? We can hunt plenty in them hills we just passed through."

"Burley wants to see the mountains to the south," said Sam. "He heard there was springs and caverns like nowhere else. I expect the hunting's even better there."

"It'll take more out of us to tote back whatever we kill."

"We won't be carrying it. These here mules will," Sam said, pointing back at the animal Burl bought at White's Fort and another they traded for in Dogwood Crossing. "I guess we ain't just hunting anyway, we're exploring."

"Exploring shit," Elisha mumbled. "We're walking our asses off."

Burl walked out of the grass onto the trail and set the stock of the musket against his boot. He pointed to the flask wrapped around Elisha's belt.

"Is that water or whiskey?"

"Water. My whiskey's packed on the mules," Elisha said, twisting the laces free and handing the flask to his uncle. Burl took a long draw and let out breath and wiped his mouth, running his fingers down his beard.

"There's Indian track on the trail just past them trees," he said, pointing behind him.

"You want to go on?" said Sam.

"We already know there's Osage all over here. We won't avoid them by staying here or turning back."

"What do we do then?" said Elisha.

"Stay alert and keep your muskets up. They're unpredictable but I don't figure they'll attack three grown men who ain't carrying much."

Sam shouldered his musket and Elisha put his hand on the pistol in his belt and Burl led them into the grove and beyond into a glade toward the long crest of the grasslands between the ranges. The taller ridges to the south blended with the pale blue and above them the worn peaks melted into the horizon. They walked for miles without speaking and camped in the open so the fire would be seen and traveled again in daylight for five days until they passed the Black River and traversed the woodlands again through creeks and springs and passes of tortured shale. Sam lost himself in the contrast between the twisted stone, broken and violent, that stood the shattered subject of what was above it, the rich redemptive soil yielding cedars and linden and oak trees, green and thick and indomitable. He could see only dimly the conflict and harmony, the death and the beauty and the life embattled and perpetual.

Burl led the way as the trail curved upward into the busted cliff sides and sharp ridges and thick trees that clung like stone fingers to the broken earth. Sam and Elisha followed until they began to hear the rush of water over rock. They continued through the trees when they saw the spring rushing out of the hillside and falling in sheets over the shale into a pool sprouting watercress with black lichen on the rocks lining the banks. Sam didn't ask his uncle any questions and stayed nearby with Elisha stopping to tend the mules. Burl climbed the dry rocks near the waterfall and Sam could taste the mist of the flowing water and the cool of the inner earth as they entered the mouth of the cavern. Burl stopped and leaned against the wall.

"Tell your brother to tie up them mules and to light a torch and bring it up here," Burl said. "Them old beasts will be fine as long as they don't wander."

"What about the Osage?"

"We won't be in here long. The woods is noisy so I don't think any of them's watching us."

Sam worked his way down the rock again and yelled Burl's words back to his brother. Elisha pulled the mules to the side and tethered them to a petrified stump and pulled from the pack a wooden shaft tied at the top with a dry cloth. He opened a skin bag on the other side and took out the flint and stone and placing them in a small shoulder pack he began climbing toward Sam. When he reached him Sam took the torch and Elisha struck the flint to the stone and set the torch ablaze. Sam handed it to Burl who held it ahead crouching low. The antechamber just after the falls was narrow and dark and Sam could feel his heart race as the torch lit a space only three yards ahead leaving the darkness looming. Burl kept on with Elisha behind until the light of the fire rose like liquid spray into the cavern. Burl stood on a ledge of dry limestone as Sam and Elisha came out of the antechamber. Sam looked out and felt his body thin to nothing stunned in wonder at the interior cathedral with grand vaulted arches and water-carved statuary and the rich and many-colored walls of layered earth. The inner structure appeared before them in a fractured fresco of dolomite and limestone, with thin plates of porous rock seeping water and sediment sheeting the sides in a flowing drapery of colored stone. Under the earth with his vision working at the will of a fading torch, Sam saw an order he sensed only in fragments under the sky, a presence oblique, a language attic and sacred and sacramental. The calcite crystals descended in divine symmetry from the ceiling dripping acid water onto the floor, trailing cold white stalactites and below them reaching to the heavens again the crystalline stalagmites rising. The whole of the inner chamber was lined in earthen figures almost human in form with even arches above them and finely cut sculptures calcified and polished. Sam leaned against the wall and took in the rich smell of sodden moisture and Burl caught him from the corner of his eye.

"I heard about these caves, but I ain't never seen them," Burl said. "I sure as hell won't forget them."

"Me neither, I guess," said Sam, still awestruck.

"Elisha, where are you at, boy?" Burl said, looking back.

"Right here," his voice husky and thin of sound.

"Pretty ain't it?"

"It is that," said Elisha, looking across the cavern.

"There's secrets writ out on these walls."

"About what?"

"About everything. About us."

"What do you mean, old man?"

"Look at how all them rock figures fold into one thing, like sung music and instruments, the water seeping out of nowhere and shaping them out."

"A beautiful accident."

"I almost wish it were."

Sam stood up from leaning and found a place between them, making sure to find solid ground to set his feet.

"They remind me of them glass pictures I seen on the parish church in Ste. Genevieve," he said. "The men all colored out in blues and reds, carrying them things I couldn't make out."

"I don't remember them," said Elisha.

"I do," Burl said. "And others like them on bigger churches in New Orleans. Them glass panels tell stories."

"There's a story here, but I can't read it," said Sam.

"You ain't meant to," Burl said.

"Burl, Sam's gone plumb out of his head. Just like you," said Elisha. "They're just rocks."

"Maybe."

"With death in them," Elisha continued as he leaned against the wall, his face drawing inward and his voice hollow. "Death everywhere. Tombs and dead matter."

Burl turned and looked long at him. Elisha stared forward as if entranced.

"I hope not, boy," Burl said.

Sam listened to them with his mind sifting words as he looked outward at the sculpted walls. Burl handed the torch to Sam and turned crouching to make his way into the antechamber with Elisha following him. Sam stayed back and stared hard at the room again trying to hold it in memory. After a time he stepped across the limestone ledge and into the passageway keeping the light in front of him until the sunlight muted it and the opening appeared in front of him. Burl and Elisha were near the bottom of the falls as he worked his way carefully onto the rocks and down to the ground. Elisha unhooked the mules and Burl found the trail again and they walked into a small clearing between the cliff sides.

It was near evening with the sun behind the thick high branches and Elisha pulled the blankets from the mules together with the torches and food packs. Sam took the food from him and pulled out two slabs of jerked pork and some flatbread. He set them down on a rock and walked over to a tree and wrapping the strap he began climbing up to hang the bag. Burl brought back some dry wood and began chipping away the bark for kindling. Elisha sat against a rock with a flask and took a drink and looked over at Sam.

"They ain't but one way to do things for Sam," he said. "Look at him tying that bag to the tree. He ties the same knot every time and looks for the same kind of branch at the same height. I think I seen him do it a thousand times."

"Some get comfort in small things being the same," said Burl as he chipped at the logs. "I knowed an old boy on the river. He was a brave man. He traveled into the Illinois territory earlier than most and fought Indians and weather and wilderness. But one time he couldn't find a rope belt he had for years, and looking for it he near cried like a baby."

"Did he find it?"

"He never lost it. I was hiding it from him as a joke. I give it back to him straight off."

Sam walked toward them as Burl dropped the kindling to the ground and took the food from the rock and sat down on the cool ground. Elisha took another drink and reached over as if to hand it to Sam. Sam shook his head as Burl took the flask and drank and handed it back to Elisha.

"You're spending a lot of time with that whiskey these days, son," Burl said. "And you don't look to be enjoying it much."

"Mind your own affairs," Elisha said dryly.

"In case you ain't figured it out yet, boy, you are my affair."

Sam reached for the flask.

"We all been wondering what's eating you lately," he interrupted.

"Nothing's eating me, for God's sake."

Elisha set the flask down between his legs and ran his hand up to his face and cupped his forehead.

"You seem on edge," Sam said.

"Ain't you on edge?" Elisha said, looking at him accusingly. "Hell, since we left home you nearly lost a kid and a wife and you buried a stillborn child."

Sam looked down at his feet and felt a rush of blood in his temples. Burl rubbed his hand against his face.

"We don't know but them things wouldn't have happened anywhere," said Sam weakly. He looked down at his feet then up at his brother, his eyes wide and limitless, even childlike.

"I ain't blaming you," Elisha said. "I just would have figured them things might have changed you some."

"Maybe they did," said Sam. "But what matters is them that's alive. What matters is that we all make it here."

Elisha took another draw and kicked his heel into the moist ground. Burl reached into his pocket and pulled out his pipe and stuffing it he raised it to his mouth.

"I'm thinking about joining up with Moses Austin's people and working in them mines," Elisha said.

Sam raised his head in surprise and looked across at his brother, his neck bending forward.

"Hell, why not sign on as a draft mule?" he said, his voice beginning to shake. "All they use in them damn holes is slaves and near-slaves. They'll work you hard as hell and pay you next to nothing."

"I ain't afraid of hard work."

"I know you ain't. But why would you want to work for them instead of with your family on your own piece of land?"

"Because you don't have to worry about the weather or the price of grain or the state of the soil one year to the next," Elisha said. "You get your pay and you live and you let them big fellas do the worrying."

"That's the kind of life we just come from."

"And I miss it."

Burl was silent and Sam looked over as if to call him in but the old man looked down and took a long draw from his pipe and then stared above the tree line.

"What about the family?" Sam said.

"What's the family got to do with it? I'm still in the family."

"A family works together and lives together."

"There's a lot of families around here that has some people working the mines and some in the fields," Elisha said. "Hell, the man that owns the dry goods in Ste. Genevieve's got a brother with a big cut of land on the *Grand Champ*."

"That's a damn strange kind of family."

Burl looked down from the dim-lit skyline and across at his nephews. In the twilight Sam could make out his eyes. He appeared to stare coldly into both of them.

"This ain't about working in no mines. It's about being happy and easy with yourself," he said, looking at Elisha. "You ain't happy no more, boy. Not like you was. And there's no easy choice you can make to change it. That jug and them women ain't helping you none, neither. You got to think it through, and you got to do that clear headed."

Saying nothing Elisha took another draw on the flask and stared into the fire. Burl let the comment stand. Thoughts twisted through Sam's mind like spinning embers and disappeared before he could frame them into words. The sound of insects rose into the night and the fireflies snapped and burned against the trees and the moon hung full and heavy under stars that stood like fixed sentinels cold and silent against a curtain of black. Sam chewed slowly on the jerked pork but felt his appetite leave so he reached for the flask. He drank the whiskey and felt the burning in his gut as the warm mist of inebriation set a mask over his thoughts. Burl settled under his blanket awake and watching and Elisha lay down and Sam leaned against the rock as a dream-filled wakeful sleep took him slowly.

He awoke to the sound of Burl packing the mules and the smell of the fire burning high. Elisha stirred slightly as Sam stood up stretching himself against the chill. The clouds set a sheet of gray above the eastern tree lines and he could make out Burl's face looking at him.

"We can set up a blind on the even slope near that draw to the south," Burl whispered. "I seen six or eight game trails when I walked through there yesterday."

"I suppose we best get set up soon," Sam said.

"Yea, or we'll be waiting until evening."

"I'd rather not. I want to head home soon."

Burl understood his change in mood and pointed over to Elisha.

"You best rouse your brother."

Elisha sat up slowly with Sam at his feet and Burl finished with the mules and took his boots to the fire, kicking the moist soil over the flames and making sure the standing embers were out. Sam walked over to the food sack and pulled out a slab of flatbread. He tore off a slice and handed it to Burl and tossed the rest to Elisha without meeting his eyes. Elisha took a mouthful and uninterested tossed the rest behind the rock. Burl yanked at the reins on the first mule and Sam took the second as they passed through the glade into a stand of hickory and scattered red oak and further into the draw where Burl had seen the trails. They worked the mules up a gentle slope and over a crest and tethered them to a tree out of sight. Burl pulled free the muskets and balls and powder together with the water and food and Sam took out an axette and ran his finger across the blade. Elisha picked up his whiskey flask as Burl handed him the provisions and Sam made his way down the slope toward a fallen hickory log that rested four feet high atop a boulder of busted limestone shale. He saw a large red oak nearby and took the axette to the low-hanging branches making sure they were thick in leaves. He set the limbs in angles from the log forming a V-like shelter of green. Burl packed the barrel of the musket and checked the pistol and handed the other to Elisha.

"Load this one too," he said.

Elisha took the musket and powder and shot and packed the barrel and sat under the cover and Sam entered the stand as well, placing himself at the other end. Sam's anger now benign and vain came out in hopeful silence but Elisha's thoughts were elsewhere. Burl knew enough not to speak.

He sat between them chewing on a slice of jerked pork and sipping from the water flask. As if to anger his brother Elisha took a long drink of whiskey and leaned against the base of the log. Sam looked at him but said nothing turning his head away. They sat in silence, Sam staring through the leaves at the opening in the glade where the game trails gathered and converged. With his eyes set downward he saw the flash of a tail as a small doe and three fawns stepped into the clearing together with a large doe fully mature and heavy with flesh. Sam lifted the musket to his shoulder, but Burl looked through the blind and touched him on the arm.

"Let these ones pass," he whispered. "There was some big track on them trails, and I'm guessing there's a few big bucks nearby."

Sam looked at him sidelong and skeptical but pulled the musket back into the stand. The sun was still low in the east and the mist drifted ghostlike through the glade and the call of a wren made the doe's ears rise as the fawns fed carelessly on the grass. Sam kept his eyes on them and Burl did as well until they drifted out of sight. The glade was empty for a long moment, but Burl kept his eyes intent.

"There," he whispered.

The tall rack of a mature buck appeared through the opening, its head firm and heavy and its neck arching high and majestic with its nose sniffing the air. It slowly dropped its head to feed and Sam could see the muscles on its shoulders flex under the weight. The grass was high and the head was lost but its shoulders and chest could still be seen.

"I ain't sure I can get a shot," Sam whispered.

"Just wait," Burl said. "Maybe he'll rise again."

Sam held the musket out and sighted along the barrel
and waited to shoot if the animal revealed his head and chest
again. The wren called out and the buck heard the sound
and rose with its gray chest now in full view. Sam set the
sight between the animal's shoulders and his vision thinned
as he pulled smoothly on the trigger. The muzzle sizzled
at the stock as the ball sliced through the clearing and as
the powder charged the big buck turned his head toward
them. Sam saw its eyes now, cold-black and full, bright still
and beaming in fear and anger, shining with a glint of the
sun's reflection like the colored glass on the parish church.
The big animal pushed out breath as the ball rose above
Sam's aim and snapped one of the points on its rack. Sam
rolled from the stand and the buck stood for a long moment
looking, the blind antagonism now present and palpable in
the angle of the neck and the chill of its eyes. Burl lifted
the other musket to his shoulder but the animal turned,
its muscles heaving and controlled and its power now fully
manifest as it lifted itself from view and disappeared into
the woodlands.

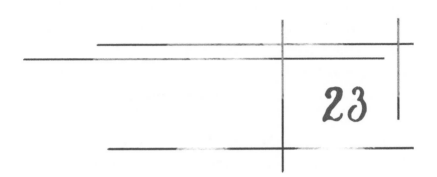

23

Charlie walked through the door of the dry goods in Dogwood Crossing and Sam heard his footfall on the porch
planking and reflected on its weight. They stepped into the
room with the high ceiling and the hanging implements and
the sacks of unsold grain. Sam could see the far wall lined
with reaping hooks and below them on wooden pegs hung
an axe and a splitting froe. There were winnowing trays on
the counter with smaller tools in random piles, a paring
stick and a boring auger together with chisels and mallets of
various kinds. The storekeeper stood with his back turned
atop a stool and lifted a hook free from its peg and handed
it to a farmer standing nearby. Charlie walked toward the
counter and Sam moved ahead of him and the storekeeper
saw them and stepped down. He looked at the farmer.

"You want anything else, Patrick?" he asked.

"No, that's all I need."

"That'll be fifty pesos."

The farmer reached into a pocket and pulled out the
coins and handed them over as Sam stood by. Charlie had

drifted to the other side of the store toward a stack of pelts lying neatly in piles arranged by size and type on a table.

"Mr. Willard, where did these here skins come from?" Charlie yelled over to the storekeeper.

"St. Louis."

"That's where you got them, but where did they come from?"

"From up on the Missouri River, I guess," Willard said. "That's where most of the trappers is working these days. At least that's the country I hear them talking about most."

Charlie ran his finger along one of the pelts and felt the heavy fur and thick hide and smelled the wildness still lingering. Sam leaned onto the counter.

"I need a barking spud," he said.

Willard rifled through the tools in a winnowing tray and handed Sam what he asked for.

"How's your crop looking so far?" Willard said. "The rain's been better than usual."

"Looks as good as any crop I seen coming in here."

"I expect you'll do enough to pay me for the seed and keep on?"

"I hope. Lord willing," Sam said, the worry present in his voice. Willard sensed it and averted his eyes tapping his fingertips on the counter.

"Rolens, you don't talk much but you seem like a good fella," he said. "I could extend you for a year or two but these big miners want the land. If they heard I was giving more than a year's credit on grain to you farmers they'd buy elsewhere. They'd put me out of business."

"You got a predicament, I guess."

"They're determined men."

"They're rich men."

Sam picked up the tool and inspected the metal then looked over his shoulder at Charlie.

"Let's go, son," he said, and turning to Willard, "How much?"

"Fifteen pesos."

Sam gave him the money and Willard stood still behind the counter as they walked out onto the porch along the plankboard walkway. Sam stepped into the mud of the street past a roan gelding hitched to the side and walked toward their mules. Charlie followed behind reaching into his shirt pocket for his pipe. He placed it in his mouth then took it out again, stuffing and lighting it as the smoke drifted into the air. Sam took in the sweetness, warm and raw against the dense smell of moisture and manure in the street. He looked across the quay toward the makeshift inn newly built next to the livery. A heavy man walked out dressed in a white shirt and a black wool coat with broad lapels and a collar rising high on the back of his neck. He carried himself above the man who followed, dressed as a *journalier* and carrying a pistol prominently in his belt. Other men milled nearby and clearly knew them as the well-dressed man stepped into the street toward a tall horse cleanly combed with breeding and musculature and ornate tack and a gold inlaid French saddle.

"That's Moses Austin," Charlie said.

"That's him?"

"One of the biggest of them mine owners next to Amable Partenay."

"You can't spend an hour in this shit town without hearing about him."

"There's some dispute between him and the commandant in Ste. Genevieve."

"What dispute?"

"The commandant don't consider his claims real," Charlie said.

"Burl told us about them false claims."

"I guess it will get resolved by the government folks in St. Louis."

"How come you knew him when you seen him?"

"Uncle Burley pointed him out last week when we was in town. Burley and Elisha been arguing about him," Charlie said. "I guess Elisha thinks he deserves them claims and Burl figures he's too greedy, that he's ruining the land and running out people like us."

"I wonder what he's doing here," Sam said. "I thought most of them boys lived up near Mine à Breton. That's near forty mile from here."

"I guess they figure there's money to be made down here too."

Sam looked on at Austin who leaned his shoulders back as his henchman took his knee and lifted him onto the horse. He looked back at Sam for an instant then past him. Sam could feel the man's indifference and knew that to men of his order farmers and workers were nothing. Sam kept looking and was fascinated by his posture and expression. The man seemed an emblem of things large and indomitable and beyond the present moment but weak when displaced from his money and his imported clothing and the tall horse that framed his wealth. There was something in his carriage as he moved the horse into the street that made Sam turn away.

They came into Ste. Genevieve in the cool of the afternoon after two days' traveling and crossed the street to the tavern and entered through the open doors. The building was new but looked old without the ornate French styling of the tavern they'd come to when they first arrived across the river. Elisha had been there three days. He had traveled ahead with six *engagés* he knew from Dogwood Crossing. The room was full and loud with men drunk and laughing and smoke hovering among the rafters. The walls were rough and unpainted and black with tar and the ceiling was low, with thick beams of solid oak set crossways holding the twisted planking daubed in clay. The tables were strewn randomly and were dimly lit with candles and the bar rested near the wall barely visible in the dim interior light. Sam and Charlie walked through the room filled mostly with *engagés* and *journaliers* just up from the mines and trappers and traders and river-men from Cape Girardeau. Sam looked across the room and his attention was drawn to a short man sitting unsteadily at a table, dirt lining the skin above his collar, his shirt worn and stained, a faded crimson chapeau resting on his head. He looked past him and saw Burl leaning against the wall smoking his pipe and Elisha near him sitting at a table, talking loudly at three *engagés* he seemed to know. As Sam came forward with Charlie he heard his brother's drunken voice and saw his blood-swollen eyes and faltering smile.

"Well, if it ain't my brother," Elisha said with a bite in his words, looking over at the other men. "Boys, this here's Sam Rolens. I'm sure you ain't met him yet. He don't get out much."

"You're drunk," said Sam, setting a hand on his shoulder.

"Drunk?" Elisha said, pulling himself free. "I ain't drunk. I ain't leaving yet, neither. I'm telling a story. Set down there, brother. You too, boy."

Sam took a chair not wanting a scene and Elisha leaned back in his seat, lifting the front legs free and losing his balance. Burl saw him and reached forward and steadied the chair. The door opened hard and slammed against the wall. One of Austin's henchmen walked through and stepped up to the bar. Sam saw him looking toward them and sensed his tension as he took hold of a whiskey bottle. The henchman leaned against the bar and spoke to the bartender but Sam couldn't make out his words. Charlie sat down next to Elisha and took a drink from his bottle and Burl continued to lean against the wall drawing from his pipe and looking at the man at the bar. Elisha didn't notice him and started speaking.

"One day there was a man and his wife lived alone," Elisha began. "A traveler come by and asked if he could stay all night because it was cold and miserable outside. They only had but a small house and one bed so they all had to lie together against the cold. The husband was a hard worker and a tired man when the end of the day come, and soon he was asleep, breathing heavy and snoring away. The woman got the traveling man to get on top of her and mount her. The old traveling man was humping away and the woman held the blanket between her teeth to keep from letting out a moan when the traveling man seen that her husband was stirring. So he began to cluck like he was driving his mules making like he was asleep and dreaming and not humping on his wife."

Elisha leaned forward resting his elbow on the table, losing his grip on the edge and slipping. Sam moved forward to steady him but stopped as he caught his eye. Elisha kept on.

"The husband just laid there but opened an eye and seen what was happening. The traveler was hollering and clucking away. Pretty soon the old man leaned up on an elbow and said, 'Stranger, my guess is you'll need to unload if you're going to get your rigging unstuck from that mud hole.'"

Sam dipped his eyes to the floor and Burl smiled only slightly but the *engagés* belted out in laughter and Elisha leaned back, howling.

"Now, ain't that some way to act?" he said. "With his wife humping a traveling man right next to him?"

Elisha took another drink from the bottle. Sam reached to touch his arm but Elisha pulled free again. The *engagés* stood up and sidled toward the bar. Burl stepped over to a table nearby to watch a card game. Elisha took the jar and lifted it to his lips but set it down again before drinking, then dropped his face to the floor in mute defiance of Sam's portentous stare.

"What do you want?" he said.

"I want to know what has hold of you."

"I done told you before when we was up in them hills to leave me alone."

"I ain't going to let you alone."

"I can't never figure you. There ain't nobody in the grip of things more than you. Why the hell do you keep at me?"

"You're my brother."

"That ain't it."

"It is."

Elisha lifted his eyes and Sam tried to take hold of them but they were glazed wet, shale black and shimmering. He looked through them down to the floor again.

"I need you," Sam said, curious and even shocked to hear the words come from him. Elisha looked up and Sam sat still.

"Burley ain't here forever," Sam continued.

"You got your piece of ground."

"It's ourn."

"I ain't got it in me to want it, brother."

A thick haze sifted through the rafters and Sam could see the dripping pitch as it caked the posts that lifted the ceiling. He looked across the room toward a table at two *journaliers* laughing over cards. He couldn't hear them speak. They seemed like they had been lifted voiceless from a dream.

"I can't see why you'd want to work for them bastards and not for us," Sam said, turning back to Elisha.

"The limbs over the bend in Hunting Creek just above Arch's outfield."

"What?"

"Do you remember how them limbs hung near all the way across the creek, so when you was walking there you had to step back and up onto the bluffs to get by?"

"I guess," Sam said.

"I never thought on them much."

"Me neither."

"I can't get free of them now. When I close my eyes I see them," Elisha said.

"We can make us a home right here."

"It ain't just Carolina. It's the boy buried there. The baby buried up on the West Fork Red. And everything else that can happen anywhere."

"I told you, we need you."

"You don't need me," Elisha said. He lifted his eyes and looked at Sam and set his face hard in a glance that was firm but mild. "You think you do, but you don't."

"We need every hand. Every heart. These bastards is all set against us."

"It ain't just flesh set against us."

"Whatever it is, then, we got to stand up together."

"There ain't no amount of standing up that can last."

Elisha lifted the jar to his lips and took a long draw and Sam saw him loosen under the heat of the whiskey.

"I ain't leaving you for them mines," Elisha said finally. "I want to, but I can't."

Sam heard the words and reached at them for comfort but lost them in the hollow of his brother's voice. The *engagés* came back to the table and Elisha's twisted joviality returned as he kicked a chair free so one of them could sit. Sam took hold of the jar and sat back as Elisha bantered with the *engagés* and slurred his words and writhed in his chair. Sam scanned the room and took in the smoke and the smell and the desperation cloaked in laughing. He saw Austin's henchman at the bar. He was still drinking, his movements tense and cinched as he looked over at them. Sam kept watching and his expression seemed to call the man out. The henchman turned from the bar toward them.

"Rolens," he yelled, his eyes bloody and his face twisted. "You're a might popular with the ladies, ain't ye?"

Elisha looked over slowly under the whiskey.

"What did you say there?" he said.

"She was mine and you knowed it, you son-of-a-bitch!"

Burl stepped away from the card table and Sam turned toward the bar. Elisha lifted in his chair and began to open his mouth and Burl came forward. The henchman reached under his lapel and pulled free a pistol and Sam could see that the hammer was cocked as he pointed it forward. Elisha held his hands up and his eyes cleared. But the henchman's face was red and his lips were set firm. Sam saw the man's finger press down and the motion of the room seemed to slow and his own movements became weighty as he struggled hard to stand. Burl pulled his knife from its sheath and held it high.

"You'll die the second that ball is spent, mister."

The man loosened on the trigger, and his face turned inward as he tipped the barrel toward the rafters.

"I can't let this go," he said.

"You best let loose of that pistol," said Burl. "You can take this outside and settle it with your hands."

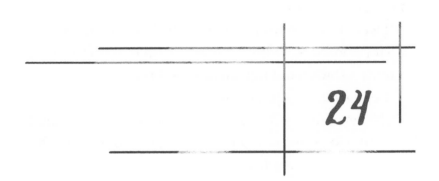

24

$\mathscr{A}$ thick mist lifted from the creek bed and seeped between the walls laying a blanket of cool gray on the porch as Sam followed his brother into the street. Elisha jumped from the planking and dropped to a knee and stood again and walked forward a few steps and turned. He lifted the back of his hand to his brow and blinked twice and opened his eyes wide. The henchman pushed through the door and Sam turned to see him. His steps were short and tense and his fists tight and his brow creased like a cut piece of dried deerskin. Sam read him. Something had taken him, and there was no reason discernible in his face only need and something like desire. Sam looked away. Others came from the tavern and lined the plank walls and Burl pushed two *journaliers* aside as he stepped into the mud. He turned as one of them began to resist but the old man's eyes blazed and the *journalier* stood back. Charlie followed him. A gust of wind flushed the branches over the tavern and the cracked leaves of maple dropped into the wet dirt of the street, lit now by torchlight and the fading sun. Elisha stood. The flames glinted in his eyes.

"I want to watch while you die," the henchman said.

Sam stood next to Burl. He felt a rush of blood and saw his uncle's thick hand tighten around his belt.

"Let's get at it," Elisha said.

The henchman pulled a blade and began to move toward Elisha who kept his own in its sheath. Sam wondered at his brother's stillness and feared it.

"No knives, mister," Burl yelled. Sam turned and saw that Burl had pulled his long-knife free and held it by the tip and was set to let it fly. "You best throw that blade aside."

The henchman turned sharply and blinked like a cat. He looked at his knife and back at the old man and tossed it aside into the dirt. In a quick moment he rushed at Elisha who held him in his eyes and as the little man went for his legs Elisha sprawled back pressing the little man's face into the mud. Sam saw that his brother held the man firm and knew he could lock his arms now and break his collarbone but wondered if the whiskey had blunted his instincts. It didn't seem so. Elisha tightened his grip around the hench-man's neck and pressed him and Sam could see the little man's face in the mud, his features pressed and his face red with the blood beneath his skin and his eyes shut like traps. Just as he seemed contained Elisha let loose and thrust him to standing as if he were a sack of dried feed.

"What the hell is he doing?" Sam said.

"I don't know," said Burl.

"He seems like he's playing with him," said Charlie.

"This ain't no game," Sam said.

Elisha began to circle as the little man rushed again too full of rage to think. Elisha took his arm and thrust him aside and sent him sprawling into the mud. The wet ground covered the little man's leggings and he slipped as he stood again, wiping his eyes clean.

"You just made a big mistake there, mister. You shouldn't have let me go," he said, as he gathered himself and set his feet ankle deep in the moist earth.

"That boy's dumb as hell," said Sam. "Elisha could finish him quick if he'd just take hold of him."

"I ain't sure he wants to finish him quick," Burl said. "He don't seem drunk no more, though. At least he don't move like he is."

The voices of the *journaliers* and *engagés* began to rise and Sam could pick out Austin's men by looking at their eyes and the wind began again and the flames in the torch lights rose under the breeze. One *journalier* held a hide strap tight in his fist and at the end of it a mongrel thick in the shoulders yapped and snarled, its long teeth wet and black at the roots and its thick eyes pressing outward cold and white.

Elisha motioned at the henchman and to Sam he seemed composed and intent and more himself now. But there was something in his face that hinted a bleak intent and took the air from Sam's lungs and quickened the pace of his breathing. The henchman circled now more slowly. Sam could see he was trying to think but there was scarcely anything to think with as he ran sliding to his knees taking hold of Elisha's ankle. Elisha kept his balance as his body took the blow and his face was firm even as he arched forward against the impact. A thin wisp of dust lifted from his leggings as the mud splashed and covered him and stepping back his face was steady and grim with purpose as he pressed the little man's face into the street again. He took hold of the henchman's hand and held him by the head and Sam knew his brother had him now. But Elisha released him and threw him backwards.

"Keep hold of him!" Sam yelled. Charlie echoed the same words.

"Let him be," Burl said. "He can't hear you."

There was a hush of movement along the walls and Sam could see two of Austin's men sift through the crowd toward the little man in the street.

"Them boys is moving toward that bastard," Charlie said.

Sam stepped into the street and Burl was ahead of him with his knife in hand. Charlie pulled the pistol free and held it at his side and Sam looked across at Elisha who stood up straight, his eyes thin now and piercing, with no trace of the whiskey in them and a resolve Sam hadn't seen in a long while. Elisha turned toward the henchman and saw the glint of firelight near his hand. It flashed against a gun barrel as it passed from one of Austin's men into the little man's grasp.

"No!" Sam yelled.

Elisha stared forward with his face full and bright and his thick chest rising. He made no attempt to move. The little man raised the pistol and Sam could see his brother's face. His jaw was set. His lips rose high and his teeth were as white as crafted marble. He seemed almost to smile. The powder cracked and lifted in a thin visible breath from the barrel and Burl let the knife go as the ball flew free. Charlie raised his pistol and shot but the pull of the gun in the little

man's hand had sent him back. Burl and Charlie missed as
the knife sliced into the planking. Sam heard the hollow
sound of the ball as it hit his brother's chest.

Elisha flew back against Little Charlie and knocked him
to the ground. Burl jumped over both of them. He was on
the henchman before he could lower his hand. He took
him by the collar and threw him against the far wall and
the henchman reached for his knife but Burl took hold of it
and wrenching it away he threw it behind him. Burl saw fear
and awe in the little man's face and the fright there fueled
his rage. He took his fists to the man's head pounding hard
at his eyes. The blood poured from the henchman's ears
and he lost breath as Burl kept on. Burl felt a searing pain
as a knife hit his shoulder and Sam reached him and pulled
him free. Burl turned and lifted his hand. Sam saw his eyes.
They were glazed and inward set and he didn't know who
took hold of him.

"Burley, it's me!"

Burl came to himself and saw his nephew and looked over
his shoulder. The man who had thrown the knife stood next
to another. They began coming forward and Burl pulled the
knife free as Sam turned to face them. Charlie slammed his
hand against the outer wall of the tavern. He had reloaded
while Burl took to the henchman. He stood looking at the
two men with his pistol held straight at them.

"Which one of you boys wants to stop this ball?"

The men stood back and Charlie held the gun as Sam
moved toward him. Burl turned to the henchman and saw his
battered face and sunken eyes and broken nose barely there.
The blood flowed in streams from his ears. Sam stepped

toward his brother who lay flat in the street. His eyes were like gemstones. He rested still and heavy. The ball had pierced his lung and he was no longer breathing.

25

*C*harlie held the pistol in front of him. The smoke was
thick and the movement of bodies sent spinning rings
of gray mist into the eaves. Sam stood over his brother who
lay still, his body flat but his head twisted against the porch
planking. His form was claylike. Burl held himself by the
shoulder but kneeled and took his nephew gently by the
neck as Sam lifted his legs and pulled him flat to the ground.
Charlie glanced to the side as a small man slipped around
the side of the tavern. Sam's head stopped spinning and the
fire in his limbs settled and his chest began to heave, his own
blood surging as he looked down at the body and across the
street at the men standing.

"Pa, we best clear out," Charlie said. "One of them miner
boys just left. He'll likely be back with more."

"I don't want to leave him here."

"We got to," said Charlie, as he held his eyes on the men
in front of him and moved into the street. Sam went to Burl
and began to help him move.

"I can walk fine," Burl said. "It's only my shoulder."

They stepped away from the men as they began to disperse, their faces dim in the twilight. Sam looked down the *Rue à l'Englise* toward the parish church past the houses washed in pale white, the boards and the siding rising to the rooflines, the windows set like eyes, the buildings themselves like harlequin masks hollow and knowing, comic, their stark geometry framing only his questions and the silence that followed them. Standing across the quay on a plank porch near the dry goods stood the old woman in black who had stopped the auction. She turned to them and Sam met her with his eyes. She was too far away for him to read them but she stood still and defiant beneath his stare. Her head was cloaked in black linen drapery and her face was drawn and lined and full of empathy. Her lips were thin and there was sorrow in the frame of her granite face. He knew she wouldn't take her eyes from him until he turned away, and he knew she would say nothing, but her expression seemed iconic and iridescent. He looked north along the face of the buildings and the weight of the air hung heavy in his lungs, the moisture itself a presence as it melted into the tree lines beyond the town. He lifted Burl onto his mule as Charlie sat mounted and waiting. The animal spun as he stepped into the stirrup. The moon rose behind Bolduc's house and the red sky bled into the cornfields of the *Grand Champ* as they passed along Gabouri Creek toward the river. White oak and cedar pressed the banks with branches reaching in odd angles and hanging languid into the stream. The creek was too low even to hold a pirogue or canoe and the sand-banks were dry as the air settled in sheets of dust on the face of the inlet pools.

Charlie led his mule onto the sand near the banks and reined her into the stream as he edged past the trees. He took no notice of the sound of the hooves in the water or the branches breaking since there was only one place on the river where they were certain to find a boat. The men that followed them would know where they were going but if they kept apace they would get there before anyone could overtake them. Burl sat unsteady in the saddle, and as Sam followed he saw a stream of blood flowing from his shoulder to his leg. It flowed slowly enough that Sam knew it wasn't from a vital artery. But the blood loss would weaken him, and by the time they reached the river he wouldn't likely be strong enough to take the current on his own. The mules worked along the creek-side traversing fallen logs and busted shale boulders jetting out dry and bladelike, the contours of their surfaces dim in the twilight, the rising darkness omnipresent and knowing, enveloping an exhale of palpable malevolence, the tree lines along the river in the distance still full near the ground in foliage but with tall and leafless branches rising as if burned and claw-like, spiraling into the red sky. Sam tried to push his brother from his mind and keep his thoughts on Burl and Charlie and on the threat of Austin's men. But in the fading landscape he could see his brother at the table lifting a jar of whiskey to his lips. He remembered the firm outline of his face near the campfire and the twist of his neck against the planking as he lay dead outside the tavern. The confluence of images compressed in his chest. Burl and Charlie turned around.

"Keep going," Sam said as he came up to Burl, who steadied himself in his saddle.

"You all right?" Burl asked.

"Yeah."

Charlie circled back around a tree and trotted the mule toward them. To Sam his silhouette against the sky seemed unfamiliar and changeless and fully formed.

"What are y'all waiting on?" Charlie said.

"There's a pirogue tied up down near the ferry stand," Burl said. "I'll need to take it up-river past the route of the ferry. These miner sons-of-bitches won't know how to figure my route if I work against the current away from the rest of the boats."

"I don't know how you're going to work a pirogue up-river with that shoulder," Charlie said.

"Can't you just go with the current down toward Natchez?" Sam said.

"That would decrease my chances," Burl said. "That's what them dumb asses will expect me to do. Some of them may already be headed down-river."

"I don't figure any judge would trouble you about killing a crazy son-of-a-bitch that come after somebody in your family," Sam said.

"It ain't the judge I'm worried about," Burl said. "The judge won't be with them when they catch up with me. You boys will be fine. You didn't do no killing."

"Let's cross through this field and catch the creek again down near the river," Charlie said.

They reined the mules into a clearing through the tall corn of the *Grand Champs*, Charlie in front and Burl between them as the rush of the stalks pressed against the ribs of the animals. Charlie kicked the mule into a trot as the faint howl of dogs rose from the town behind them. Sam saw the movement of his son's back and the thickness of his neck and he knew him but didn't know him, remembered him not as he was now but as a pair of child's eyes looking at him with questions and trusting he could answer them. Now the boy took to the river to save Burl with the same fierceness the old man had shown with the Cherokee on the Trace. Charlie knew what to do. The instinct in him was base and real. There was no thinking in it.

They reached the tree line near the river and skirted along the edge until they happened upon a small game trail leading to the banks. Charlie took the trail through the thin stand of white oak onto the dry sand. Sam could see across to the American side as the moon behind him refined the lines marking the far shore. The brown water pressed against the hard green of the trees and Sam could pick out shades of color among the leaves and branches, the pale yellow of the new growth and the black of the girdled stumps near the ferry stand. Above the trees a sheet of gray pressed down. Flashes of lightning turned the sky a blinding white and forced him for an instant into a colorless void of absence so chilling that he turned away. The carping of the hounds was getting clearer, and as they arrived at the waterline he looked down the bank where a mud turtle lay resting with its neck extended and its chin lying in the sand. At the sound of the mule's hooves the animal lifted its head and turned, its thin black eyes blinking slowly and its strong jaw moving in rhythm. Its mouth was hooked and the folds of its neck were twisted and sinewed. The turtle saw them as it moved into the river, eyes vigilant, skimming the waterline, watching the men and mules as it moved outward into the deep and disappeared.

Charlie pointed toward three pirogues lined up randomly near the ferry stand. Burl leaned over in his saddle. Sam stepped from his mule and took his uncle by the shoulder and taking the bulk of his weight helped him to the ground. Burl dropped to his knee. Sam pulled a knife from his belt and cut free the blood-soaked hide of Burl's jacket to see the wound.

"The bleeding's stopped," Sam said.

"I can't get my breath," Burl said. "I ain't got no strength in my legs."

Sam knew Burl couldn't row the pirogue very far without collapsing, or any distance at all with the shoulder wounded. Charlie jumped from his mule and ran downstream and rifled among the pirogues, selecting what seemed the surest one. He lifted the oars then pushed the vessel into the water and jumping in rowed toward them. As he arrived at the shore Sam lifted Burl into the pirogue and Charlie took him by the shoulders and they rested him against the bow.

"Pa, you know I got to go with him."

"Give me one of them oars," said Burl.

"You couldn't even lift the damn thing," Charlie said. "You lost too much blood."

"Just lie back there for a minute," Sam said, looking at Burl. The crisp high barking of the hounds was clear now as they crossed the cornfield toward the trees. There was a murmur of voices behind them as two single musket shots rang out.

"Pa?" Charlie said again.

Sam looked across at Charlie and through him to Burl, and then beyond them to the family and the green earth and the busted dirt marked by them all in the imprint of what seemed a single hand. But now it wasn't earth and blood together but blood alone that called for his allegiance or his betrayal. Burl lay silent. He was unconscious, his breath rising heavy but steady in his chest.

"Get that other oar, son," Sam said, as Charlie reached behind him and placing the oars in the locks spun the paddles into position. "Keep low and get to midriver as fast as you can. Make sure you're more than fifty yard offshore, out of musket range."

"Pa, I'll---" Charlie began.

"Get out there, now," Sam commanded, stopping his son short of a promise the boy had no power to keep. Sam pushed the pirogue into the current and pressed his palms against his knees as it drifted free. Charlie leaned into the oars as the boat moved swiftly into the river. Sam met his son's eyes as the hounds broke through the trees. Then he turned into the torch lights glaring.

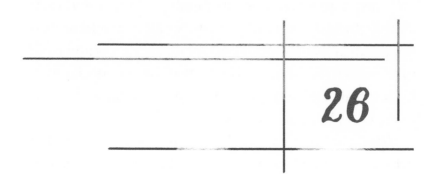

26

The makeshift courtroom was dimmed gray by the sweltering thickness in the air. François Vallé sat behind a table with the sleeves of his robes loosely draped and the collar of his shirt rising as the sweat gathered under his quiet eyes. He motioned to his attendant.

"Je suppose que Monsieur ne parle pas français?" he said.

"J'en suis certain." said the attendant.

Sam faced the table with his hands in front of him tied in leather straps. Moses Austin stood nearby with his face like cut slate and his shoulders prim and high. His jacket reached to the floor in a sweeping mass of dark maroon. The dust gathered on his wig and drifted to his shoulders as the sweat burned dark lines of brown along the creases of his sleeves. His wealth was apparent but incongruous in the moist heat and human texture of the room. People gathered along the wall. Some were *engagés* and *journaliers* in leather breeches and gray chapeaus and others were merchants with aprons removed and tossed across their shoulders and others were traders who knew the parties

involved. The women were mostly the wives of mine owners, and their faces were indignant and confused. Moses
Austin stepped toward the commandant at the table as the
attendant stood by.

"I'm sure the commandant is already familiar with the
circumstances of this case, with the events as they occurred
in the tavern last night," Austin began. "These behaviors
challenge the authority of your honor, and indeed of the
civil society we're trying to create here."

"Mr. Austin, these proceedings will be conducted impar-
tially," Vallé said.

"Of course."

"Am I to understand you are a party in this case?"

"The murdered man was one of mine."

"He was a slave?"

"No," Austin said. "He was one of my workers."

"Then you are not a party?"

"I am here to represent his interests."

"That is the role of this court and its officers," Vallé said.
"Were you a witness to the events?"

"No, they were recounted to me."

"You understand that the court must consider only the
testimony of witnesses?"

"Yes. But it should be made clear---" Austin began.

"You're welcome to remain," Vallé said firmly, "but you
must join the spectators. This court will call its witnesses."

Sam stared at the commandant. Vallé looked past him
to the crowd. Their eyes darted from wall to wall and to the
floor and away from Vallé's face. Austin shook his head and
moved backwards.

"Will anyone step forward as an eyewitness to these events?" Vallé asked.

No one answered, and Austin looked forward as if to take hold and command the scene. Vallé turned his eyes to the tavern owner.

"Of course, you were there, Travignon," said Vallé. "Can you recount for us the events that transpired?

"If I must," Travignon answered, in heavily accented English.

"Please step forward then."

The tavern owner lifted his arm and wiped his brow as he moved to the table. He stood with his head bowed slightly and his hands clasped in front of him.

"Proceed," Vallé said.

"Many of the men were drunk, of course," Travignon began. "The tavern was crowded and the tables were full. There was no violence at first. Austin's man Ackerman came and sat at the bar. Then I noticed him move quickly toward the table where this man was sitting with his people," he pointed at Sam. "I didn't expect anything to happen."

"What did happen?" said Vallé.

"Words were exchanged, and the men went into the street. They fought there. It was all very confusing. I heard the gun discharge. Ackerman was holding it. This man's brother fell to the ground."

Travignon paused to take breath and shifted his weight nervously from side to side. He lifted his sleeve to his brow and wiping himself took his chapeau from his head and gripped it in his fists. He glanced quickly behind him, and to Sam it seemed he caught Austin's face with a glance.

"Then what transpired?" Vallé said.

"The escaped man rushed forward," said Travignon. "He had no weapon but he took to Ackerman with his fists. It all went very fast. There was blood."

He paused again for breath with his face held down. Sweat dripped from his brow and his eyes opened wide and his lips pushed forward as if in surprise. Then he began again.

"A knife flew, but I don't know from where. I could see Ackerman dead and the old man wounded."

Travignon began to shake at the knees and his breath became short and audible.

"Step back, Jean Michelle," Vallé said. "Are there any eyewitnesses who would like to challenge this account?"

"Someone must speak to the brutality of the crime," Austin said.

"The nature of the act isn't germane to these proceedings. The perpetrator is fled. My concern is with the culpability of the man accused."

Vallé stopped speaking and leaned backwards in his chair and raised his arms letting the thick sleeves of his gown fall free of his wrists. He looked at the crowd again.

"Can anyone speak to Mr. Rolens's guilt or innocence?"

"He helped the murderer get to the river," one of Austin's *engagés* yelled forward.

"That's where we caught up with him, knee deep in the mud," another added.

Vallé leaned forward and looked at Sam. He rested his arms on the table and folded his hands. His face was searching but benevolent and his voice was steady and without the modulation of severe emotion. Sam lifted his chin and met the commandant's face squarely, knowing his power as power only.

"Is this true?" Vallé asked.

"The man killed my brother and my uncle killed him," Sam said. "I'd have killed him myself if it weren't already done. I helped the old man get to the river and my oldest boy went away with him."

"Where are they now?"

"Somewhere on the river," Sam said. His jaw tightened as his eyes gleamed wet. "They won't be back."

Austin's face lifted as he leaned against the wall. There was a murmur among the men around him and a low and whispered gasp of relief from the women. One middle-aged lady lifted her shoulders at the sound of Sam's voice. She wore a large hat of dark pink with a loose brim draping to her neck and a broad feather sinking in the heat of the room. Her face changed and her eyes beamed confidence as she waited for Vallé to speak. The commandant looked downward at the table then lifted his face at Sam.

"It's not good to assist a man who may be guilty of a crime. Even if that man is family," Vallé said.

"He weren't guilty of no crime."

"Your uncle killed a man."

"He killed a murderer."

"Do you understand that the court must make these determinations?"

Sam stood silent. Vallé looked across the room and fixed his eyes on the windowpane and through the dark glass into the street.

"I'm unhappy with your manner, sir," Vallé said firmly. "You must respect the government's authority in the affairs of law."

Again Sam was silent. The commandant's face was mild, incongruous with his words. He leaned back in his chair and paused.

"Events like these are rarely seen with any clarity of mind, even if witnessed," he said. "There are always ambiguities."

"My man's death must be answered," Austin said.

Vallé heard him and held his breath in silence as the voices in the room began to rise. Then he straightened himself in his chair and leaned forward.

"Sir, I'm not blind to your purposes here."

"Civility demands retribution," Austin said.

"I'm by no means sure we share the same notion of civility. We are both landowners and men of business. But your methods have become dubious. In point of fact, civility does not require retribution. It requires justice."

Sam turned to Austin who tried to look past him but couldn't. The fabric of dresses and leather breeches pressed the wall and scratched the whitewash. Austin looked hard at Vallé but said nothing more.

"I can't in good conscience punish someone who defended his family against the threat of a mob," Vallé said. "The man who did the killing wasn't pursued with the authority of the law, nor was he under its protection when he escaped."

He shifted in his seat and lifted his sleeves again. "Mr. Rolens was justified in seeing his uncle to safety," he said.

He looked at Sam directly now. "You're free to return to your farm. But I must counsel you against violence. I must admonish you also to trust the law and its institutions."

Sam's face softened. Austin turned from the room and was followed by four *engagés* and the women. Vallé looked at his attendant.

"Unbind this man's hands," he said.

Moist clay covered his boots as he walked through the merchant lanes toward the parish church. Dim contours of sifting light wafted aimless through the front pane. The air in the street was heavy as the smell of green worked at his lungs and the trees hung weary over the eaves. But for the occasional side glance he saw no threat in the people on the street. He wondered that they were still breathing, their common gestures a cold insult with Elisha dead. He knew he was safe from them but not from the brute reality of his own enveloping sadness. He tried to even out his breathing as he passed the dry goods and the tavern and the private houses of the wealthy and made his way into the square. The church pierced the disenchantment and threaded the trees with its spire black in the falling light and the plankboard roofline reaching. He moved from the street into the building. The center aisle was narrow and the pews dark and straight and two cedar pillars sealed in pitch rested square and solid near the altar. He walked between the pews past the vestry and stepped lightly beyond the rising candles into the heart of the sanctuary. A pale beam of gray shone through the window and in the interior light his eyes still faltered, but the dim shape of a body rose near him as the crucifix came into view. The dark wood of the cross was pressed hard to the wall and set secure in trusses and the body of the oaken Christ was nailed true to the planking in a torment carved and palpable. Sam washed his eyes in the figure, taking into memory its feet and the rise of its chest and the sculpted depths of its attic face. The woodcarver knew the contours of bone and sinew, and to Sam they seemed the living movements of *engagés* and *journaliers* and tenant farmers and slaves. Sam saw the heft in its arms and knew they were rightly figured as the arms of a carpenter. They were his brother's arms as well, framing the gray-painted figure in supplication, lifelike in the shadows, with eyes staring in psalmic reverence into silence and suffering. Sam moved back as the cross became larger and the Christ image disappeared within it. The stained glass cast a colored drape of shade across the altar as the room became dark and the carving faded into the sifting light.

He worked his way through the square beyond Vallé's house to his borrowed wagon. His brother lay in the back wrapped in thick woven linen. Sam climbed into the seat and lifted the reins and moved the oxen forward into the shallows of Gabouri Creek. The wet sand was firm beneath the water and the wheels took hold as he rose to the far bank and upward onto a road leading west away from the river. The rains had moistened the clay and the wheels caught and slid and the oxen pressed at the yokes. The air clung to the leather and softened the harnesses as the reins slipped in his hands. He pulled them tightly and leaned back raising his hat brim above his eyes. He passed by a stand of red maple and through them to a clearing on the edge of the *Grand Champs*. The sunlight on his face was blinding and he tightened his eyes against the grief and knew too well its pathway, the exquisite shock on waking and the mild acceptance before midday and the tired and merciless despair in the afternoon. His mouth was full of acid and his gut churned snakelike and his mind was too weak for questions. He worked the wagon through the fields and beyond the broken woodlands toward the surface mines, and he paused the wagon at the edge of a pit. He stepped sideways down the embankment near the busted shale scattered in fragments on the floor. From inside the pit seemed a miniature of a creation removed from all beneficence with walls and high banks naked and descriptive, the whole of it a demonic axiom of chaos with gaps and recesses filled out in a rich precision of pain. He began lifting the hand-sized stones to his chest and carried them toward the wagon and tossed them up the bank. He moved from the rock pile to the wall and carried it piece by piece to the wagon as the shale gathered on the road. He climbed the embankment and walked to the wagon and gently moved his brother's body to the far side of the bed. Then he began lifting the stones into the wagon filling it as high and as heavy as the oxen could sustain. They would line the road he would carve near his crop line and buttress the fence posts along the outfield and crease the floor of the spring behind his implement shed. A breeze worked at the sweat on his neck as his gut loosened and his mind drifted to where he would set the stones. When the wagon was full he climbed again onto the seat and beat at the reins as the oxen struggled forward on the road. Piles of square planking lined the roadside with some placed crossways and the oxen climbed them and moved with greater ease. Clouds began to gather beyond the tree lines and the breeze took to swirling and the branches twisted in the air. The thunder cracked in the distance and the rain began washing the glades in front of him and he drove the team forward as the water hit his face. The road opened into a meadow and he could see Elisha leaning near a tree, intense in his stare but laughing as he talked ahead at someone listening.

The rain fell in windswept waves as he pulled the wagon into Dogwood Crossing. The wheels sunk in the shallow mud but caught the hard surface layer beneath as the oxen worked their way to the center of town. There were people in scattered bunches huddled under porches waiting out the storm, looking on as he drove the team. He could see from the way they stared that the bad news had arrived before him and he tried not to look at anyone too long. He knew there were faces carrying messages that weren't his to read. A Creole *habitant* near the dry goods leaned against the wall. Next to them stood a young woman. Her hands gripped hard at the fabric of her shirt as she cast her unwavering eyes on the wagon, and Sam could see them and he turned away. He reined the oxen to the side and stopped the wagon in front of the tavern. There was a new sign resting at the base against the wall near the door, and Sam saw the bright red lettering lined in cheap gold leafing. It read simply, "*TAVERN*" and under it, "*Beer and Whiskey, J. T. Greenhall, Proprietor*". He wrapped the reins and jumped from the seat onto the porch planking and straightened himself as he walked inside. The room was empty but for two black men working on the legs of an upturned table and the owner lifting clay jars full of spirits from straw-lined wooden crates. The old man heard Sam's footfall and turned.

"I come here to settle any accounts my brother left unpaid," Sam said.

"There ain't none except on some whiskey already drunk," Greenhall said. "It ain't much. We'll call it paid."

"I'll want to pay off anything he owes."

"I figure you're already paying it," said Greenhall. "You're burying your brother."

"Did he leave an account?"

"No, not by my calculation. Mister, you see a lot a different kind of folks in this place. They try to pay me all kinds of ways for whiskey. I mostly ask cash money. But some men bring something to the place that pays for what they take away. Your brother was one of them kinds."

"He was known for being a lively talker," Sam said quietly, lifting his eyes to one of the standing tables. "Especially when we was back in Carolina."

"I can guess."

"He was mostly pretty mean when he left to come here," Sam said.

"He weren't mean once he got here."

Sam pulled his purse from his jacket and began to loosen the drawstring.

"Rolens, I ain't taking no money from you."

Sam looked at him. Greenhall lifted his hand to shake and Sam took it firmly.

"Take a drink every now and then, friend, in between working," Greenhall said. He smiled at Sam and turned back to his crate.

Padgett was leaving the new land office as Sam stepped from under the porch roof into the street. He walked toward him folding a piece of parchment in his hand and shoving it into the inner pocket of his coat. They met near the head of the team.

"I guess you know everybody heard what happened," said Padgett.

"I figured that from looking at them. How did it get here so quick?"

"The news come from some of the *engagés* that seen it. I guess they figured Austin would take hold of your land."

"Why were you over at the land office?"

"Checking the maps."

"How come?"

"You never know when them bastards will draw up new ones and burn the ones that have your land marked out right. I aim to make sure they know I'm watching."

Sam kicked his boot at the base of the wheel. The oxen shifted under their harnesses. Padgett reached into his pocket and pulled out a block of tobacco. He offered it to Sam who shook his head. The rain had thinned to a drizzle and the people were moving in the streets and the hard smack of leather against hide could be heard from the makeshift tannery. Padgett took a wedge between his teeth and pushed it into the recesses at the back of his jaw.

"I hear your oldest boy ain't with you no more," Padgett said.

"He went upriver with my uncle."

"You all right for hands out there at your place? Corn's high this year."

"My younger boy's still here. We'll manage."

"The crop's good. Looks like you'll make it."

"This year, anyway."

Padgett spit in the mud at the feet of the team and rubbed his hand at his shoulder then leaned his head back loosening the muscles.

"Your brother didn't want to come here, did he?"

Sam looked past him to the tall buildings fronting the street and rising in thin-coated whitewash out of the wet dirt.

"I guess he didn't," he said.

He left the town and passed into a stand of hemlock and the high call of a scarlet tanager sifted through the branches. Beside the road wild geranium foliage and large-flowered trillium lifted the trees and beneath them the black moss and ferns and strands of yellowroot covered the soil. A thin string of spruce lined the edge of the stand and nearby a tall dogwood stood separate with branches dark and broad leaves coloring. Sam held its seasonal dressing in his mind, with its stark and wasted branches finger-like and demonic in winter and its blossoms disembodied and fragrant in spring. He looked under its leaves to its branches. Then he stared past them into silence. There was something beyond articulation in the twisted limbs and browning leaves, in the ashen features of the oaken Christ, and in himself, in the fear and hope and anger with which he loved even the dead. He drove the oxen into the meadow toward Padgett's farm and further until the tall roof of his own house curled like a grasping hand over the top of the ridgeline. Looking toward it he saw Lucetta standing and facing him in the yard.

He bent his shoulders and held the brim of his hat as he stepped through the low door of the implement shed. The air was cool as the days had passed with the sun behind the high fields in the west and the colors now crisp against the fence line. The outfield below the house was tall with corn and the wheat field was a yellow sheet dimming brown under the thinning clouds. He followed the narrow footpath toward the house and watched his feet as he walked. Ewan was struggling to carry a post and Sam saw him but couldn't make out where he was going. Lucetta walked slowly from the truck patch beside the house and waved her hand at Eve Mary who saw her and looked away as she entered the house. There was a slow ache in Lucetta's chest as she looked beyond the house at the gravestone. But fearing her own depths she chose against them and looked ahead at Raymond who took to his feet and edged his way along the wall. She climbed the porch and lifted the Creole shawl around her shoulders and turned looking across the yard at Ewan near the fence. Sam followed the pathway toward the house and Lucetta met his stare and walked down the steps again. She could see his eyes were open and his brows suspended with something visible in his expression she wanted to call sadness. She spoke the word and heard its hollow echo and let it go. His face was a broken mosaic of questions.

She met him in the middle of the yard. He looked at her.

"Where was I in all this?" he said. "The boy back home, the baby, my brother?"

"Where were any of us?" she said, pressing her hands against her thighs and staring beyond him.

She lifted her hand to his face and traced her fingers from his eyes to his lips. "Living breaks you down," she said. "It makes you weak. It's the only pathway to purity I know."

She rested her hands at the base of her shawl and wrapped it more firmly then stood back from him, looking into him.

"There are answers, Samuel. I think you know there are answers to your questions."

"Where?"

"I don't know."

"You don't know?"

"No."

He took in her face. Her expression was full and rich.

"You're trying hard to forgive yourself," she said. "You can't do that alone."

He could feel the weight of his chest rise against him and his knees give way as he dropped to the ground. She came down to meet him and took hold of his face and pulled him to her breast. He could feel her breathing and hear in dim murmur the pulsing of her blood. His eyes burned wet and the breath left him in hollow waves. She held him as he kneeled before her like a supplicant. Then she lifted him by the shoulders and raised her shawl to his face.

He turned and looked across the outfield beyond the hemlock and maple stands and into the horizon dusted red and then he walked forward toward the fence line. He stepped into the hemlock up the steady rise that lifted to the ridgeline that crested above his farm. He worked his way into the trees and past them into a clearing and walking to a stack of wood he took hold of an axe that leaned on a newly hewn cedar. He took it as if to use it but instead rested his palm on the handle. He looked out over the tilled land enmeshed with the wild of the woodlands and saw the budding order there and wondered at its meaning, and he knew it lay itself before him like shape notes on a page of sacred music he had never learned to read. It was an order not his own but his now to claim and it draped itself like a blanket over all he had intended. The sky was awash with fading light and the trees were crimson and purple in a sifting breeze that was cool and soothing on his face. He could imagine at least that one day his mind would rest and his heart would slow to pace, when time gave way to essence and the white faces of the dead faded into mist. Then maybe Elisha's fear and quiet pain and busted hope would fall like shards of carved stone onto the floor of the universe, and the marbled face of the architect would lift free from the bas-relief of a sculpted world. He looked down at his son. Ewan set the post flat and climbed the low railing and lifted the sledgehammer from behind. Sam could see his face in silhouette against the falling light. Lucetta sat down and lifted the Creole shawl from her shoulders and placed it on her legs. Sam cast his eyes across the trim pastoral, carved and shaped as if to answer death. The cut fields were angled against the trees and the walls of buildings stood out in lines drawn from wild recesses and the creation itself seemed an artifice drawing toward perfection. He walked down the slope of the yard out of the woods onto the carved land. Ewan saw him coming.

Lucetta leaned back in her chair. She looked on at them as the wind sifted through the trees. They met against the fence line and raised the post to standing and Sam took hold as Ewan lifted the sledge. He felt its weight as it met the post. He set his grip again as it came down in a singing rhythm that echoed down the glades. Ewan finished and turned toward him. Sam rested against the fence. Washed in the dimming light, he closed his eyes.

THE END

Acknowledgements

I would like to express my heartfelt thanks to a host of people and institutions who contributed to this novel from its inception. My appreciation to the administrators and staff at the Center for Appalachian Studies and the Belk Library W. L. Eury Appalachian Collection, both at Appalachian State University. This book doubles as a cultural history, and I found various historical studies of immeasurable value, especially David Hackett Fischer's *Albion's Seed: Four British Folkways in America*, Carl J. Eckberg's *Colonial Ste. Genevieve*, and Jonathan Daniels's *The Devil's Backbone: The Story of the Natchez Trace*. Folktales and jokes emerging from the oral tradition were adapted from Vance Randolph's *Pissing in the Snow and Other Ozark Folktales* and Richard M. Dorson's *Buying the Wind: Regional Folklore in the United States*. Warren Moore's *Mountain Voices: A Legacy of the Blue Ridge and the Great Smokies* was of great help in informing me of other aspects of a rich and varied folk tradition.

I am especially grateful to the many fellow seekers who read the manuscript in its early stages and helped in other aspects of its creation: Laura Myers, Eve McVicker, Jim McVicker, Gail Mahar, Hal Mahar, Howard Gellinck, Kathy Gellinck, Leon Lessinger, Janet Lessinger, Alice LaDeane, D. Brian Mann, Frank Nickell, G. R. Thompson, and especially Greg Trine and Eric Carl Link. Eric and Greg, writers themselves, were indefatigable in their encouragement from the first word to the last, and their final readings were incisive and invaluable. Thanks also to the faculty and staff in the English department at California State University, Bakersfield for their support and assistance.

My special appreciation goes to my departed parents, Ed and Joann Frye, who tirelessly reviewed the manuscript in various stages, focused their efforts in retirement on finding it a home, and who have always been an infinite source of inspiration and hope. It was their stories of our family history that brought life to the narrative and its characters. As always, to my partner in life and best friend, my lovely wife Kristin, who for many years has blessed me with security, joy, and love. Her efforts in improving this novel were essential and beyond any estimation of value. Finally, thanks to my two grown children, Melissa and Thomas, who with their insight and unguarded appreciation of everything beautiful, lend humanity and grace to my thoughts and days.

ABOUT THE AUTHOR

Steven Frye teaches writing and American literature at California State University, Bakersfield. He has published short stories, articles, and essays in such journals as *The Southern Quarterly, The Centennial Review, The South Carolina Review,* and *The Kentucky Review.* He has written three books of nonfiction and edited five volumes of collected essays, which are published by Cambridge University Press and the University of South Carolina Press. He works from his home in the high desert of Southern California, where he lives with his wife Kristin and his brown Labrador Retriever, Sam.